WHERE FURNACES BURN

Also available from Joel Lane and Influx Press:

The Earth Wire
Scar City
From Blue to Black
The Witnesses are Gone
The Blue Mask

JOEL LANE

WHERE FURNACES BURN

Influx Press
London

Published by Influx Press
The Greenhouse
49 Green Lanes, London, N16 9BU
www.influxpress.com / @InfluxPress

This edition 2023.
Printed and bound in the UK by TJ Books.
First published in the UK in 2012 by PS Publishing.
Paperback ISBN: 9781914391095
Ebook ISBN: 9781914391101

Cover design: Vince Haig
Interior design: Vince Haig

CONTENTS

For Mark Valentine – a true connoisseur of the unknown

AN INTRODUCTION TO
WHERE FURNACES BURN

R.M. FRANCIS

I grew up in the region Joel Lane takes his readers to. I've lived here most of my life: the Black Country – real and imagined. I recognise the eerie and weird in its landscapes and mindscapes. Lane's horrors could only ever come from this place. A place of breakages, borderlands, disjunctions, and displacements.

The Black Country is a strange place. It's not found on maps and its borders are under constant contestation. A region known for its Industrial heritage; we're now haunted by the residues and ruins. Old railway lines and bell pits punctuate an off-kilter landscape built of green and grey. Rewilded spoil heaps cosy up next to large housing estates. Wildflowers and rare insects share space with litter, graffiti, and clandestine behaviours. Not a conventionally beautiful place, but one Joel Lane saw the beauty in and helped me reconfigure my love for.

I came across Lane's work in my early adult years. I'd just finished my English Literature degree and had returned to my homelands. Like most twentysomething dweebs, I thought everything that was interesting in the world happened somewhere other than my neck of the woods. Then I stumbled on some of his stories and poems in Dudley Library. Oh shit! I thought, I've completely overlooked this place and completely underappreciated its strangeness. One of literature's strengths is its unique ability to remind us and give language and image to that which we'd forgotten we knew. Reading Lane taught me that too. He taught it viscerally.

I'm reminded of Jacques Lacan's psychoanalytical landscapes here. Like Lane's regions, conflict and ambivalence are at its core. Distinct parts of our selfhood wrestle, lose traction, crack, and then reform. Self is a site of breakages. Lacan refers to the mirror stage, where one recognises their reflection in the process of becoming a subject. We recognise a distinct individual. We also notice an imaginary, perfect self which is then quashed as we become socialised. This imagined reflection of self is something that one wishes to regain, because it is pure self. We're afraid of it too – it is our pre-socialised unruliness. This unruly yet beautiful thing is Lacan's Lamella. Lacan says:

> Whenever the membranes of the egg in which the foetus emerges on its way to becoming a new-born are broken, imagine for a moment that something flies off, and that one can do it with an egg as easily as with a man, namely the hommelette, or the lamella.

This thing is a part of our self which is constantly around, always chasing but cannot be fixed upon. It is the result of the very act of passing through the mirror stage, jettisoning the abject or orientating our castration complexes – it hides, haunts, seduces, and sickens. Like Freud's id – it is the primal, unruly part of our psyche. You'll catch glimpses of this almost-untraceable, infinite and infinitesimal, equally attractive and repulsive being, which is you and not you, throughout Where Furnaces Burn. Like me, you might be reminded of things lost or best forgotten. It might reignite things long repressed in the dank recesses of your mind.

In Stambermill, my five-year-old self raced bikes through housing estates and around the backs of homes where patches of woods make dens for rodents and gangs of naughty kids. Here, the river Stour's polluted currents meander past scrap yards, small holdings, and old, barren pubs. The waters run under the blue brick arches of a Victorian viaduct where mosses and lichens rhizome and the ghosts of freight still rumble if you know how to listen for them. A similar in-between and off-kilter landscape is found in 'My Stone Desire' and 'Still Water'. In these tales, rural, urban, organic, and machine conjugate to form erotic and abject hauntings. This refrain runs through this collection, tracking the old case notes of a West Midlands police officer, as he charts his own alienated and disquieted career and personal life, full of unusual sex, dislocated experiences, and a strange sense of lack. A lack that springs out of the liminal and the residues of place-identity.

My fourteen-year-old self wanders up the Thorns Road to meet mates on the top of Quarry Bank. No one knows where the borders are here; we are between different subsets of the DY postcodes. Looking up I see Merry Hill Shopping Centre, a hyperreal, indoor town built on the remains of Round Oak Steelworks. Looking down, the industrial estates and webbed terrace streets of The Lye. This is the land Lane called Clayheath in 'Black Country', a place revisited from the looping narrative of 'The Lost District' in his earlier collection. The hoard of thefts and vile juvenile criminality in this story springs forth in the liminal and the dreamscapes – literally and figuratively. It seems the culprit is a John Doe, built from the layers of lost childhoods and liminal lives that were never allowed to reach out and fulfil anything.

My nineteen-year-old self drives out to the Worcestershire countryside on the edges of my region: Hagley, Kinver, Bewdley. These sites seem natural but are more cultured than first appears. These are spaces where the rural and urban mingle – one threatens to overtake the other. Lane uses these edgelands and plays an explicitly Weird card in 'A Mouth to Feed', drawing on the primal critters of Bram Stoker's Lair of the White Worm or Robert E. Howard's Worms of the Earth. His Lindworm is the phallic lamella, sitting on the rural edge of the urban and modern; the sleeping threat of an encroaching primal force that might envelope and erase our existence.

My thirty-year-old self stumbles home from Turner's pub to the Sledmere estate in Netherton. I cut through the allotments and down the canal tow path. I navigate the ruins of an old engine house and the dried-up hole of a now defunct reservoir. Spoil heaps have been rewilded by pollen-heavy weeds. The rust of corrugated roofs from the dark industrial estate puncture the skyline. Netherton tunnel eats through one-and-a-half miles of dolerite hillside. Here, it's easy to envision the shamanic and erotic machine-god of 'Wake up in Moloch'. In 'the unique patchwork of urban villages and gravel meadows' that mark out Netherton, is something 'like a giant steam engine turned inside out' which is the centre for a vampiric and pagan orgiastic worship. At the start of this tale, we're warned that this place 'grew out of the Industrial Revolution [...] It was inevitable that sooner or later, we'd have to give something back'. Again then, this fusion of organic and machine, animate and inanimate, past and present brings forth some peripheral yet overwhelming and inexplicable threat.

In the final case, our detective discusses his retirement. 'There isn't a why,' he says, 'There's just what happened. But everything falls apart, so perhaps it doesn't need much explanation.' But there is some explanation – inexplicable as the answer may be. The trouble is, as Morton suggests in 'Slow Burn', 'THEY DON'T BELONG HERE. What belongs here doesn't belong in the world.' It's in the ground itself. It's in the mineral-rich elements that produced the industrial heartlands of the UK. In the deep time and the geological residues of the place.

My thirty-seven-year-old self walks a Staffie around the damp and desolate grounds of Wren's Nest Nature Reserve. I lived here for six years and know it in all its tiny details; a quintessentially Black Country space. The nature reserve is a lush and beautiful site of protected flora and fauna, home to fossilised ripple beds and Silurian outcrops. It's also full of industrial relics – mineshafts and old railway lines. One of Dudley's infamous council estates wraps around the whole thing. This is a place where domestic, industrial, natural, and geological create strange confluences. We are safe and unsafe here, familiar and unfamiliar, attracted and repulsed. The hallmarks of the abject and uncanny. The story 'Slow Burn' deals with this explicitly. In Lane's hands, these Wren's Nest confluences produce a harrowing genius loci: 'It had a thin, spineless body, but its hands were wide and reaching towards us with bloodless fingers. Its face was a swirl, a thumbprint, without eyes or mouth'. This spirit of place hollows the community and the people making this queer space their home.

The land is toxic. Its history is toxic. The Black Country is a country blackened. It diseases the area and its inhabitants. Bodiless beings, broken and lacking, are summoned by this. Now, nearly forty, I taste the bitter brambles that thicket the canal tow paths of my homelands. I'm looking for my own lost districts – I cannot help myself.

Jacques Lacan, *The Seminar, Book XI, The Four Fundamental Concepts of Psychoanalysis*, trans. Alan Sheridan (New York: Norton, 1998)

R. M. Francis is a lecturer in Creative and Professional Writing at the University of Wolverhampton. He's the author of novels, *Bella and The Wrenna* (Wild Pressed Books) and poetry collections *Subsidence* (Smokestack Books) and *The Chain Coral Chorus* (Play Dead Press). His essays have been published in journals and edited collections and he co-edited the book, *Smell, Memory and Literature in the Black Country* (Palgrave MacMillan). He is reviews editor for the *Journal of Class and Culture*.

MY STONE DESIRE

Some people join the police force to try and make a difference to society. Some do it to try and keep things the same. Some do it because they like beating people up—and they're the only ones who don't end up disappointed. I'm still not sure why I joined the force, or why I stayed in it for twenty-four years. But I think it had to do with needing to understand. Police work was about finding evidence and explaining. There was no room for the unknown, or for the complications that lead from one thing to all kinds of other things. I was young then, of course.

When I started training for police work in Wolverhampton, I left home for the first time and rented a truly dreadful flat in Coseley, a few miles outside the city. It was part of a converted house that had once belonged to a fairly wealthy family. The exterior was still quite impressive, but the interior was largely plasterboard held in place by woodchip wallpaper. The water pipes had the ghost of a murdered child trapped inside them. The fuses regularly blew if two people in the house were cooking at the same time. Not that you could cook much on the tiny, sluggish Baby Belling cooker in the corner of my living room.

In the early days, I spent as much of my off-duty time in Wolverhampton as possible. There was a lot of good live music around at that time; blues and folk as well as the grinding industrial rock that would eventually be called heavy metal. I was on my way home from some gig or other, waiting in a frost-coated bus shelter for the last bus out, when I met a dark-haired girl called Kath. The next weekend, we met again for a drink. Kath lived with her parents in Tipton, a few miles south of Coseley, deep in the estranged heart of the Black Country. She could speak the Tipton dialect, which no-one outside the town understands.

By early spring, Kath was spending the weekends at my place. We'd sit up late, smoking cigarettes and drinking cheap vodka, sleep into the afternoon and make love until nightfall. It was my first experience of intimacy— whether physical or emotional—and I couldn't seem to get enough of her. The bed stank of tobacco smoke and flesh. What I liked best was the dreamlike recovery from the climax, when we held each other and slowly got our breath back while the shock of joy went on echoing in our veins. At those times Kath seemed like a recently fallen angel, her skin glowing, her eyes filled with a mysterious bitter light.

When we met during the week, there was rarely time for us to go back to Coseley together. We'd see a gig or a film in Wolverhampton, then walk out together along the bus route heading south. Just where the factories gave way to fields and woodland, there was a low railway bridge of blackened stone and criss-crossed iron girders. At night, the underside of the bridge was murky and cold. Young couples went there to smoke dope, drink bottled beer and screw. Sometimes there were people hanging around, and we wouldn't stay. But often we were alone, holding each other in the blurred half-light and kissing desperately as the cars sped past. Or looking up at the intricate, barely visible iron lattice as if it was a stained-glass window, some kind of design we needed to interpret.

One night when it was raining, we sheltered under the dripping bridge to warm our hands on each other's skin. Droplets of rain flickered in Kath's hair. I kissed her closed eyelids, and her mouth twisted with some emotion she didn't have words for. Her nipples were rigid under her thin shirt. Being quite small-breasted, she often didn't wear a bra. Our mouths locked together, sharing breath. I felt the distant pulse of an approaching train. Then its passing shuddered through us, and the quiet was torn apart like a tarpaulin over a nail bomb. Kath pressed against me, breathing hard. My fingers found her open.

Kath bit my lips as I shared her with the lime-smeared wall, fumbling to remove the barriers of fabric between us. The air was cold, too cold for this. Kath's muscles locked me inside her. It felt unreal, or perhaps more real than I was. We struggled, cried out, froze together. The night was suddenly very still. Kath found a tissue and wiped her thigh. I felt as though I had violated her, or something had violated both of us. We walked to the bus stop in silence, holding hands, a little shaky from the violence of it. Thirty years on, I still remember how that felt.

A few weeks after that, Kath told me she was late. 'I must have forgotten to take the pill,' she said. We were sitting in a café near the bookshop where she worked. In those days, there were several bookshops in Wolverhampton. She lit a cigarette but stubbed it out after one draw. I noticed that her make-up was clumsily applied, the eyeshadow not quite masking the effects of a sleepless night. Her fingernails pierced the back of my hand. 'Can I move in with you?' she asked.

I felt my head shaking before I'd even thought about it. Panic gripped me. 'You did it on purpose,' I said. 'Getting pregnant so you could leave home.' I apologised almost at once, but the damage was done. Things unravelled quickly after that. A few awkward phone conversations; one more shared night, bitter and restless; then nothing.

As a child, I had a recurrent dream of a hidden place. It was part of a waste ground, not far from my school. No such location existed in my waking life, but each time I dreamed of it the memory was clear. I wandered through brittle ferns and the grey fringes of willow trees towards a ruined wall, on the far side of which someone was waiting for me. When I reached the wall, I could hear traffic going past rapidly on the other side. I remembered that only the road was there.

Kath got another job and didn't come into Wolverhampton any more. I think she had the baby, but I don't know if she kept it. More than anything, I felt tired—as if the sleep debt from the past four months needed to be paid off all at once. The rainy spring dried out into a stale, metallic summer. I concentrated on passing the police entrance exams.

By the end of the year, I was a constable in the Missing Persons team. Off duty, I kept to myself for the most part. They built a new expressway going south out of Wolverhampton, and closed down the road that passed under the railway bridge. I walked out there one freezing afternoon and saw the bridge had already deteriorated: a dense black mould was spreading on the walls and blurring the overhead girders. There was a smell of decaying stone, if stone could decay. I never took another girl there.

The Missing Persons work was fairly demanding, though I soon became frustrated by the lack of answers. Almost every week, someone in the region would disappear—and not only loners but young couples, pregnant women, even people with families. My more experienced colleagues seemed to take it for granted that no-one would ever turn up. 'Either they're alive and hiding, or dead and someone has buried them,' my supervisor commented.

The local paper ran a few stories about the missing people, but it made no difference. I began to realise how fragile the links between people really were. Like a necklace that broke at the least strain, scattering beads everywhere. I tried not to think about Kath and the baby. Eventually they became unreal to me. Muddy Waters seemed to have the relationship thing sussed.

One night in early spring, I took a girl back to my flat. She complained about the smell in the bedroom— 'It's like there's something dead in the wall.' I hadn't even noticed, but when Susan pulled the mattress back I could see a black skin forming over the woodchip wallpaper. It had crept up from a discoloured piece of skirting board. I touched the mould with a fingertip. It was smooth and yielding, like a bruise.

We took the mattress and blankets into the living room that night and slept with the gas fire on. I dreamt the house was burning down, and woke up sweaty and confused. The orange light glowed through crumpled tissues on the floor. There was a dark shape huddled in the blankets beside me, smelling of blood and perfume. I didn't want her to wake up.

The next day, I scraped all the mould off the wall and dabbed bleach onto the raw plaster. Then I dried the surface with an electric fan heater. The next morning, it was already growing back. I scraped it off again. Once separated from the wall it became flaky and brittle, like ashes. I moved the bed into the middle of the room. In the morning, the wallpaper in the corner was grey and puffy. By the next evening, the mould was back again.

I stuck a poster over it and went out to phone the landlord, then stopped at the pub on the way back. By the weekend, the poster had split down the middle. I could see the blackened plaster behind it.

I'm not sure what made me go back to the railway bridge that weekend. Perhaps I wanted to be forgiven, allowed back into the past. And I was naïve enough to imagine I could reach it on my own.

As I walked along the disused road in the moonlight, the bridge looked different even from a distance. I thought it was because the streetlights weren't working any more. But as I reached the bridge and stood just outside its shadow, I could see that the stone and brick of its exterior were entirely covered with uneven black mould. The pale streaks of lime that the rain had leached from the brickwork were no longer visible.

The moonlight revealed another difference too: something the mould had hidden from me before. The structure of the bridge was made up of tightly packed, naked human bodies, twisted together in the warmth of slow decay. They looked as if they were about to move, but they were still. I was close enough to smell them.

My hand reached out, but I was afraid to touch the wall. Afraid that I might not be able to leave. In that moment, I realised they hadn't been killed and left there. They'd gone there of their own accord. A train ran over the bridge then, and the vibration made me start to shake.

STILL WATER

It seemed funny at the time, but in retrospect it wasn't funny at all. A gang of jewel thieves who'd gone missing in Stoke had turned up in the Black Country, hiding in a street with no name. It was the late seventies, and there were quite a few anomalies in the local street map: remnants of lost districts that didn't belong to anywhere and the council hadn't given them postcodes or kept track of who lived there. In this case, it was a string of old railwaymen's houses in the poorest part of Aldridge, uninhabited for thirty years at least. A pearl necklace that had been stolen in Derby turned up in a Walsall pawn shop; we traced it to a prostitute who'd got it from some men living out there. She said it was a derelict house.

At that time, I'd been in the force for a year. I was working from the Green Lane station in Walsall. There wasn't much going on except drunkenness and domestic violence. This was my first taste of organised crime. We planned a nocturnal raid on the ruined cottages, with at least four arrests anticipated. According to the prostitute, the gang were like a family. They shared everything. Some of what she told us didn't end up on the interview record. My superior, DI McCann, had a sense of decency that was unusual for a policeman.

Four cars full of police officers descended on the nameless street shortly before dawn. The houses were built on either side of a railway bridge that had been condemned in the fifties, but never demolished. They backed onto a patch of wasteland where old canals had leaked into the soil, giving the landscape a fertile variety of plant growth and a pervasive smell of stagnant water. It made me think of unwashed skin. We'd been told to go to the third house; it looked just like the others, uninhabited and impossible to inhabit. Black lichen and moss caked the crumbling brick walls; the windows were boarded up, the front door covered with rotting planks. Some tree-dwelling bird called to us mournfully in the night.

behind the house, the marshy ground and thick brambles made an approach difficult. The rear windows were unprotected, though no light was visible through them. What first appeared to be a dense curtain was revealed by our torches as a black mould covering the inside of the glass. It was hard to believe that we'd come to the right place. But in the silence before we broke in, a faint sound reached us. A man's voice, muffled by brick and glass and layers of filth. He was singing: *Baby, you're out of time*. So was he.

McCann crashed through the back door, and five of us followed him. The rest waited outside. Our torches made crazy snapshots of the interior: rotting wallpaper, a cracked ceiling, broken chairs. Some new-looking food cartons, bottles and candles on a table were the only sign of occupancy. In all probability, this place had never had electricity. The singing continued in one of the upstairs rooms. Was it a tape recorder? What kind of trap were we walking into? On the staircase, my foot went through a rotten step and I fell, cursing. When I got up I was alone on the stairs. Ahead of me was only the song. The blues.

Apart from police, there was only one man in the upper room. He was kneeling on a filthy mattress, in front of a small suitcase. The lid was up. The suitcase was full of jewels: pearls, rubies, silver, emeralds. Some were strung or inlaid, some were loose. He was running his hands through them, and singing to himself. His hair was knotted and filthy; his once-white shirt was streaked with filth and sweat. He didn't look away from his hoard or stop singing, even when McCann clamped the handcuffs on his wrists.

We kept him at the Green Lane station for a week. His name was Jason Welles, and he was a member of the Stoke gang. An experienced fence, despite being only twenty. Among the station officers he was known as Mr Pitiful— and not only because of the singing. For two days he did nothing but complain that we'd taken his jewels from him, because 'She won't come to me if I don't have them. She's an old-fashioned girl. No gifts, no loving.' His eyes were a pale, tormented blue.

One night, when I took him his dinner, he remarked to me as calmly as if we'd been talking about her all evening: 'That first time, she came out of the wall. Plaster clinging to her like a shroud. I was holding an emerald

11

bracelet, trying to judge its value. She stood there naked and reached out for it. Then she took me into the garden and showed me where her family live. I wanted to stay with her, but she said it wasn't time yet. When will it be time?' The last question was asked as if everyone knew the answer but him. I didn't know what to say.

Every attempt to interview him produced the same story. He lived in a twilight world of ghosts and angels, a delusional shell that could have made him a cult leader if he'd had a better haircut. It seemed likely that the gang's adolescent games with drugs and prostitutes had triggered some kind of buried madness in him. Or else there'd been some hallucinogen in the moulds and lichens that decorated the ruined Aldridge house. A search of those houses and the surrounding waste ground had yielded no trace of the other gang members. If he didn't tell us where they were, we'd probably never find out. But how do you interrogate a madman?

I attended three of the interview sessions. Each time, he sang to himself and muttered random nonsense, ignoring our questions. To be fair, we ignored his. His world and ours rarely seemed to touch. Typically, he'd rock in his chair and run his hands through imaginary jewels—or through the hair of an imaginary woman. He'd sing 'Out of Time' or 'I Can't Help Myself', then start talking suddenly, as if resuming a conversation we'd interrupted. The interview tapes and transcripts are doubtless long since thrown away, but I can remember some of his words.

'As soon as I saw the house, I knew it belonged to a family. A real family, not like my mum and her boyfriends after my dad went to prison. Nathan, Mark and Rich, they brought call girls into the house, but I knew the family wouldn't like that. Then she came to me one night. Wearing a gown of rotting wallpaper that fell from her and her body glowed brighter than a candle. She showed me where her family sleep under the water. And the thin grey tubes they breathe through, like a baby's umbilical cord. I gave her jewels to wear in her long dark hair. To hang in the tunnels under the ground.

'The other three guys… well, they were just thieves. They had no idea what anything was worth. It was just money to them. Money to spend on cars and clothes and cunt. I let her family take them.' He giggled like a child. 'Not much left of them after a while. Poetic justice. What they had was stolen. But she never stole from me. I gave her everything. I opened her and wrapped her around me. They say when you come off, it never lasts. But I know how to make it last forever.

'Then the morning comes, and she's gone. *Baby, you're out of time…* Where are my jewels? The earrings, the bracelets, the necklaces. I need them to give to her. Why have you taken them from me?' He stared angrily at McCann and me. We said nothing. 'She can't reach me here. It's too far from the water. *You're out of touch, my baby…* Why don't you let her find me? Why'd you put me in a cell with no plaster or wallpaper, so she can't get through? I've nothing to give her now but myself. Why do you always have to break up the family?'

We weren't getting anything useful from him. And he was a liability as a prisoner. He yelled, kicked at the door, wet the bed, needed a suicide watch. We were glad to get rid of him. The Stoke police thought he was probably unfit to stand trial, but he'd be on a section for quite a while anyway.

It was hard to imagine him getting involved in organised crime. He couldn't even feed himself.

While Jason Welles was dreaming in a secure unit somewhere near Stoke, I took my annual leave. I'd been going out with a girl called Joanna since the previous year, and this was our first holiday together. A self-catering week in Dorset. The days were close and rainy, so we spent a lot of time in bed. I kept dreaming about him reaching up for something he couldn't touch, saying 'I opened her and wrapped her around me'. His obsession had convinced me there was something dangerous about love. We split up not long after we came back to Walsall.

Joanna came from Blackheath, and had a rather bleak sense of humour. That was something we shared. She used to repeat bits of Dolly Allen monologues, an elderly comedienne who was well-known in the Black Country at that time. Like the story about the vacuum cleaner salesman. *I opened the door, this young fellow in a suit was stood there. He poured a little bag of dirt onto my hall carpet and said 'If my vacuum cleaner can't get that dust out of your carpet in one minute, I'll eat the dust.' I said 'Here's a spoon, there's no electric in this house.'*

One day when the sky was clear, we went for a walk inland. The footpath took us through an abandoned farm. The old farmhouse was in ruins, its roof beams open to the sky. The sun was burning and we needed shelter, so we slipped into the barn. Gaps in the roof showed where the rain had got in and rotted the bundles of hay. Something moved at the edge of my vision—a snake or a mouse. Joanna turned to me and we kissed hungrily in the shadows. We made love with some violence, our fingernails and teeth leaving marks in each other. Afterwards, we struggled for breath and held each other more tenderly than we had all week.

At that moment, I recognised the cold fever-smell of stagnant water. Looking over Joanna's shoulder, I saw a barrel standing behind the haystack we'd used as a bed. It was nearly full of water. In the dim light, I could just see a number of pale tubes hanging down from the water surface. But I couldn't see what they were connected to. I reached over and let my fingertips brush the water. At once, the tubes convulsed. They were connected to long, translucent maggots that jerked in the water. My finger touched one of them. I threw myself backwards and stood there, breathing hard and trying not to vomit.

Joanna started at me as if I'd gone mad. 'What's wrong with you?' I gestured at the water barrel. She turned and stared at the murky surface. 'Oh, some rat-tailed maggots. Horsefly larvae. Not very pleasant, are they?' Her biological knowledge was more wide-ranging than mine, as I'd noticed on other occasions. 'The long tubes are for breathing. They live in foul water where there's no oxygen. If you see them, you know the water's not fit for anything much.'

I'd been back at the Green Lane station for three hours before DI McCann saw fit to tell me the news. 'By the way, that nutter of a jewel thief has escaped from the secure unit they were keeping him in. Broke a guard's leg and ran for it. They said he'd been such a good prisoner, they weren't expecting it. You think they'd be used to the insane.

Anyway, can't imagine he'll come back here. There's nothing for him, now the jewels have been returned to their rightful owners.'

I stared at him. 'You're joking, aren't you?' He looked confused. 'Of course he'll come back here. The house. His woman.'

'But that's just madness. There's no woman there.'

'To him there is. Look, you interviewed him five or six times. The woman was more real to him than you were.'

It took me another ten minutes to persuade McCann to drive out to the railway bridge. Night was falling, and I wished we'd brought more officers along. This time, we had a key for the back door; but there was no singing inside. The house was empty of life, except for the secondary life of rot and decay. We used our torches to search the waste ground behind the house. He was where I'd known he would be: in the shallow pond close to the back door. There didn't appear to have been a struggle. He'd used stones to weigh himself down. When we pulled him out, he was curled up, his arms crossed, his knees close to his chest. Like a kid in a school assembly.

Later, we drained the pond and found nothing more, apart from a mass of weeds and insect life. But I wonder about the layers of marsh and silt beneath those houses. How easy it might be to make tunnels, or to close them down. It's in the nature of life to adapt. If you don't have food, or oxygen, or love, you find a way. It might not be a good way by someone else's standards, but it's a way.

The autopsy confirmed that Jason Welles had died by drowning in shallow, dirty water. The only external damage was some fretting or eroding of the mouth, caused by small fish or water snails. The only other significant detail had no bearing on the cause of death, and was described by the pathologist as 'demonstrating the feverish reproductive activity of aquatic life at certain times of the year'. When they opened up the dead man's body to remove the viscera, they found that the wall of the body cavity was lined with thousands of tiny pearl-white eggs.

MORNING'S ECHO

It was the strangest kind of dating I ever experienced. But at the time, I was quite young. I hadn't been in the police force long, and I'd only just moved to Birmingham from the Black Country. In a way, it was how I got to know the city. Years later, when I was getting serious with Elaine, I told her a little about that. I said Carla had still been in love with her ex. Which was true, but it wasn't the whole story.

One evening, a girl of eighteen or so turned up at the Digbeth station in some distress. She wanted us to help her find her boyfriend. When we asked where he might be, she said: 'He's in the ground.' Denny was the head of a local teen gang, the Falcons, that had some minor criminal involvement—a couple of my colleagues knew him. He'd recently been threatened by an older and more dangerous gang, the Jackals, about whom we knew a lot more. Now he'd disappeared.

We spoke to the leader of the Jackals, a vicious little scrote who was probably capable of murder if someone else cleaned up after him. He claimed not to know who the missing boy was. We had no evidence. Carla wasn't able to say where the body might be, though we went round a few parks and waste grounds with dogs. We suspected Denny had done a runner and Carla was covering for him. But we didn't have the heart to accuse her of wasting police time. She was a thin, dark-eyed girl with spiky hair and a fragile loneliness that encased her like a shell.

A fortnight after we'd stopped looking for the missing boy, I had the first dream. I was with Carla in a ruined factory somewhere, open to the sky. There was a new moon. I dug with a spade through weeds and loose soil, took out a few shattered bricks, found a package wrapped in newspaper. In the moonlight, I began to unwrap it. Carla's fingernails gripped my arm. I woke up shivering, though it was only October.

That night was the beginning of something for me. I knew that it would be stupid to tell my colleagues about the dream—but at the same time, that I had to do something. Carla's passive face glimmered at the edge of my vision. The next day, I phoned her. She knew the place from my description: it was in Tyseley, just off the Grand Union Canal.

We went there after midnight. I was living alone, so there was no need for an excuse. Just as I'd dreamt, I dug up a buried newspaper package. This time, I unwrapped it. Thinking of 'pass the parcel' games in junior school. It contained the hand of a young man—drained white, but not in the least decayed. Carla took it from me, wrapped it again, and kissed me on the mouth. Then she walked away, leaving me to replace the soil and fragments of brick in the ground.

About a month later, I had a second dream. Another place I didn't know. Trees on the edge of a flooded running track, behind a decaying wall of red stone blocks. The same pale sliver of moon. Carla watched me dig in the marshy soil and uncover another small package. I felt her breath on my face.

Once again, I called her and she knew where it was. Near the university, behind some tenement houses where students lived. Because the running track was in a valley, the rising water table had made it a swamp. There was a strong odour of decay and unclean growth. But once again, what I found was perfectly preserved: the pale, narrow foot of a boy. Carla's kiss left me as frustrated as if I had woken up, though I was still in a moonlit landscape that seemed unreal. I wondered if it belonged to her memory.

The next time was a railway bridge in Digbeth: another foot. Then where a narrow river came above ground: a buried arm. It was always an abandoned place, and there was always a new moon. I was so keen to dream that I wasn't sleeping well, and Carla was in my mind all the time. But she wouldn't see me except when I'd dreamed about finding more of Denny. I asked her if she was keeping the pieces together. She said: 'They're not just pieces. He's coming back.'

Carla had a baby son she said was Denny's. I heard him crying a few times when I phoned her, and I saw them together one time when our paths crossed in the Bull Ring market. It was strange to see her so bound up with normality. The only thing that kept my obsession with her in check was how desperately busy we were that year.

There was a rising level of street crime, some of it linked to the Jackals. Their leader was killed in a fight, but an even nastier piece of work replaced him. Things seemed to be on the edge of a chaos no police work could unravel.

Every month, another bitter dream. Another date with Carla in a place that she knew and I didn't. Another newspaper-wrapped part of her boyfriend. Another brief kiss that brought me no closer to her. I thought of something I'd read in college: the hermeneutic circle of learning, how you reached the whole through the parts and the parts through the whole. The hands, feet, arms, calves, thighs, and then a torso with the penis cleanly severed. Almost a year of madness.

Finally, it was October again. She led me through the Vyse Street cemetery to a half-circle of stone ridges that was strangely like a Greek theatre. I could hear water running underground. There was a disused air raid shelter here, I knew. Long rats crept through the grass between headstones. At the heart of the structure, I saw a ruined vault. This time I didn't need to dig: the package could be reached through a break in the stone. No creature had interfered with it. I peeled away the layers of newsprint from the unblemished face. His eyes were still in place, seeing. This time I walked away. Not wanting to see how Carla looked at her lover's head. Then I felt her hand on my arm. I turned. She embraced me, pressed her open mouth against mine. We stood together for a few seconds.

Then she said: 'There's still one part missing.'

'I don't think that's going to turn up,' I answered. Carla shrugged. 'It's always the way.'

A cloud slipped over the moon like a scarf over a

damaged face. 'What's going to happen now?' I asked.

She paused, uncertain. 'Denny and I will go away together. He's back now. The balance is restored. But we can't stay here.' She looked back to where Denny's head was waiting in its cradle of local news. Then she turned back to me. 'You'll meet him again,' she said. 'And he'll be fair to you. Because you helped.'

At the time, I thought she was talking about the police's dealings with the Falcons. It wasn't until years later that I realised she might have meant something quite different. She was, after all, mad. But I think about what she said more and more these days. Sometimes it's all the comfort I have.

THE HOSTESS

Not long after I moved to Birmingham in the 1980s, a family feud led to one of the worst crimes in my experience. It happened in Digbeth, an old industrial district now taken over by warehouses and wholesale businesses. The narrow backstreets and rotting factories hid a multitude of stolen goods. But most of the actual crimes happened elsewhere. The Digbeth police station was busier with drunks fighting in the Barrel Organ and the Railway Tavern than with professional villains.

For two decades, the O'Kane family had been significant players in the black economy of Digbeth. They were a family of craftsmen: one could hide the pieces of a stolen car in another dozen vehicles, another could work stolen gold and silver into brand new jewellery. Three of them had done time, but they were a close family and we'd have needed something much nastier to put them out of business. I think the Digbeth team had a sneaking respect for their dedicated work on the wrong side of the disused tracks.

The Marin family were something else again. New money, well-spoken, an attitude you could break a glass on. The three brothers formed the core of an under-achieving but vicious gang that specialised in drugs and prostitutes. Its informal office was the back table of Bar Selona, a dive frequented by people who'd been banned from the Little Moscow. There were some severe beatings around that time, of men we knew to be involved in similar business. But the victims weren't talking even when their mouths healed.

I saw the youngest Marin brother one night in the Railway Tavern, when I was relaxing off duty at a rhythm and blues gig. The band finished late, and when I came out of the function room a lock-in was in progress. I might have been tempted to buy a drink, but just at that moment a thin-faced man in a suit entered the pub in the company of a young policewoman. Who wasn't, of course. It was some lad's birthday, and the girl put handcuffs on him before starting a strip-tease. I walked out, but the girl's minder shot me a look that could have frozen vodka.

We had an informer at that time who warned us that the Marin and O'Kane families were at odds. There was a fight outside a pub near the Parcel Force depot that resulted in a close ally of the O'Kanes being glassed: a classic 'Belfast kiss'. He lost an eye. Then the house of the elder Marin brother burned down when he and his wife were away for the weekend. We found the charred remnants of a petrol-soaked blanket inside a broken rear window. Just after that, something scared our informant so badly that he relocated to the Netherlands.

THE HOSTESS

While we were struggling to get to grips with the situation, Theresa O'Kane went missing on her ninth birthday. She was the only daughter of one of the family's more law-abiding members. He and his wife didn't hesitate to call us. Theresa had been walking home from her school in Highgate with a friend when a car had stopped and two men had got out. One of them had hit the friend with a cosh, and she'd blacked out. When she'd recovered consciousness Theresa was gone.

That night, we put out an appeal on local TV and radio. Nothing. A day of frantic searching and questioning followed. The Marin brothers didn't have perfect alibis—that would have been too obvious—but we had nothing on them. Another night fell with Theresa's parents—both of whom were under thirty—in a state of numb desperation. Then another dark November day. Another night.

The call came at six in the morning. A homeless man, looking for a place to sleep, had wandered through the viaduct off Digbeth High Street after a troubled night. The mewing of seagulls had caught his attention. Behind one of the arches, near the porn cinema, he'd found a heap of dead rats and a few dying gulls. There was an acrid smell in the air. Using a stick, he'd pushed the rats aside—and then run to a phone box.

Theresa O'Kane had been garrotted with wire. Her body cavity had been opened up, packed with rat poison and sewn shut again. Poison had also been forced into her mouth and throat. We were shown post-mortem photos. The body had only been under the viaduct a few hours, but our pathologist estimated the time of death as the evening of the abduction. She hadn't made it through her birthday.

27

Of course, the murder was in the papers for weeks—though we managed to keep the rat poison quiet. The O'Kane family had to go through the standard press cycle of bogus sympathy, suspicion, revelation, blame, abuse and final indifference. Twenty-eight-per-cent of *Daily Mail* readers thought the O'Kanes were tragic victims, while seventy-two-per-cent thought their criminal record was directly responsible for the child's death. It was business as usual: the memory of a dead child being falsified, mass-produced and put to work on the streets.

Small wonder that the O'Kane family sold their homes and were scattered overseas before the end of the year. The Marins continued their operations. We never managed to prove their connection to the murder, let alone the vicious symbolic gesture that followed it. But within a couple of years, we had some luck with their drugs racket and put the two elder brothers away. They weren't sufficiently big-time to own the police or local authorities. Then the youngest brother died of a septic ulcer, and the gang was finished. Other bastards replaced them, of course.

Years passed. I moved to the Acocks Green station and lost interest in Digbeth. The area slipped further into silence, with old houses and even churches being used as storage space for construction materials. As rents fell and concern for preservation became increasingly absurd, the ground was laid for the area's colonisation by offices—but that was still a decade off. Turf wars were still going on: pubs were set on fire, building projects were subject to overnight 'accidents'. The only people living in the district were in hostels or on the streets.

I'm not sure when it started. Some time in the early nineties. We thought it was one of the new gangs making its presence felt. An old man who'd been drinking in the Eagle and Tun was found dead in Lower Trinity Street, a few yards from one of the arches of the railway viaduct. Two days later, a homeless woman was seen dying in convulsions under the railway bridge by the Taboo cinema. Both deaths were the result of strychnine poisoning. Which could be rat poison, though we found no sign of it in the area.

A week after that, three children aged nine or so were found dead. They'd been playing with a ball in a disused car park near the Digbeth viaduct. Again, it was strychnine. Some of the powder was smeared on their mouths. The local police station went into overdrive, trying to find a drug dealer who might have sold them (or given them) a wrap of painful death. They arrested every addict they could find. It was late October. A few days before Theresa O'Kane's birthday.

Childhood memories are strange things. Who can predict when a buried memory will come to the surface and cause harm? It could be at puberty, or on leaving home, or after a broken marriage, or after the loss of a child. And when the trauma is profound enough to tear you out of the world... what then? I'm not de Richleau, I don't have those certainties. The best I can do is guesswork. There was no way I could banish Theresa, unless I could stop the ruthless from controlling others. But maybe I could make her back off. We kept a police watch on the viaduct, and no-one was going there at night any more. At three a.m. we packed up and left the poorly lit brickwork to whatever crept in the shadows, picking over scraps of litter. An hour later, I came back alone. Wearing a black tracksuit, surgical gloves and a scarf over my face. Under the scarf, I was wearing a flesh-toned latex mask I'd got from a Soho colleague with underground contacts. The eyes and mouth were narrow slits.

A half-moon was just visible through a skin of cloud. There was frost on the pavement. Miles away, fireworks were slamming doors in the night. I paused under the bridge where the homeless woman had died. Rain had drawn spikes of lime from the brickwork. Then I walked slowly on, past the private cinema to the viaduct.

From the pub in Lower Trinity Street, you can see three railway arches. I stood in one of them and lit a cigarette, then dropped it and stamped it out. A trace of smoke filtered through the cold air. The smell of rotting brick was overwhelming. About twenty yards away, against the wall, a Victorian iron urinal had been closed up for decades. She was standing there, watching me. Her face was slightly out of focus, as if one of us was shivering.

I waited under the viaduct, cupping my hands over my mouth to trap the warmth. She was hesitant, but determined. It was her birthday and no- one else had come. *Did they tell you it was a surprise party?* I thought. Her hair was dark and tangled. Her face was as white as the frost. Her school blouse and skirt were torn and smeared with oil or tarmac. As she moved towards me, looking sick, I held out my arms. Then I turned my face so her lips would touch my cheek.

Her small hand pressed into mine. I felt her grip more as a purpose than as a sensation, since her hand was as weak as fresh snow. Her mouth fastened on the slick non-flesh of the mask. Then she let go of me. Her face closed in on itself, flickered like old celluloid. I watched her turn and walk slowly away, back into the shadows of the industrial estate.

When there was no further sign of movement on the street, I peeled off the mask and gloves and slipped them carefully into a plastic bag. I'd dusted them with strychnine powder before putting them on. I wasn't sure if I'd told her a kind of lie or a kind of truth. Either way, she'd got the message.

There were no more unexplained deaths in the Digbeth area for a while. A few more children died from poisoning, but that was just a result of the amount of toxic waste in the ground. If police work teaches you anything, it's that gradual death is very rarely a crime.

BLUE SMOKE

You expect homeless alcoholics to disappear. They die in hidden places, die and are not identified, or move on and start again. In any district, the drunks come and go. But when a lot of them disappear at once, you start to worry. The younger ones might be recruited by pimps or the Jesus Army. But the older ones have no market value. Their harvesting would mean the unknown, which is never good.

In the winter of 1989, when Eastern Europe was in turmoil and the papers were declaring the end of Communism, we noticed a sudden fall in the number of street incidents involving drunks. At first, we assumed the winter was forcing them to take shelter, or killing them. But the hospitals and social services told us they weren't turning up anywhere. And it wasn't a national thing. The Salvation Army confirmed that something was taking away the city's drifters.

That was the last year I worked in Digbeth, the old industrial district just south of the city centre. At that time, before the cheap offices and the media companies, it was a lifeless place: derelict factories, empty canals and a disused railway. Buildings were cheap, so people just took over what was available: I remember houses filled up with bricks, a ruined church used to store loose scaffolding. Many of the streets had Victorian urinals, all sealed up.

Apart from night shift workers and a few prostitutes, the only people there at night were homeless. So, when they began to disappear, the sense of desertion was hard to ignore. We went out looking for them, walking in a ghost landscape coated with frost and ice, with dark patches under the bridges. The mounds of wrecked cars in the scrapyards could have been Egyptian tombs. For some reason, the streetlights reflected from the frosted pavement had streaks of blue. I spoke to a tiny old woman sheltering under a corrugated iron roof; she told me 'the monks' had taken all the drinkers for 'their church'.

Then an off-licence on Digbeth High Street was robbed in the early hours of the morning. Only bottles of spirits were taken, including many from the back of the shop. The robbers drove a car through the front window, scattering glass over the roadway, then loaded up the car and raced away before the alarm summoned the police. It was hard to believe they'd gone to so much trouble just for some alcohol. The shopkeeper said a group of men had spent some time in the shop that day—'looking around, like they was in a dream'. They hadn't bought anything, and he suspected they'd had enough already. 'Smelt of booze. Four of them. Wearing old clothes, with shaved heads. Didn't say a word.'

Perhaps these were the 'monks' the old woman had seen. If so, it was a new kind of gang. It felt like something I'd been waiting for. There'd been a few too many nights down the pub recently—and cans emptied while alone, listening to the stereo, in my tiny flat. Since coming to Birmingham I'd met Elaine, who would later become my wife. It was the first time I'd experienced how being in a relationship can leave you feeling unreal whenever you're on your own.

We'd had an argument after visiting her parents (they didn't like me having a 'dangerous' job, I resented their influence over Elaine) and agreed not to see each other for a few weeks. I was caught between anger and pain. My body seemed more determined to remember her than my mind was. The only thing that could dampen the fire was alcohol, because it let me dream while I was awake— or rather, it turned the world into a dream, something beautiful and silent and long dead.

A few times, I got drunk with a colleague called Terry. He was an Irish Brummie, and his outlook was a dark blend of faith and disillusionment that struck a chord with me. He was fond of saying that the only purpose of this world was to make us ready for the next. We drank in the Irish pubs scattered around Digbeth and Highgate: quiet places where white-haired men listened to rebel songs and the air was stained with loss.

One night in December we were drifting from one Digbeth pub to another, ending up in a lock-in at the Railway Tavern. We recognised half of the drinkers from recent arrests, but no-one said anything. There was a strange mood in the pub: no fights, no loud arguments, just people sharing memories or staring into the past, not even seeing the glasses they drank from. A few people sang old songs I'd never heard before, about murder and ghosts. I told Terry I'd seen a few things I couldn't explain over the years. He said everyone did, but they made themselves forget.

When we finally left the pub, snow was falling. Gusts of wind threw handfuls of sharp flakes at the cars and streetlights. Every surface was covered with the same raw white skin. I could see the blue light trapped under it, like a bruise. The drinkers staggered off in twos or threes, holding each other up. The falling snow erased their footprints. I tasted a flake on my tongue: it was frozen vodka. I fell to my knees and raised my hands to catch the falling snow.

A voice behind me said: 'In the next world, the snow is vodka. The rain is gin, the dew is wine. Come with me, I'll show you how to find it.' I turned my head. A short man, either bald or with a shaven head, was staring at me. His eyes were so dark they could have been missing.

Terry was kneeling by the gutter. He wiped his mouth and stood up. 'Follow me,' the monk said. 'I'll show you the blue light, the light hidden from the world.' His lips weren't moving, but I could hear his voice clearly in my head. Terry looked at me, nodded. The monk turned and led us away from the high street, towards the end of the road. My breath was freezing on my lips. I felt sure this was a journey I wouldn't return from. It didn't matter.

We walked for a long time, through narrow streets that only damage opened up. Snow drifted like confetti through broken windows and exposed roofbeams. The wind picked up, carrying the smell of rotting brick. We passed a boarded-up pub, the Blue Moon, whose sign was a blacked-out circle.

On the steps of an abandoned hostel, a heap of blankets had frozen to an empty cast. Tarpaulins flapped on scaffolding frames, holding up faces of mould.

We saw other people on the streets: men in shabby clothes, with shaven heads where snowflakes gleamed like scars. They were walking clumsily, as if with great effort, all headed in the same direction. Under the still waves of snow, the pavement was badly cracked and pitted. I blew into my hands, felt nothing. The monk was walking a few steps ahead, patches of snow crusted on his dark coat. Terry and I followed. We didn't speak.

The landscape we were walking through seemed less and less like a place where people had once lived or worked. There was no traffic on the roadway; the only cars were rusted hulks filling up with snow. The buildings looked somehow unfinished, with no loose bricks or exposed structures to suggest a past. The only road signs I saw had been burned to anonymity. Monks were all around us now; as we merged with a group of them, I realised they were not completely silent. Very weakly, as if lacking vocal cords, they were chanting.

At last, we came to a shelter: an old church that still had most of its roof, though there was no glass in its narrow windows. Ahead of us, monks were going in through the open doorway. As we stepped through into the nave, where candles were flickering on the mould-streaked walls, a monk handed each of us a small empty glass. Most of the pews, which were splintered and swollen with damp, were occupied by dark-coated men with shaven heads. Their eyes were fixed on the altar, where some kind of paraffin lamp was burning: a shimmering blue flame rose above the stained wood. Behind the altar was a table covered with sealed bottles.

Snow was falling through the gaps in the roof, settling on the heads and hands of the worshippers. It didn't melt. I could hear the chanting more clearly now, but I couldn't see any breath freezing in front of their blank faces. The glass in my hand seemed full of my own failure and loss. I needed a drink more badly than I had ever needed anything. How long would I have to wait? The last few monks took their places in the rotting pews. I stared at the blue flame, wondering why no warmth seemed to come from it.

We waited for a long time. Terry and I were shivering. Then the same two monks who'd stood inside the doorway picked up bottles and walked up and down the pews, filling the outstretched glasses. They ignored a man near the front, who I noticed did not have a shaven head, though he was balding. They walked past me and Terry as well, though they served the monk who'd been our guide. I felt like screaming for a drink. It was some kind of blue-tinted spirit; I could smell it, despite the general reek of paraffin and decay, and it made me ache inside.

Finally, all the monks raised their glasses in unison and steadily drained them. The two officiants, who looked no different from the others—this was a nonconformist sect, I realised—returned to the altar. One of them beckoned to the man near the front who'd been denied a drink. He stood up and made his way stiffly over the snow-covered tiles towards them. Then he knelt before the altar.

An officiant raised a glass of the blue spirit to the edge of the flame. As the liquid started to burn, he poured it over the worshipper's silent face. Blue flames ran over him, charring his clothes, burning off his hair. When he stood up, his face was eyeless and blackened. One of the monks filled a glass and placed it in his hand. He poured its contents into the lipless crater of his mouth. Slowly, the ashes turned white and flaked away like fresh snow. The face beneath them was smooth, bald and without expression. Only the eyes still held the darkness of what the fire had left behind. He went back to his seat.

One of the celebrants looked towards me and Terry, then gestured. Behind them, the blue flame trembled like a pure mountain stream. I felt myself standing up, beginning to move towards the centre aisle. Terry grabbed my arm. 'No.' He pulled me back. We swayed for a moment, in balance. The monks around us sat dead still, facing the altar. I felt a thread of bile rising through my gut; its bitter taste filled my mouth. 'Come on,' Terry said. I couldn't move my feet. He linked his arm with mine and half- steered, half-dragged me to the door, lifted the latch, pushed me out into the snow-covered street. I fell to my knees and was violently sick. A line from an old song played over and over in my head: *Though our eyes were open, they might just as well have been closed.*

Three days later, before the snow had melted, a police squad raided the derelict church and found over fifty bottles of gin, vodka and white rum, all adulterated with a blue substance that turned out to be a mild hallucinogenic drug, stashed away under the altar. The bottles had probably been stolen from the off-licence or elsewhere, but that was impossible to prove. Terry and I had reported finding an unlicensed drinking den. None of the monks were found.

In the spring, Elaine and I got married at the Broad Street registry office. Terry was among the guests. He moved to another station not long after and we kept in touch for years, but never discussed what had happened that night. Bad things are difficult to share. Later that year, the church was demolished.

After the long walk in the snow, I had frostbite and spent a day in hospital. There are white scars on my feet where the skin didn't grow back. That at least proves it happened, though I sometimes doubt my memory of what I saw—both that night and a week later, the first night I was back on the beat. It was four a.m. in Fazeley Street, by the canal. I hadn't been drinking.

What happened was simply that I saw a train go past, on the old railway line. It was a freight train, but people were standing in the carriages, packed together. The moonlight glinted from their bony heads and the bottles in their hands. They were leaving the city. Then I remembered that the railway line was derelict, had been for quite a few years. I stood there and watched the train fade into the distance. Dawn was a few hours away, but I could see a faint blue glow on the horizon.

For Alan Beard

BETH'S LAW

The face of a missing child on the front page of a newspaper is the most powerful symbol in the world. The mute appeal of that fragile smile lies in the scream we don't hear, the terror and pain we can't see. It proves the violation, in a single act, of every kind of privacy we know: the home, the family, the body, the mind. The text warps around the perfect image, becomes a kind of hieroglyphics. No other story merits a read. The rest of the newspaper becomes merely a hiding place for the abductor, a gallery of suspects and accessories.

And behind it all, there's what we know but can never say: that for every nameless predator lurking on the edge of the playground there are a hundred brutal assaults in the home, a hundred respectable fathers with their daughters' blood on their pricks. You won't learn that from the front page. What you'll learn is how, from the light in a missing child's eyes, to construct an identikit photo of the outsider who has taken her. Then, if you study the newspapers hard enough and listen hard enough to the word on the street, you'll learn the name of the dark god to whom the child was sacrificed.

Ten-year-old Elizabeth Kindling disappeared from outside her own house in Yardley, one Sunday morning in early November. She had no brothers or sisters. By lunchtime, her parents had called the police. Four of us spent the afternoon searching for her. It had rained overnight, and the streets were blotted with the imprints of dead leaves and newspapers. By evening, there were over forty police officers in the district. We searched the cemetery, the canal walkway, the Swan Centre. We alerted the local press, TV and radio. Every hour that passed took us further from hope and deeper into the well of media panic.

I knew the family liaison officer working on the case, and he was pretty sure the parents were genuine. Some leads involving school friends who sniffed lighter fuel or hung around with older kids got us nowhere. And there were no boyfriend issues. You'd be surprised how many ten-year-old girls these days are going through puberty, but Eliza hadn't got that far. By the start of the week, it was hard to believe that she would ever get the chance.

The local papers put out a recent photo of her with a request for anyone with information to contact the police. But when the tabloids picked up the story, they got an earlier photo from her school that showed Eliza with longer hair and a bright smile. They also decided that Beth sounded more English, hence more likely to win the hearts and minds of their readers. And it was the tabloids, not the local press, who first suggested that the child might have been abducted with some longer-term purpose in mind—slavery, ritual abuse or sacrifice. The police's failure to discover her body was taken as evidence in favour of this speculation. As a belief, it had the obvious advantage of implying that she might still be alive.

All of this had some impact on me personally, as I was one of the team trying to find Eliza's body. Other investigating officers pursued leads that might track down her killer or kidnapper. My team were more concerned with abandoned places. We dredged the local canals and the River Cole, searched the waste grounds and parks and forests with sniffer dogs, prowled around dumps and viaducts and disused railways. We found, in total, nine dead vagrants, two dead addicts (frozen in a last embrace under leaves and bracken on the Clent Hills) and—in one particular Edgbaston lake—the skeletons of more than a dozen newborn babies that had been there half a century or more. But we didn't find her.

At that time, Elaine and I had just bought a flat in Hall Green. Our daughter Julia was six months old. There didn't seem to be enough of anything: sleep, time, money, attention. Every night was a struggle, in more ways than one. I used to wake up twisted in the duvet, sweating, unable to remember what I'd been dreaming about. A few times, Elaine said I'd pushed her out of bed in my sleep. We were both on edge, forgetting things all the time, so reliant on sex as a narcotic that we fucked even when we'd argued and regardless of whether it led to any reconciliation. It was a long, dark winter; the snow didn't settle, but the frost cut deep.

Early in the New Year, a small gypsy encampment in Warley began to draw the attention of the local press.

There were the usual stories of theft, drug dealing, seduction of local girls. The local council asked us to keep an eye on the encampment while they got rid of them through the court order and social services route. They didn't want a big showdown that would win public sympathy for the gypsies.

Nobody seems to know where the human sacrifice idea came from. A clever journalist? An impatient CID officer? A paranoid school governor? The sheer vagueness of it stopped anyone worrying about the lack of evidence. Sacrifice. For what reason? In whose name? The idea was in circulation for weeks before Beth's name was mentioned in connection with it. And when one of Warley's vicars gave a statement to the paper about the threat of paganism in music and TV, the rumour reached critical mass. Suddenly everyone knew that beth had been abducted by gypsies or other vagrants and sacrificed to the forces of darkness. That no real evidence pointed to this was as irrelevant as the fact that the child wasn't really called Beth.

Then the national press got involved. The *News of the World* published an eight-page feature on the ritual murder of children. Colin Wilson wrote an article about the links between anarchism and devil-worship. All over the country, members of Wiccan groups were named and their photos printed in the press, along with calls for them to lose their jobs and be prosecuted. Pressure was brought to bear on the West Midlands police, and we were in no position to resist. We broke up the gypsy encampment, made every drug-related arrest possible, constructed a DNA and fingerprint database of travellers that was correlated with national data. We found nothing significant.

By early spring, the press had focused their suspicions into a demand for what they called Beth's Law: a policy of zero tolerance towards Romanies and other travellers, enforced through internment and the seizure of caravans. The Midlands paper that was most passionate in its advocacy of Beth's Law was owned by a man whom we were investigating for links to sex traffic. We had to drop our case against him because the key witnesses, a few dozen young women from Russia, were threatened with disfigurement if they appeared in court.

In June of that year, a traveller group in transit was attacked one night and their caravans set on fire. Nine of them died, including two children. Some of the papers hinted that the children might have been prisoners. But they weren't. The police investigation into the attack fizzled out, and I heard at the time that a few millions in hush money had been paid to the local authorities by landowners who were campaigning for Beth's Law. After that, things quietened down. But by then, I'd seen the ritual and understood what was going on in a different way.

I've never liked the clocks going forward. It always feels like waking up after too much drinking and not being able to remember what happened. For me and Elaine, the lack of sleep and inability to relax just reached a crisis at that time.

Between us, we'd forgotten to put the clock forward and I was late for a Sunday shift. We had no time to make love. Elaine slipped over me in bed, trying to hold me down. I pushed her away so hard her shoulder struck the headboard. Then I took hold of her, saying I was sorry, but she wouldn't look at me. I kissed her and suddenly we were locked together, and then I was inside her.

In the next room, Julia woke up and began to cry. She sounded panicked. Elaine tried to pull away, but I wouldn't stop or let her go. She froze, as if I'd assaulted her. I stopped, got out of bed, showered and dressed, then left without a word. She never quite seemed to trust me after that.

Sometimes I think police work is all about trying to make up for what we don't understand or can't cope with. But of course we twist it back to front, try to model our own lives on police work. And so we go from living in fear to thinking fear is the world. The cry of a child is echoed in the wailing of sirens, and in the droning of military aircraft.

Near the end of April, we heard a rumour about a ritualistic cult meeting on an inner-city estate. One of our junkie informants, a man called Jensen, was claiming knowledge of a planned May Eve sacrifice. But his personal credibility wasn't high enough for us to treat his word as gospel. He was OK on specific things, like who had sold how much smack to whom, for how much, and at what degree of impurity. But when it came to the bigger picture, he was in a world of his own.

DI Scully asked me to meet with Jensen on the night in question and find out what, if anything, was going on. I suspected he was asking me because I'd been involved in a couple of 'weird' cases, and could be trusted to take the whole thing seriously. Perhaps he expected me to prevent the sacrifice by shouting the last two lines of the Samsara ritual. I said that if anything were really going on, we'd need a team to break it up. He said that would be too conspicuous.

We compromised by assigning three plainclothes officers, including me, to turn up armed. That would be enough to interfere—and a squad car would wait a couple of minutes away. If the whole thing turned out to be bullshit, we'd stop using Jensen—which meant he'd be fair game for prosecution by the drug squad. We knew he wouldn't set us up. A word from us in the wrong ear, and he'd be fulfilling a lifetime ambition: to swallow his own cock.

My preliminary meeting with Jensen took place in the Lickey Hills, at his insistence: a walk along the stubbled cheekbone of Rednal, far enough from his usual territory to avoid being seen or heard. Even so, he kept stopping and looking around as if his enemies might be stalking us from behind the trees. Jensen was a skinny, bald man in his thirties who worked in a Nechells pub as a glass-collector and bouncer. He giggled when nervous, which was all the time. We walked through a landscape in which moss-coated trees held up curtains of foliage, studded with glittering raindrops.

'It's on the Lee Bank estate,' he said. 'One of the condemned buildings. The niggers and Pakis use it for pimping and drug dealing. They got mattresses there so you don't have to lie on all the broken needles and used condoms. Some of the nigger whores have left their newborn pick'nies there for the rats to chew on. That's how the place started to pick up an aura of blood. A power born of corruption. Certain people found out about it, and money changed hands.'

I'd been warned that Jensen usually talked like this. None the less, as we passed a stinking pool on the edge of the slope, I had to make a conscious effort not to shove him in. 'This is the big one,' he said. 'They've got an Aryan

47

virgin. You know who I'm talking about.' He smirked. 'Couldn't be an estate girl. No Aryans on Lee Bank, and no virgins either.'

I bit my lip. 'Where are they keeping her?'

'Who knows? Some caravan somewhere. Back room. Narrow-boat. A safe house full of asylum seekers. If I find out, I'll tell you.'

'I bet Dyson wishes he had you as a contact.'

'That fucker owes me money,' Jensen said without missing a beat. 'That reminds me, tell DI Hargrave I wants payment in advance for this.'

'I'm not sure she trusts you. Can't imagine why.'

Jensen shivered and clutched his ribs. 'I don't like it out here. But at least it's safe.' I glanced at his face; he was beginning to sweat. 'Never mind the advance,' he said. 'Fifty will do for now.'

I gave him a twenty. We walked down the steep incline to the road, where I left him waiting for the bus. He wouldn't want a lift from a copper, and I wouldn't want him in my car. 'May Eve,' he said as I turned away.

May Eve was the Sunday night before the bank holiday. A cold, rain- drenched pit of a night. Even the infamous King George pub on the edge of the Lee bank estate wasn't bothering with a lock-in. I had two junior officers, McMahon and Bestwick, with me. They weren't heavies— we weren't keen to attract attention—but they could be handy in a crisis. Jensen was giggling almost silently between his teeth. Most of the tower blocks on the estate were blacked out, tarpaulins over their windows, ready for demolition. They'd been like that for years.

The tower block Jensen had identified as the temple of sacrifice was called Marvell House. It was barely identifiable as a building. Scaffolding was crusted over the lower floors, holding up a tattered skin of tarpaulins. The upper floors had been gutted by a fire some time ago. Jensen showed us the concealed point of entry, where some loose boarding covered the doorway to the lower fire escape. A few bare stone steps led down to the basement. There was a faint smell of Domestos and rat urine, a combination I recognised from my years in cheap lodgings.

Having shown us how to get in, Jensen fucked off home to his needles and his stories. I felt slightly envious. Why couldn't I be at home tonight, mending my relationship with Elaine? Or if I had to witness a pagan ritual, why couldn't it be in a starlit field rather than a reeking basement? Even without the rain, you'd never see the stars above central Birmingham. There's too much light pollution.

The plan was remarkably simple. Wait in the basement. If anyone else came, stop them. If necessary, phone for back-up. What we would do if nothing happened had been only lightly touched upon, but McMahon had sensibly brought along a flask of black coffee. No biscuits, but the atmosphere wasn't conducive to hunger. As Jensen had said, there were mattresses down there. It was easy to believe that birth and death had taken place there with the same mechanical regularity as the heating and cooling of the dusty boiler in the corner of the room.

A couple of hours, at least, went past. We crouched by the boiler, listening to the faint static of the rain. From time to time, we smoked to overcome the smell that filled my head with multiple, confusing images: a litter of rats, a human foetus, a mop soaked in bleach, a torn condom, a bloodstained hand, a decaying gull. A quick check with a pocket-torch early on had revealed nothing too grim; but now I wondered what had been hiding under the rotten mattresses, stiff blankets and scraps of tinfoil. Perhaps the darkness had been shifting around the light. Guarding its secrets. There were a few whispered attempts at conversation, but all our voices sounded like Jensen and after a while it was less disturbing to keep silent.

I remember thinking the damp had got into my bones, because I felt painfully tired and weak. I could see flickers of blue in the darkness, as if a number of lights were moving a long way off. And then there was a sound, only yards away from us: something moving awkwardly over the floor. I reached for my torch, expecting to see a dog. Minutes went past while my hand refused to move. The lights slowly brightened, forming a ragged circle in the middle of the basement. On either side of me, my colleagues were awake, watching.

In the centre of the circle of lights, a small figure was trying to hide between two ripped and swollen mattresses. It had the form of a naked child, but its flesh seemed to be made entirely of torn and wadded newsprint. Blurred photos gave its head something like eyes and a mouth. I had the feeling it was trying to cry out, but had no lungs. It cringed, waving a grey arm above its head, as the wavering blue lights closed in.

I could make even less sense of the thin glowing figures whose light exposed the child. Something in their bent posture suggested hunger; but there was no substance to them, nothing but edges. They lifted the child between them and slowly tore it apart, cutting away layer on layer of newsprint to reveal only smaller versions of the same thing: an infant, a baby, an embryo. The blue light faded slowly, until complete darkness filled the basement.

I felt my hand rising with the torch, switching it on. The two mattresses at the centre of the floor were covered in shreds of damp newspaper like a rat's nest. A few random, indecipherable scraps of a headline were stuck to the fabric like a nearly-erased epitaph. The image came to me of the papier-mâché head I'd made in infant school: features clumsily shaped over a wire skull and left to dry. Dark print showing through a whitish skin of water-paint.

We talked in the dark for a while, but none of us had anything useful to say. The only thing we were sure about was that we had no basis for a report. Somehow we stayed there until dawn, taking comfort from our shared inaction. Then I phoned the station, and we took off. The gaunt windowless buildings of Lee Bank seemed unreal when you could see the city centre beyond them: cars streaming down the expressway, cranes reaching into a sky tinged with an unexpectedly deep blue.

Our cars were parked near the Bull Ring. Bestwick and McMahon went back to the station. I went home to a hungry child, a frightened wife, and a sense of deadness that took years to wear off.

A CUP OF BLOOD

Recovery of stolen goods is difficult enough, without asking awkward questions about who the goods really belong to. And the places some things turn up, you wouldn't believe. Back in the early nineties, when I was a Detective Sergeant based in West Bromwich, we had a burglary reported by a man who was a known handler of stolen goods.

We thought it was a great joke; but really, the joke was on us.

His name was Craig Furniss. We knew he was involved with a theft ring, probably fencing stolen antiques for European collectors; but it was hard to make anything stick. We were keeping an eye on his Warley home, so it was a bit of an embarrassment to us when he phoned the station. Apparently, someone had broken in and taken the contents of a display case. Antique pottery, glassware and stuff, mostly foreign. He was upset.

Two of us went out to his house. Furniss was a little fat man whose face needed a moustache but didn't have one. The thief had broken in through a skylight, probably at night, and used the loft to store things collected from downstairs during the morning. He'd cut himself breaking open the display case, since blood was streaked on the carpet; but by the time he'd gone back up the stairs, the wound had been covered up.

For a collector, Furniss was pretty vague about some of the stuff he'd lost. He said the most important things had been in his family for two or three generations. Especially a crystal drinking goblet which he described as 'quite heavy, like hollow quartz—maybe Greek or Armenian, I'm not sure'. My superior, DI Heyward, asked if he'd had them valued. He said they were insured for ten thousand pounds—'but it's not the monetary value, you understand. It's their meaning: history, continuity. Things these thieving scum will never understand.' His swollen lip wavered. We said we'd let him know.

Back at the station, Heyward asked me: 'What do you think he's up to?' I gave him a blank look. 'That cunt probably knows every dodgy antiques and jewellery racket in the West Midlands. If he hasn't got a state-of-the-art security system, it's because he thinks no-one would dare to rob him. But now some gormless local kid who's never heard of Furniss has broken in and taken some stuff. Not even that valuable. Do you really think, with his contacts, he can't get it back? We're being used for something.' He rubbed his nose thoughtfully. 'But if we keep our eyes open, maybe we can turn it to our advantage.' I tried to look like nothing would get past me.

In those days, Elaine and I were still in love. Our daughter Julia was two years old. We had a house in Handsworth, just off the Soho Road: a mostly Asian area. Every day, I drove up the long tree-lined road past the Hawthorns (the West Bromwich Albion ground) and through the huge elevated roundabout that linked two major expressways. Hawthorns, Albion, crossroads: no doubt it had all seemed magical once. West Bromwich itself is a small industrial town with a long history, though its centre has been stripped out and replaced with the kind of identikit shopping mall you can find in any new town. What people think of as the Brummie accent actually comes from West Bromwich.

One bright morning in April, three days after the theft of Craig Furniss' glassware collection, I turned off at the high roundabout and followed the expressway north-west into Oldbury. The skyline was dominated by grey tower blocks that housed any number of ex-cons and problem families on the Social Services crisis list. But I was looking for the older part of town.

Hart lived in a cosy Victorian semi with leaded windows. He was nearing retirement age. In the doorway, he glanced anxiously past me. 'The car's parked half a mile away,' I reassured him.

'Unlike your face.' He led me through the naphthalene-scented hallway to a living room full of bookcases. 'Is this a social call? Only I'm fresh out of Earl Grey. Old Mrs Cherrington next door has had most of it.'

'Good fences make good neighbours.' I pulled a list from my coat pocket. 'You wouldn't know anything about glassware?'

'Well, I'm not an expert. But I know what I like.' He put on a pair of reading glasses and scanned the list. 'Mmm-hmm. Have you tried a car boot sale?'

'This lot was insured for ten thousand. Sentimental value.'

'You've touched my heart,' the old man said. 'I don't remember any crystal goblet. Decanter type thing, or just a cup?' He scribbled a couple of names on the back of the list and gave it to me. 'Must be something. The rest wasn't worth a grand.'

'Family heirloom. Apparently.'

'Didn't think Mr F had much idea who his parents were.' Hart looked thoughtful. 'Maybe it's not exactly what he says it is. It's got to be worth a lot more than the insurance for him to come running to you. Maybe he wants you to find out where it went, and he'll do the rest.'

'What do you think it might be?'

'Well now. Didn't the original World Cup go missing?'

'The Albion not doing so well then? There's always a link between deprivation and fantasy.' I pocketed the list. 'Cheers. We'll be in touch.'

'I'll get some more tea in,' he said, a little sourly. 'Do you know, I don't know why I do this. Every time the phone rings, I feel like I'm in prison.' He looked out through the leaded panes; the narrow street was flooded with sunlight, like a chain of gold.

Four days later, a fisherman discovered a body in the canal between West Bromwich and Oldbury. It turned out to be a teenage boy called Steve Wain. There were two bullet wounds in his chest. His blood type matched the sample found in Furniss' house. His name was one of the two that Hart had given us; we'd been looking for him. At once, we pulled in Furniss for questioning. He told us nothing.

Part of the problem was we couldn't be sure that Wain

had burgled his house. One thing seemed to prove that he hadn't: the burglar had evidently cut himself on broken glass, but there were no recent cuts on the body. He had a thin scar down the side of his face, but scars don't form in a week. His parents didn't remember the scar; but they hadn't seen him since Christmas. He had a record for shoplifting and petty theft, spent six months in a juvenile detention centre just after leaving school. 'Maybe he had it coming,' Wain's father said.

The other name Hart gave us was an antiques dealer in Stourbridge. Some of the stuff in his shop would have given Hugh Scully heart failure: gold-leaf etching or motifs that were totally inappropriate to the original makers. We found almost all of Furniss' stuff in a crate in the dealer's attic, some of it damaged. By now, I could have predicted what piece we wouldn't find. If it existed at all.

We kept Furniss under arrest for two days, but it was a waste of time. Most of what we had on him, we didn't want him to know about. 'I don't get it,' Heyward said to me in his office some time after midnight. 'If he sent his men after Wain, why did he go to us first?'

'Maybe he didn't plan to sort it out himself. But then force of habit took over. And I still don't think he's got what he wanted. Those two bullets are a sign of frustration.'

'Mmm. I thought this missing cup must be full of heroin. But if so, why the fuck does he want *us* to find it?'

'Maybe it won't let itself be found by him.'

Heyward stared wearily at me. 'What are you talking about?'

'I don't know,' I said. 'I'm tired. Need some sleep.'

*

It was a frustrating summer. The Wain murder enquiry was going nowhere, and Furniss seemed to be cutting down his enterprises and breaking his links with the bigger boys. Maybe we'd already missed our chance: if we tried to break his operation now, we'd sacrifice a whole network of contacts and informers. There was no point. It wasn't like we had time on our hands. Every time I came home from a shift, Elaine would have a go at me about not helping with Julia. 'It's not enough to pay the mortgage, you know. This isn't a business, it's a family.' We weren't spending enough time together, but somehow the time we shared wasn't good. Some nights I'd sit up drinking until I was sure Elaine was asleep.

One morning she woke me up with a hard shove. 'What the fuck's happened?' I'd dropped a glass in the living room, left the spilt wine and broken glass on the carpet like a tapestry of a rose with jagged thorns coming out of it. 'This isn't just your house, you know,' she said. 'It's mine too. When you damage it, you're damaging my property.'

'It's not mine or yours,' I said hopelessly. 'It's ours.' Something in her eyes turned from bitter to sad. We looked at each other for a few seconds; then she crumpled a newspaper and handed it to me. I started collecting the fragments of glass.

Around that time, the *West Bromwich Courier* ran a series of articles on how the police were losing the war against crime. The fact that we'd arrested Furniss in connection with Wain's death was brought up. Furniss was quoted as saying: *It's always the victims of crime who get harassed by the police. My house was burgled, so I had to end up in custody.* Of course, Furniss and the editor of the *Courier* were big pals: they ran the local Conservative Association together. Most villains are Tories—most successful villains, anyway. You could imagine Thatcher writing fan letters to the Kray twins. Their ideologies were a perfect match: the only community was the family, with its private manor, its rules and its walls.

In September, an elderly vagrant called Peter Woodheath was found stabbed in the Sandwell Valley. He was known for getting into fights, and his grey-stubbled face was familiar to the A&E staff at Dudley Road Hospital. Which was where I drove one dark afternoon, puzzled by some details in his autopsy report. The clouds overhead were purple streaked with red, like wounds.

After looking through Woodheath's file, I spoke to a red-haired nurse with a badge marked KEVIN. 'He was in here twelve days ago,' he told me. 'I stitched up his face. Someone had glassed him. He was cut under one eye, upper lip, right cheek. Twenty-nine stitches in all. We were expecting him back this weekend to have them taken out. Though it was hardly a fixed appointment, given his situation. Poor old bastard. Any idea who did him?'

'Maybe.' I showed him the autopsy report. 'Read the bit about his face.'

'Fucking hell.' Kevin stared at the description: fine scars under the right eye, down the right cheek and across the upper lip, at least three months old. 'It's like he got months older in a few days. Can't be the same guy.'

'He was still wearing this.' I showed him the plastic hospital bracelet we'd found on Woodheath's wrist. Kevin shook his head slowly, then rubbed his eyes. He looked shattered.

Two hours later, I was in Hart's living room. He was still out of Earl Grey. 'I think they're onto me,' he said. 'I've been getting funny looks from Mr F's boys. Awkward questions. You'd better take me back with you. Arrest me. Then I can get the fear and tell them I'm out of it.'

'Fine,' I said. 'We'll throw in a few bruises and contusions if that will help. But there's a condition.' He shrugged, looking more apathetic than ever. 'I just want to know: is Furniss still chasing that missing cup?'

'Like it was his girlfriend's... punany, I believe is the current phrase. Nobody knows why. I've heard it ran away with a bunch of travellers.'

'Or maybe that was his girlfriend.'

'Don't know. Don't care.' He glanced at the window; rain covered it like a plastic sheet. 'He's had people beaten up, even killed. It's an obsession. You know Mr F. Strictly a small-time operator. Mr No-Mark. Mr Big in West Brom. This bloody cup of his has caused more trouble than you'd think he was capable of.'

'It's not his,' I said. 'And it never was. That's the problem.' Hart wasn't listening. He was pulling on a tweed jacket the colour of toxic waste, in preparation for his trip to the station.

As we drove off through pale curtains of rain, I thought I could see a fire under a canal bridge below street level. But it was probably the light in a factory basement, reflected in the dark surface of the water.

I was expecting Hart's body to be the next one found. But the fake arrest seemed to work. The next death wasn't one any of us were expecting. In late October, the Birmingham police discovered a man floating face down in a Hockley canal. He was dressed for sleeping rough: two old shirts, a ratty cardigan and a mackintosh. But he was carrying a driving license; the photo matched his face. It was Craig Furniss. He was clutching a gun in one hand. There were four bullets in it; the safety-catch was off. The cause of death was drowning, pure and simple.

The police who found him had been tipped off by a homeless man called Paul Cross, who was in hospital with a gunshot wound in his left arm. When they identified Furniss, they contacted the West Bromwich station. I came into brum and interviewed Cross in hospital. My official verdict on his statement was that he'd been confused by alcohol and the trauma of being shot, and that he was trying to make sense of the behaviour of a psychotic man. DI Heyward endorsed my judgement; there was no further investigation.

Paul Cross was a small, dark-haired man with a trimmed beard. An alcoholic with a history of depression. He'd admitted himself to hospital, the sleeve of his overcoat soaked with blood. This is what he told me. Since the end of summer, stories had been going round among Birmingham's homeless people that there was a man living in the canal network who had some kind of gift. He could heal wounds and make sick people well. Cross had an infected foot that he thought might be turning gangrenous. He decided to seek out the healer. It was something to hope for.

There was quite a community down in the canal system. Beggars, prostitutes, travellers. Cross was offered various forms of magical healing—none of them free, or new. His foot was getting worse. Then, after a couple of days, he met a fat guy called Barry who said that he, too, was looking for the healer. He suspected it was Barry's mind needed healing: the guy had an insane look to him, a calm stare that could turn your blood to ice.

The night Cross was shot, they found a group of travellers stranded by the theft of their van. There were five of them: an old man, a younger man, a couple and a baby. They shared their fire and some tinned food with the two newcomers; Barry passed round a bottle of white rum. It was cold, winter settling in, the stars bright overhead. They were somewhere north of the city centre, under a viaduct flanked by derelict factories.

After they'd finished the bottle, Cross started moaning about his foot. The middle toe had gone black. He was afraid that if he went to hospital, they'd cut it off. The mother whispered something to the old man, who looked at Cross suspiciously. Then he seemed to come to a decision. 'I've got something might help. Might not. Done me some good, though I don't know why.'

He rummaged among a pile of clothes in his rucksack and unwrapped a heavy drinking-cup made from some kind of frosted glass, with handles. It had a pale glow about it, as if there were a candle inside. 'How'd you come by that?' Barry asked. The old man glared at him as if to say *None of your business*. Then he stood up, took the cup to the canalside and dipped it below the surface. As he came back, the water in the cup reflected the firelight: it glowed a kind of deep red, not quite real.

'Show me your foot,' the old man said. Cross unfastened his left boot, but kept the sock on over the dying flesh. The old man winced at the smell, but he tipped the glass over Cross's foot. 'This is good for what ails you.' Barry laughed nervously. Cross felt the sensation returning to flesh that had been numb for days. It was like being a child at the seaside, feeling the current flow between your toes for the first time.

The silence was broken by a harsh crack. It echoed from the viaduct. Barry was on his feet, waving a short revolver that he'd fired into the air. His eyes were like bullet holes in glass. 'Give me the cup,' he said quietly. 'It's mine. Give it back to me.'

The old man backed into an alcove of the viaduct, holding the cup in front of his face. Barry leapt at him, jabbing the gun into his belly. The others were backing off. The old man lifted his hands and spread them, letting the cup fall towards Barry. Who grabbed at it and missed. It fell to the ground, cracked, and shattered.

Barry knelt to pick up the pieces. He cradled them in his hands. Nobody moved. The fat man was making some terrible sound in his throat, as if he'd swallowed the broken glass. Cross stepped towards him, meaning to help. His hand was on Barry's shoulder when the fat man whirled around, lifted the gun and shot Cross through the upper arm. 'Keep the fuck away. It's mine.'

This is where Cross's testimony starts to become blatantly unreliable. He fell to the ground, near the dying fire. What he saw from there was the glass in Barry's hands beginning to shift and flow, making a complete shape. It was the original cup, but with the cracks where it had broken running through it like scars on a damaged face. They divided the cup into a thousand facets. Barry held it up to the firelight.

For a moment Cross could see many tiny images of the fire, reflected in the pieces of glass.

He didn't know what Barry saw. But the fat man put the cup down in front of him, stood up, and walked away from it. He walked to the edge of the canal and leaned over. His face was gleaming with sweat. Very quietly, he crouched down by the water and slipped in. The oily canal surface covered him like an old coat. He didn't move. Cross blacked out.

When he came to, he was alone. The fire was a dull glow in a nest of ashes. The travellers had gone. They'd left the cup, which was standing just where barry had left it. Cross struggled to his feet, almost blacking out a second time. His arm was burning; the whole of his left sleeve was red. He glanced over at the canal, where a dark shape was lying a few inches below the surface. He didn't dare touch the cup. Maybe someone else would find it.

As Cross finished his statement, he motioned to me to refill his glass from the jug of water by his bed. 'Cheers. You know, mate, I could do with a real drink.' I shook his hand, slipping a couple of tenners into it. He looked surprised. 'Cheers again. See you.'

'Maybe.' The ward was flooded with a blank, medicinal light. The first shift of day nurses were changing the sheets for patients who were still trying to sleep. As I made my way back to the exit, it occurred to me that I could do with a drink myself. But not in a crystalline vessel that belonged to no-one. A plain pint glass, property of my local, would be fine.

EVEN THE PAWN

Early on a February morning in the city centre, two refuse collectors found a human body wrapped in double-strength bin liners. It had been dumped in one of the tall bins at the back of a Chinese restaurant, with no serious attempt at concealment. As if whoever put it there had wanted it to be found. The refuse collectors had chased a few crows away from the bin, and immediately seen what they had attacked. Before the rush hour, the body was in the city morgue next to the law courts.

Fortunately, the crows hadn't reached her face. Though what identification we managed was of limited value. She was aged eighteen or so, white, possibly Slavic. Her hair was cut short, spiked and bleached. She had complex injuries, external and internal, that pointed to sustained beating and sexual abuse. What made headlines was that she'd died after being left in the bin, though probably without regaining consciousness.

The photo that appeared in the papers showed her face after the mortician had toned down the bruising. It was a strong face with dark-blue eyes and good teeth, a few loose. She was somewhat overweight. When dumped, the body had been wearing a T-shirt and shorts that were too small for her, probably not hers. We failed to match her face, teeth and DNA with anyone on record.

In the week following local press coverage of the death, we received three anonymous phone calls from men who claimed to know the dead girl. All of them said her name was Tania, and she'd worked in a massage parlour in the city. Two of them named a place in Small Heath, one a place in Yardley. Both parlours were owned by the Forrester brothers, two local businessmen whose affairs we weren't likely to be investigating soon. They had important friends in the force and the local council—by 'friends' I mean people they owned. There are other kinds of friend, though it seemed that Tania hadn't had any kind.

The hostesses at both parlours told us the same thing: Tania had been sacked because she was unreliable. A colleague some distance up the food chain from myself had a word with the Forrester brothers, who claimed no knowledge of what had happened to her. We'd already established by default that Tania—which almost certainly was not her real name—had been trafficked from Eastern Europe, but since the Forresters were above reproach we had little to go on.

My involvement in the case started with something the hostess at the Kittens parlour in Yardley had said. There was a 'regular' at Kittens who always phoned to ask if Tania was there. If she was busy when he arrived, he waited for her. Since most of the punters chose other girls, this fanboy had made quite a difference to Tania's confidence. Since her departure—the hostess claimed to be unsure whether the dead girl was really Tania—he hadn't been back.

Yardley being part of my regular patch, I was asked to monitor Kittens and try to track down this possible stalker of the dead girl. It was one of several parlours near the Swan Centre, a convenient stopping-point for sales reps and long-distance drivers. The hostess—'receptionist' was her official job title—was a tired-looking woman in her forties called Martina. She promised to call me on my mobile if Tania's former admirer turned up. Before I left, Martina showed me the waiting area, where two girls were watching TV and drinking coffee. They were both wearing blue cat masks.

I didn't stay, but the image bothered me for days afterwards. At least the sins you commit in your heart don't expose you to blackmail.

The call came a few weeks later, but not from Martina. The man on the phone said he sometimes visited Kittens, and had been friendly with Tania. He hadn't been there in a while. Today, when he'd turned up, Martina had warned him the police were after him. 'I thought I'd better contact you myself.'

We interviewed the punter, whose name was Derek, for two three-hour sessions. He was aged nearly forty and lived alone. It soon emerged that he was an alcoholic. The interviews were very dull. He wanted to talk to us about Tania and his distress at her death. But he seemed to know nothing that could help us. The weekend of her death he'd been in Stafford, helping his parents move house. We checked the alibi and it held. He was harmless, ignorant and about as interesting to listen to as woodlice in the loft.

'We were close,' he said more than once. 'Tania liked me, I could tell. The way she reacted when I touched her. Sometimes I'd make her come. Sometimes we'd make love fast, then just sit together and talk until the time ran out. We didn't meet up outside the parlour, but we would have eventually. I could tell she didn't have a lover. Sometimes I know things without being told them.'

His sensitivity didn't extend to knowing who had killed her. 'I could tell something was wrong, that was all. She was frightened. I think she got sacked, then some pimp made her an offer she couldn't refuse. I wish she'd called me. I gave her my number, you know. Asked her to phone me if she was in trouble. Maybe she didn't get the chance.'

The one unexpected thing he told us was near the end of the second session, when we pressed him for any hint she might have dropped regarding who she knew, how she'd got here. 'She just wouldn't talk about that,' he said. 'I saw what happened. In a dream. Kept seeing it. Hearing her scream. The blows. It was driving me insane. All the men were wearing masks.' For a moment his face looked much older. 'I don't suppose that's evidence.'

"Evidence of what?' my colleague DI Hargrave said wearily. She'd had about enough of Derek's inner life.

The last question I asked him was: 'Why have you started going back to Kittens?'

He looked at me, and there was no hint of self-dramatisation in his face.

Only blank despair. 'What else have I got?'

The investigation stalled. It was partly the block on

anything that might inconvenience the Forresters, and partly our failure to trace anyone connected with the murdered girl. The name 'Tania' was a mask. For us, the case was symptomatic of a wider pattern. Birmingham needed something to replace its rapidly collapsing industrial base, and the city's financiers had decided the answer was business conferences. That meant convention centres, mammoth hotels, expensive restaurants and a blue- chip sex industry. Not girls on the streets, but girls in private clubs and parlours. Even without blackmail, the silence of the Council would have been guaranteed. It was business.

One question we spent some time looking at was why Tania had been dumped in the city centre. It was clearly a message to someone. Most probably to the girls working in the lap-dancing clubs, porn cinemas and massage parlours scattered between Holloway Head and Snow Hill, the hinterland of Eastern European flesh kept behind closed doors and guarded by discreet pimps on the payroll of local businessmen. A simple message: *Don't get lazy.* The Chinese restaurant was two blocks away from an 'executive gentlemen's club' owned by the Forresters. But Tania wouldn't have worked there: she wasn't the right physical type.

Within a year, we were given a solution to the case. But it wasn't one that would cut much ice with the CPS. A local filmmaker called Matt Black, backed by Skin City Productions, had made a film 'reconstructing' Tania's life and death. A heavily cut version of *The Last Ride* was screened at the Electric Cinema in Birmingham, and a few other art cinemas across the country. A 'director's cut' was sold to adults via the Internet, and screened privately a few times.

The police team investigating the murder, including me, watched the full version on DVD at the Steelhouse Lane station. It showed a girl called Katja working on the streets in Romania, then being trafficked to Birmingham and given a new name. Her pimps were an Arab gang, nothing like the Forresters. Another prostitute told her better money could be earned doing private parties for businessmen. She was given a number, but didn't call it until she lost her job at the parlour. The rest was violence.

It was a sleazy, brutal film. There were images that combined hardcore sex with prosthetic simulations of injury. Matt Black clearly thought himself a talented auteur with urban lowlife as his canvas. But the wooden acting and flat dialogue suggested that he saw the character of Tania only as a temporary barrier between the camera and her wounds. *The Last Ride* was as weak on external circumstances as it was strong on forensic detail.

Matt Black was interviewed for an arts review programme that went out on Central TV, late on Friday night. I watched it at home. He was about thirty, with a retro-style tailored suit and a nervous smile. The interviewer asked him what the main purpose of *The Last Ride* was. He said: 'To deal with Tania as an icon. A media construct. We don't know who she really was, where she came from. The film explores how her identity was constructed through the same transformations that destroyed her as a person. It's also an examination of the Madonna-whore image in Western culture.'

The interviewer nodded in a slightly bemused way,

then asked why two versions were being released at the same time. 'It's a statement against censorship,' Black said at once. 'There's a false distinction in our culture between art and pornography. *The Last Ride* deliberately blends the style codes of art cinema and gonzo porn. We're breaking down boundaries.'

'That leads to another question people are asking. Why did you use hardcore porn techniques in a film about sexual violence and abuse? You're pushing not only what can be released, but what can legally be filmed at all.' Black smiled. 'This film challenges the censors to admit the audience out there are really adults. They're saying you should not be allowed to see these images. Skin City is all about breaking boundaries. Including flesh boundaries.' His smile momentarily became a grin. 'The anal space has traditionally been taboo in all cinema except porn. We're saying, liberate the image. Open all the doors.'

'Does the image have a life of its own, apart from the human reality?'

'You're asking the wrong question,' black said. 'You should be asking, does the human reality have a life of its own apart from the image?'

The programme cut away from the interview there, just as I saw my hands reach out towards the TV with the intention of strangling it. I switched it off and went upstairs to bed. Elaine was already asleep.

Months went past. Our vague hope that *The Last Ride* might stimulate someone who knew the murdered girl to get in touch came to nothing. Other crimes and more accessible villains took our attention. It was November when I got a call from the Steelhouse Lane station to tell me that Matt Black had disappeared. My immediate reaction was: 'Have you tried looking up his arse?'

We assumed the filmmaker had gone on an unplanned trip somewhere, for research or recreation. But when Christmas came and went and no-one had heard from him, black was added to the list of missing persons. A film he'd been working on, about the dark side of Internet dating, was shelved indefinitely. His absence provoked a renewal of interest in The Last Ride, and there was speculation in the press that he'd been swallowed up by the world his films explored.

In late January, I phoned the Kittens parlour and had a chat with Martina. She'd already been made to realise that co-operating with us was sensible. The Forrester brothers might be safe from police action, but she wasn't. I asked her whether Derek had been in lately. 'We saw him just before Christmas,' she said. 'He comes in every few weeks, sees a different girl every time. But you know what they told me? He won't put his hands on them. And while he does it, he keeps his eyes shut. They call him the sleepwalker.'

Several days later, Martina called me in the evening. 'He's here,' she said. I was off duty, but I apologised to Elaine and left my dinner unfinished. I parked across the Coventry Road from the parlour and watched carefully from my car. When Derek emerged, I crossed over and followed him at a distance. He was walking slowly, his head tilted, as if drunk.

I caught up with him as he was passing the children's playground near the canal walkway. 'Hi Derek. How's it going?' He didn't look surprised to see me. 'Could we have a chat?' I asked. He nodded.

We crossed the canal bridge into the Ackers, a patch of semi-wasteland used regularly for cruising and shooting up in warmer weather. Just now it was deserted. The damp grass brushed the ankles of my jeans. Derek lit a cigarette, didn't offer me one. It was dark, but the moon was out and the lights of the Coventry Road weren't far away. 'Do you get out much?' I asked. 'Go to the cinema?'

'I bought it on DVD,' he said. 'Didn't think much of it. Is that what you wanted to know?' I didn't say anything. 'It was empty,' he said. 'No truth. I don't mean facts. I mean it wasn't her. I don't blame the actress. But the bloke who made it. Smart little fucker. Mouthing off on TV like he knew it all. He knew nothing. What I could have told him…' He stopped and drew hard on his cigarette.

'He didn't know anything about Tania,' I said. 'Someone had to put him straight. Make him understand.'

Derek stared into the murky distance. 'You think I killed him, don't you? but I didn't. I don't know where he is now. Neither does he.'

There was a long silence. I wasn't armed, and didn't look forward to arresting a desperate man. He turned slowly and looked at me. In the half-light his face was a mask with holes for eyes. 'What did you do to him?' I asked.

'This,' he said, and touched my face.

The scream that tore her mouth apart. A baby on fire in her womb. Everyone she had ever loved maimed, infected, destroyed. The men who used her four, five, six at once, making new holes when they ran out. The crows that pecked at her hands and feet. The city that broke into fragments, stone rats that scarred every child they could find. The pain that never stopped, spreading through the past and the future, the grey mist, the sea of blood, the cloud of sperm, the bone-faced men, the cries for help, the broken cat mask.

The next few days are a blur. I don't know exactly where I went. The images in my head were the only reality. I spent a night under a railway bridge, another night in a derelict house. I used the cash in my wallet to buy vodka from a few off-licences and heroin from someone I met on the streets. I smoked it under bridges in the dead of night. For a week or more I was trapped in someone else's memories. And the pain of those final hours never left me.

One frozen morning, I followed a misty thread of forgotten life into a police station. While I sat inert on a bench, they checked my wallet and contacted my department. I was diagnosed as having suffered an acute nervous breakdown. They gave me tranquillisers, silenced the terror, wrapped me in chemical bandages. I spent a month in hospital. Elaine visited me, and when I heard her voice a little of myself came back.

I assume Matt Black is still out there somewhere, numbing the pain with alcohol or narcotics, on the run from something he can't leave behind. I don't like to think about it. It took me a long time to recover, and not all of me got through. Years later, there are still words I can't stand to hear. And I don't like to have anything touch my face, not even rain.

A MOUTH TO FEED

Various people over the years, including my wife and my superintendent, have accused me of having a 'negative attitude' towards things in general.

There are reasons why, and this is one of them.

It happened about halfway through my career in the West Midlands Police, when I was a newly-promoted DS. My friend Jason—then DC Westwood—had gone up for the same promotion; neither of us was that much better than the other, but there was a moodiness about Jason that made people uneasy. We saw eye to eye on most issues, from the Gulf War to the increasing scarcity of good curry. So, when he asked me if I'd like to go for a drink after work, I hoped he wasn't going to accuse me of stabbing him in the back.

By the time I came off the evening shift, Jason had been in the Black Eagle for a couple of hours. He looked worn out. We'd had a pretty average day—topping up the supply of fake confessions, cleaning the electrodes, nothing too stressful—but his hand was trembling with stress as we clinked glasses. We settled in a twilight corner where no-one could overhear us without being seen, and I asked him 'What's been going on?'

'It's Diane,' he said. His girlfriend had moved in with him about six months before, and he'd been talking about starting a family. 'She's sick. Been throwing up a lot, fell over a few times. She went for a scan. They've diagnosed a brain tumour. She may only have a few months.'

'I'm so sorry,' I said. The words fell into the silence like a coin into a very deep well. I gripped Jason's hand, felt the chill of the glass through his fingers. 'Is there any way I can help? With work or…?'

'I'll let you know.' He smiled. 'You might as well do something useful with your new authority.'

We drank in silence. I was thinking about Chernobyl, the wave of cancer deaths across Europe in the year that followed the disaster. Whatever Jason was thinking hadn't yet thawed into words. His bloodshot eyes were fixed on something beyond me, the pub or the world, yet close enough to trap him in his seat. 'Sweet Child O' Mine' was playing on the jukebox.

Then Jason said: 'Does your family own you?'

I raised my eyebrows. 'Do you mean the family you came from, or the family you've made?' One or the other usually did.

He pointed to my empty glass. 'Same again?' While he was at the bar, I noted how the pub was filling up. Young men with shaven heads, young women with their hair tied back hard. Pale, shiny faces.

Jason placed two pints of London Pride on the shaky table between us, then sat down. 'I haven't met Diane's family,' he said. 'She's never seemed close to them. But since she got ill, she's mentioned them a few times. About her needing to go and see them. And them needing to know where she is.'

'Why? Are they helping to look after her?'

Jason shook his head. 'It's got something to do with… if she dies, what happens to her remains. Must be some religious thing. Of course, I told her not to be so daft. *Remains*. I didn't think about what it meant.'

There was a pause. Then I said, 'What *does* it mean?'

Jason looked at me and shrugged. 'I don't understand. Diane said something about a place. She was crying, I'm not sure… it sounded like *the valley of broken stones*. She said she'd have to go there.'

Neither of us could make any sense of that. Jason was starting to retreat into himself, and beyond the usual bland assurances of support I had little to offer. I could get the last round in, and did. Jason wasn't holding his drink as well as usual; I suspected he was still in a mild state of shock.

We left the pub before closing time. The pavement around the bus shelter was littered with chunks of broken glass like hailstones. There was an unexpected chill in the air; after a warm September, the autumn was kicking in fast.

All the next week, I was busy with an investigation into some local food distributors who were reprocessing and selling spoiled meat. I haven't been near a burger van in all the years since. Jason was working on the Bar Selona case—too many men being glassed in the same way, outside the same pub, over a period of years—and our paths didn't cross.

Until the following Monday morning, when I turned up at work to find him waiting outside my office. He looked like he hadn't slept much, if at all; but his suit was clean. It was all in his face. I got him a coffee, trying not to look smug about having my own office; we sat on either side of my new, but already cluttered, desk. 'Diane's gone to her family,' he said. 'Her parents' house in Bewdley. She hasn't phoned in three days. Last night she was supposed to come home. Her mobile's switched off.'

'Do you know their address?' I said, trying to sound calm. Jason's dark eyes were like sores, raw with their own inner friction.

He shook his head. 'Never thought to ask. Somewhere in the Wyre Forest, I think, outside the town. I wanted to go with her, but she said it was family stuff. I shouldn't have let her go. I guess if… if I'd stopped her, it would have been like saying the tumour was affecting her mind. She wasn't Diane any more.'

The phone rang; it was DI Hargrave. I put her off, then sat staring at Jason. 'We can find the address, then put out a missing person enquiry to the Bewdley station,' I said. 'If you feel that's a good idea.'

'I don't know. Don't like to go charging in…'

'How bad are her family? Are they up to anything? Any history? You know what I mean.'

Jason sighed. 'If that was it, at least I'd know what was going on. It's more like… some things she told me after she started on radiotherapy, when she was shaking and throwing up all night. She looked forty years older, but she was talking like a kid. They've messed with her head. Some crap about *a valley of broken stones*. And the *child of the family* needing to grow. She was out of it.'

'How's she been the last few days?' I asked—and then, disliking myself more than a little, added: 'Are things okay between you?'

Jason didn't take offence at that, which scared me. 'Physically she's a little stronger. They say the tumour has shrunk. The next step is chemo. In herself… I don't know. She's been watching cartoons on TV, reading kids' books. Trying to hide from it.'

He gulped his coffee, making a visible effort to keep his hand steady. I kept my eyes fixed calmly, not accusingly, on his pale face. He'd cut himself shaving, more than once. 'Her and me,' he said in a small dry voice. 'No rows, no falling out. But it's not the same, it can't be. I try not to think about it. We don't… Everything is different. What she feels… I don't know. How she is. Where she is.'

The phone rang again. It was Hart, one of our informers. Stolen goods man. I told him to wait, unless it was life or death—and not just his. Then I put the receiver down and stared out the window, because Jason was weeping hard, and we weren't close enough friends for me to hold him.

Late on Friday night, I was at home when the phone rang. Elaine was six months pregnant at that time. Our second child. We had just made cautious love, and I was lying with the side of my face pressed against Elaine's belly. She was lying on her side, drifting into sleep. Only the baby was moving.

I knew at once who it was. 'Diane's brother phoned me,' he said. 'She died at her parents' house. Two days ago. He said they'll take care of the funeral. I'll be invited. Nice of him. But… what about an inquest? He said their doctor has signed the death certificate. How can they just… I asked to see her. He said I can't. How can they treat me like... an outsider? I'm living in Diane's home. For God's sake. What am I supposed to do?'

'I don't know,' I said. 'They should have called you. I'm sorry... really sorry. You don't deserve this.'

'What about Diane? What did she deserve?'

I looked across the bed. Elaine was sitting up, brushing her tangled hair. Behind her, I could see the darkness through the wall. It was like a storm cloud, or an ocean.

'There's nothing you can do about that,' I said. 'She's gone. It would be terrible whenever it happened. You can insist on an inquest, but it might antagonise her family.'

'Do you think I give a fuck about that?'

'Maybe not, but you need to think about what it will achieve.'

'Show them they don't own her.'

I shut my eyes. 'They don't now. Whatever they might have thought before. She's gone. I'm sorry, Jason.'

There was a long pause. Then he said: 'Will you come with me?'

'When?' Elaine had put on her nightgown. I could hear rain brushing gently against the window.

'Tomorrow morning, early. I want to surprise them. Make them talk to me.'

I took a deep breath. 'Are you asking me to go with you as a friend—or as a senior colleague?'

'Both.'

The night was bleeding through the wall now. It clung to the telephone cable, thickened the curtains. It promised a sleep it could not deliver. 'All right,' I said.

Even in retrospect, there are no words for how futile the next morning was. We started out before dawn, driving on rain-blackened roads through jittery traffic. I drove. Beside me, Jason alternated between grim silence and confused ranting. I wished I'd had more sleep.

'They're not going to release the body,' he said. 'Diane knew they'd get her. She wanted to be cremated, you know. She said the local graveyard was too near the valley of broken stones. It must be some warped folktale her parents used to fuck up her mind. They told her she'd end up there.

'And she had this birthmark, a dark shape on her thigh—a bit like a worm with two ragged wings. They'd made something out of that. Told her it was the child of the family that needed to grow. Maybe they were trying to introduce her to religion or something, but she was terrified of the image. I offered to pay for her to have it lasered off, but she said the family would punish her if she did.'

'Sounds like she's been abused psychologically,' I said. 'Frightened in a way that stayed inside her, then surfaced when she became seriously ill. At least, I hope that's all they did.'

'Doesn't make much difference now.' Jason stared out the window at a landscape blurred by rain and mist, like a watercolour painting smeared by a wet cloth. Streaks of daylight melted into the trees and buildings ahead.

The ground was uneven: parts of the Wyre Forest disappeared from view as our car approached them, while other parts solidified out of thin air. Although the windows were closed, I could smell decay.

We drove through Bewdley, an old-fashioned Worcestershire town of the kind that rich West Midlands businessmen retire to. Antique shops, designer cafés and expensive bakeries were busy turning off their security systems as we passed through. I paused outside a hat shop, checked the map, then drove over a bridge and down a steep hill to re-enter the Wyre Forest. A weak sunlight was struggling through the trees.

The Monkton house was somewhere on a long road that twisted between clusters of trees and boarded-up workshops. We passed a pub that looked modern but was coated with pale ivy, and a church whose windows were blackened with smoke. The ground under the trees was littered with remnants of brick and glass. This hadn't always been a forest.

House numbers were difficult to make out, and I wasn't even sure we were close when Jason said 'Stop.' A thin figure, dressed in a black shirt and jeans, was standing on the doorstep of a well-kept little house with a bag of shopping, about to go in. He or she had a dark pony-tail. 'Diane?' Jason said faintly. The figure began to unlock the door. Jason cried 'Wait!' and the figure glanced back at us. It was a man. Jason opened the car door and walked fast towards the house, with me a few steps behind. By the time we reached the gate, the front door was closed and the man we'd seen was inside. 'Her brother,' Jason said. He was shaking. I knocked and waited, but there was no response. So I knocked more emphatically, for quite a while.

The thin man jerked the door open and said: 'What the hell are you up to?' His voice was incongruously calm.

'Mr Paul Monkton?' I said. 'Sorry to disturb you, sir. It's the police. Could we have a word with you?' Jason and I produced our ID; he inspected the cards as if wondering how we expected to get away with this. Then he turned away and marched back into the house, leaving the door open.

We followed Paul into the hallway, where he stopped at the foot of the stairs. On our left were two closed doors. On our right, the wall was entirely covered with a livid painted image that stretched up the stairway, as if caught in downward flight. It was some kind of creature—a dragon or giant worm, with ragged wings and a dark growth around its head like a crown of flesh. The morning light, coming through the porch window, picked out a reddish mouth and blue-black veins in its pale gleaming surface. There was a smell of damp.

'What… what the… How long has that been here?' Jason said, appalled. I knew what he was thinking. Had it been here when Diane was a child?

Paul shrugged. 'Is that any business of yours? Or is this a police investigation into interior décor? Why don't you and your boyfriend find a queer pub if you want to bitch about people's houses?'

Jason drew in his breath. 'There's no need for arguments,' I said as calmly as possible. 'This is just a routine investigation. We have a few questions. Can we sit down somewhere and talk?'

'It's not convenient,' Paul said. He was staring at Jason. 'There's been a death in the family.'

'That's why we're here.' I looked at him until he shrugged and opened the living room door. Inside, an elderly couple were sitting in armchairs the colour of old bruises. There was a smaller image of the worm-creature above the fireplace, a silk-screen print of some kind. Its wings were fully spread, like the raised arms of a triumphant football fan.

'This is Arthur and Janice Monkton, my parents,' Paul said. 'Diane was their daughter. They'll be wanting to know why you've disturbed us.' *No chance of a cup of tea, then?* I thought grimly. No-one offered us a seat, so we remained standing. The parents barely acknowledged our presence.

I introduced Jason, first as my colleague and then as Diane's partner. There was no visible reaction. 'We're not here to make trouble,' I said. 'But Mr Westwood has some legitimate concerns. I felt it would be better to drop in for a chat and clear a few things up, rather than have some protracted correspondence.'

'What do you want to know?' Paul said. His mother excused herself and disappeared into the kitchen, from where I heard her moving objects during the remainder of the visit.

'Firstly, can you talk us through what happened to Diane? I apologise for distressing you, but it would be helpful to have a clearer picture.'

Paul hesitated. 'She was climbing the stairs and her heart stopped,' he said. 'She fell down, but Dr Ferris—our family GP—said the fall wasn't the cause of death. The death certificate says a stroke. Of course, she'd been seriously ill for some time. That's why she came home.'

'This wasn't her home,' Jason said. 'She was visiting.' Paul bit his lip and gazed at the picture on the wall. Then he looked back at me.

'Can you give me Dr Ferris' address, please?' I handed Paul a notepad and he began writing immediately. 'Why didn't you contact Mr Westwood when it happened?'

Paul finished writing, then handed me back the pad. I waited for him to answer. Jason tapped his foot on the thin blue-grey carpet. I took a deep breath and said: 'Mr Monkton, it's not an unreasonable question. Mr Westwood is Diane's partner. Why did you leave it so long to tell him?'

The reply was a snort of laughter followed by the word 'Partner'. His laugh was like a sick man's cough. 'If Diane mattered to him, why didn't he marry her? Diane belongs with us. We're her family.' His flat Worcestershire accent was stronger than before.

'Whatever your feelings, Mr Monkton, other people have to be considered.' I looked at the father, but he didn't react. 'It's normal for partners to be consulted about funeral arrangements.'

Paul snorted again. 'Is he your partner now?' While I was struggling to come up with a response that didn't involve violence, he fished in his wallet and handed me a dark-edged business card. 'Talk to the funeral directors. Don't come bothering us. We've got enough to cope with.'

'Are you aware that Diane said she didn't want to be buried here?'

'According to who?' Jason stepped forward, but I put a hand on his arm.

Paul looked away. I followed his gaze to the grotesque print on the far wall. More than before, its mixture of off-white, livid blue and dull red made me think of injured human skin.

I was still looking at it when Jason tugged at my sleeve and muttered 'I'll wait outside.' He left quietly. Suddenly I realised what the picture was missing, at least in comparison with traditional dragon pictures. There were no eyes.

'For God's sake,' I said. 'How can you treat him like that? Your sister lived with him. She loved him.'

At that, the old man spoke for the first time. Fixing his dark and possibly sightless eyes on my face, he said quietly: 'Get out.'

Dr Ferris was one of four GPs registered at the address Paul had given us: an old practice on the far side of Bewdley. The waiting room was full of silent, immobile people. I showed the receptionist my ID and asked to see Dr Ferris when his morning surgery ended. She made a phone call, then told us to come back in two hours. 'He knows you're coming.'

Jason and I had a quick coffee and a sandwich in one of the town's less impressive cafés. He was close to breaking point. 'She told me Paul was obsessed with her,' he said. 'They're an appalling bunch. That picture in the hallway... can you imagine what that would do to a sensitive child? It's no wonder she...' It was raining heavily; the window in front of us was blurred with pale tracks.

The funeral parlour was on the high street, in between a bank and a recruitment agency. We spoke to the funeral director's assistant. He said Miss Monkton's body was being prepared for the funeral, which was due to happen in three days' time. Jason hadn't been told that. We asked to view the body, but the assistant said that couldn't happen without the permission of the next of kin—unless we had a warrant.

Jason's desperation was starting to get into my head. In spite of there being nothing really suspicious about the death, I let him talk me into going to the local police station for a search warrant. The superintendent we spoke to listened politely to my description of how unhelpful Paul Monkton had been. Then he asked me what the fuck we were trying to do. 'This isn't Birmingham, you know. This is a quiet town. City police marching into people's houses, firing questions at them, trying to turn a family's loss into an episode of *Cracker*... frankly, from what you've just told me, they've got grounds for a serious complaint against you two. And I won't hesitate to back them up.'

'I'm sorry you feel that way,' I said. 'But we don't just get involved where there's been a crime. Sometimes we get involved because people don't know how to behave. It's more about preventing crime than solving it.'

The officer gave me a cold smile. 'Maybe it's you who don't know how to behave. I suggest you go back to Birmingham for your search warrant. They'll be happy to assist you.'

By now, it was nearly time for our appointment with Dr Ferris. The rain had eased off, but the sky was still a mass of bruises. In the half-light the town seemed less a genuine antique, more like an industrial district that had had a makeover. We stopped for another coffee; the lack of sleep was beginning to catch up with both of us. It was difficult to talk.

Dr Ferris met us in his consulting room. He was a small, balding man with nicotine-stained fingers but white teeth. I explained that there had been some difficulties in the reporting of Miss Monkton's death. Could we see his copy of the death certificate? He unlocked the top drawer of a filing cabinet, rifled nervously through the contents and produced a card. It gave the cause of death as a cerebral haemorrhage, certified by Dr Ferris at Miss Monkton's home.

Something near the top of the card distracted me—a spelling mistake? I read through the opening words and realised what was wrong. The date of death was given as October 5th, but that was the day Jason had got the call. Diane had died two days earlier. 'There's a mistake here,' I said, and explained. Dr Ferris closed his eyes for a moment, then looked at me. 'I'm sorry,' he said, 'there's been a misunderstanding somewhere. I was called to the house to find Miss Monkton had collapsed. She was unconscious. Over the next day and a half she twitched and even raised a hand, but didn't wake up. At 9.30 p.m. on Friday, she passed away at home.'

'Why wasn't she in hospital by then?' Jason asked in a dangerously quiet voice.

'She'd asked not to be revived. No life support. There was a living will. Her father showed it to me.'

I had to bite my lip then to keep from laughing out loud. Living will had nothing to do with it.

An hour later, we were sitting in the Mermaid Tavern. I'd phoned a report back to the Acocks Green office, and the day's work was officially over. Jason was on his third glass of Scotch. I was driving us back, so I contented myself with a Coke and a sandwich. We were sitting well away from the other drinkers, and the metal-fixated jukebox absorbed our voices like a stained river.

'We can get them on withholding information from us,' I said. 'but it's small stuff really. They might get away with a warning. Paul not calling you in time—this 'living will' gives him an excuse. Being a callous piece of shit isn't a crime. You could bring a civil action, of course.'

'What's the point?' Jason winced as he swallowed the last of his whisky. 'The action we need to take isn't in a court.' He stood up. 'Another one?'

'No thanks. And I'd rather you sat down and explained what you mean. I'd rather talk to you than listen to the drink.'

'All right.' He sat back down and picked up an empty shot glass. 'That picture we saw, above the staircase. The last thing Diane saw.'

'Like you said, a way of terrorising children. And more—some kind of sick family emblem. A worm turning into a dragon.'

'Diane said it was the child of the family. Obviously they don't think it's a dragon yet. Some kind of… folk-religion, cult, that kind of thing. There might be more local people involved.' He stared into the glass. 'Most religions, people don't just pray. They do things.'

I began to see what he was driving at. 'If there's something to investigate, Jason, it'll take time.'

'We need to do something before Diane's funeral. At least have a look. Then we'll know what we're dealing with.'

'Have a look where? We can't go back to the house without a warrant.'

Jason shook his head. Behind him, rain was brushing the window. 'The valley of broken stones.'

'Where's that?' I said. 'In Narnia? It's a part of their crap.'

'Of course it is. But… I was brought up a Catholic. Belief is all about props. The altar, the cross, the wine and wafer.

They're what makes the crap real. We need to find the props.'
As the jukebox crashed into 'Ace of Spades', he muttered:
'And I know where to start looking.'

We'd passed the church on the road that led to the Monkton
house. By night, the roadway seemed narrower and the
ground more uneven. Veils of rain shimmered faintly in the
headlights. I missed the church, a dark building set back
from the road, but Jason saw it. He seemed calmer now he
had something to do. I felt detached and tired, as I usually
do in a crisis.

The graveyard wall was topped with broken glass;
but it was barely six feet high and we were able to help
each other over it, using a raincoat to protect our hands.
I'd brought a torch from the car. Inside the wall, our shoes
plunged into mud and leaf-mould. None of the headstones
looked recent, and most of them were tilted or partly sunk
into the ground. Flaps of yellow fungus glistened in the
roots of a collapsed oak tree.

It was hard to believe this graveyard was still in use.
But Jason said this was where all the family were buried.
'There might be a carving, or an inscription, or something.
A reason to stop the funeral.' I didn't bother saying that we
had little chance of doing that. Even then, I knew that trying
to prevent a burial was one of the strategies of grief—a way
of denying the person was really dead.

The effects of subsidence were much worse higher up
the slope, away from the church and the road. Perhaps the
recent bad weather had contributed. Whole graves were
reduced to mounds or mud-filled pits, with fragments of
grey stone poking out at random. A sound like the pulling

of a giant tooth made me turn around, just in time to see a stone angel fall slowly backwards.

The smell of dead leaves and bracket fungus was mingled with something worse, an odour of disease. I tracked the torch beam back and forth between the collapsed graves, then grabbed Jason's arm. 'Look!' The subsidence formed a pattern: a rough channel bisecting the graveyard. 'It's a collapsed sewer. The whole fucking area should be condemned.'

'Yes, it should,' Jason said. He didn't move as I started to head back to the church. Just stood there with his torch pointing down into the torn earth, but his face staring into the darkness behind the last standing graves. When I came back, he was muttering 'The valley of broken stones.' The rain was streaming down his face; he didn't seem to notice or care.

I more or less dragged him out of the churchyard, shouted at him to make him follow me over the jagged wall. But I couldn't get him into the car. As I struggled with the lock, he turned back and ran along the side of the wall, his face twisted away from the rain. Muttering some quite imaginative curses under my breath, I chased after him. At the back of the churchyard, the wall had collapsed. Jason stumbled over the scattered blocks of stone, miraculously not falling, and ran on through the weeping trees.

His search ended abruptly. My torch showed me a clearing just ahead, with the hunched figure of Jason moving towards it. Then there was just the clearing, and no sound from ahead. As I broke through the trees, my torch beam showed only darkness where the ground should have been. I stopped just on the edge. It was a small quarry, no more than thirty feet across. The hacked rocks tapered in to the centre, too far down to jump. I could just make out Jason lying in the cleft, blood around his head like a dark crown.

I stared at him by the light of my flickering torch beam for a few seconds, trying to see whether he was still alive. The stones he was lying on didn't come from the quarry. They were broken headstones, mingled with the fragments of long wooden boxes. I was still trying to make sense of that when I saw him move. But I don't think he was alive. It was movement under him. I know that because a moment later, a soft bluish-grey sleeve fastened onto his head.

Maybe I should have jumped down there, risked a broken leg or worse, faced the thing on its own makeshift altar. I didn't. I threw rocks down into the quarry, and a few of them tore its flabby skin, but it didn't react. The sleeve covered the whole of Jason's head and neck, stayed like that for a while, then withdrew. What it left behind could not possibly be alive. Then it reared up and wavered, as if sniffing the air. It had no eyes; its face was just a mouth. I threw the torch at it then, vaguely hoping to set it on fire, probably missing, and ran away through the bare trees and the cold rain.

The thing I'd seen could hardly be called a dragon. It had no limbs and no spine, and its skin was marked with discoloured lesions. The metamorphosis would never happen. Perhaps it had never had the potential to reach maturity; or perhaps what it fed on had retarded it. Why should it be different from any other god?

When I got back to the car, the rain had stopped. A gleam of moonlight lit up the drowned landscape. An owl flew across the road, spraying water from its pale wings. In a patch of soil by the car door, two earthworms were locked together in a hood of mucus, writhing slowly. I stepped over them.

QUARANTINE

DC Morgan looked around the bare room. There was nothing new to see, in here or outside. Then he looked at me. 'If a killer returns to the scene of the crime,' he said, 'does that make him a SoC puppet?'

It was two days since the hostel manager had phoned 999. Now the forensics had been gathered and the remains taken away, we still didn't seem able to leave. As long as yellow tape protected the broken chair, the scattered books and the dark crust of blood on the wall, the occupant was still with us. Soon the room would be cleared and scrubbed, and he'd be entirely beyond reach.

Morgan's question provoked a nervous smile from me rather than the groan it deserved. Another violent death in the same hostel, within a year, didn't say much for our investigation the first time. Yet the pathology team were sure the second death was also suicide, no matter how difficult it was for a man to beat himself to death against a wall. This room and the room of the first death both had a square brick wall at one end, no neighbour beyond it. It was a pity we couldn't take the building itself in for questioning.

The hostel was in the Snow Hill district, close to the city's oldest train station. It was a refuge for transients and DSS misfits, immigrants looking for work, mental patients looking for a foothold. Most of the tenants were under thirty; some of them worked in the local factories and warehouses and would end up renting flats near the city centre. Others would just stay here until they had to leave.

Each of the rooms had a single bed, a desk, a chair, and a couple of two- pin sockets that you'd need special plugs for. There was a kitchen and a bathroom on each floor. Each kitchen had two ancient electric cookers and a fridge that stank of decay. The bathrooms were so badly damaged it was hard to imagine anyone using them, other than the woodlice that lurked under the cracked washbasins. Everything was painted a rather disturbing shade of underwater green.

The dead man, Terry Moore, was only nineteen. He'd moved here from Bromsgrove, working as a cook, then lost his job and been unable to find stable employment. As far as we could gather, he was a fairly typical youngster, fond of pills but with no criminal record, and wasn't expected to stay long. The hostel manager, a bearded man in his fifties, said Terry had seemed nervous lately. 'Kept to himself a lot, wore gloves, like he was scared to touch anything. He was always cleaning his room.'

The girl who lived below Moore had heard sounds of a violent struggle in the night, but hadn't been sure which room the noise was coming from. The room on one side of Moore's room was empty, and the room on the other side was occupied by a man who worked night shifts. It wasn't until the next morning, when the cleaner was doing his rounds, that the door was opened. The boy was lying against the far wall as if he'd been thrown there. The room was in chaos; there was blood everywhere. It seemed likely that he'd had some kind of fit, injured his head repeatedly, broken his left hand and died before he could get help. Either that or he'd been beaten to death by someone who'd left no traces.

There was a window near the left-hand edge of the wall that had been painted with roses of blood. The window was small and didn't open, and there were bars outside it to block intruders. Like the rule banning overnight visitors, the barred windows improved security but made any sense of normality impossible for the occupants. Looking out the window, I saw fragments of dead leaves streaming upward in the air vent from the next building: a factory with black iron grids across its long windows.

DC Morgan was the only one of our team who'd investigated the first death, nearly a year before. 'It was even worse, but quieter,' he'd told us.

'Different room on the same side of the hostel. The dead man, Ian Saunders, was in his early thirties: an ex-junkie who'd been diagnosed with HIV and liver failure. Apparently he had a phobia of contact, wouldn't let anyone into his room. He'd locked it on the inside, and they had to break down the door. They found him naked, covered in powdered bleach, with more in his throat and the lining of his stomach. Like he'd tried to disinfect himself. His skin was dead white, like paper.'

Despite the cold of the November day outside, the air in the room that had been Moore's was oppressive. A few tiny beetles were creeping on the wall, probing at the dried blood. Violent death leaves an atmosphere that isn't easy to describe, one that lingers after the bodies have been removed and the fluids mopped up. It's the cold smell of violation, of human dignity being torn apart. I was desperate to get home, have a bath, put on some clean clothes. But still we stayed and talked about things we couldn't do anything to change.

That winter wasn't an easy one for me. It was a year since our second daughter, Rose, had died of a respiratory infection in the third week of her life. Elaine and I both felt a physical shock, a loss of energy and warmth, on the anniversary of her death. It had the effect of making us more anxious about the welfare of our living daughter, Julia, who was seven years old and getting used to junior school. Whether Julia sensed a partial withdrawal of our affection from her, I don't know; but our increased protectiveness seemed to make her angry. It was as if we'd denied her ability to function, and thereby provoked her own fears.

The worst argument was my fault. Julia's hair caught the light when she was sitting by the fire one night, and I thought I saw a pale speck moving in it. I seized her and began examining her scalp. It took Elaine a further examination to convince me that the child didn't have head lice, by which time Julia was white-faced and trembling with rage. She called me a cocksucker. I would have slapped her, but Elaine caught my hand. She put Julia to bed, while I sat alone in the dark.

The inquest on Moore's death returned an open verdict, but we had no evidence of homicide. Over the winter we kept in touch with the hostel, dropping by regularly to look out for any signs of trouble in the building or the surrounding area. I grew used to the outsized viaduct of Livery Street, each tunnel a window into a sodium-lit waterway where part of the city hung upside-down. Occasionally there were things to report, though nothing criminal disturbed me as much as the silent rats that infested the backstreets and canal walkways.

My anxiety about infections seemed to get worse as the nights grew longer. Lying awake beside Elaine, sometimes aware that she was awake too, I could hear the tapping and creaking of a thousand tiny forms of life. Sometimes I felt that was the only real life—without the parasites and diseases, there would be nothing but cold stone and dripping water. Human beings were the outsiders. Every morning I made myself late for work by scrubbing every inch of my skin, wiping or brushing everything I would wear, packing my briefcase with tissues and wet-wipes and tubes of Savlon. Every cut or bruise was a trigger for panic.

Christmas was hard. I went to work in the morning, interviewing a drug dealer who'd cut off the finger joints of his competitors. We'd found traces in his waste-disposal unit. I put some bleach in the toilets at the Acocks Green station and scrubbed my hands raw, but they still didn't smell right. At home in the afternoon, I managed to get out of pulling a wishbone with Julia. I didn't know where it had been. For that matter, I didn't know where my wishes had been.

And then, in the last days of December, the hostel on Snow Hill had another death. This one wasn't much of a mystery.

A young Chinese guy studying for a vocational certificate in food technology had taken a massive overdose of painkillers. He died in hospital after the night staff found him unconscious in the toilets. He'd left a handwritten note in Chinese which we assumed to be a suicide note, but when it came back from our translator she said it was a poem. As far as I can recall, her translation of it was something like:

> There's no way out of this room
> except through the poison district
> that reaches with hands of disease
> to drag me through its streets
>
> where the stones are infected with life
> and the doctor waits to treat me
> but his eyes are full of blood
> and his cure is madness.

William Lu had occupied a room next door to the one in which Terry Moore had died, and below the one in which Ian Saunders had died a year before. All three rooms were at the same end of the building, with a brick wall at the back and a window giving a view of the factory. Standing in his room on a cold Friday morning, I tried to imagine what might have gone through his mind when he sat on the bed, patiently swallowing death a little at a time. Nothing occurred to me. The small window was crusted with loose flakes of sleet, overlapping and falling away like dead skin.

Elaine wanted us to go to her mother's for the New Year. I cried off, saying the pressure of seasonal violence made it necessary for me to be at work. I'd never made such a claim before, but she didn't argue. We shared a glass of whisky as the last light of day faded, and she told me to take care. I said I always did. Julia hugged me for a moment before following her mother to the car. Then I dropped a few things into a weekend bag, caught the train to Snow Hill Station and walked on up the frost-scarred hill to the hostel. I'd booked a room for two nights.

I could hear music from another room, Massive Attack or the like, maybe a small party. There wasn't space for many people in one of these bedsits. I thought of one of the corridor parties from my college days, people going from room to room with bottles and spliffs. They wouldn't allow that here. The rules designed to prevent drug use left people with nothing to do but take drugs. Or sit here, listening to the sounds that filtered through the thin walls. Imagining each tenant's life as part of a greater life that inhabited the hostel. A life of isolation repeated over and over, in space and time.

The only light in the room came from the red two-bar heater set into the wall above the desk. Despite what I'd told Elaine, I was off duty tonight. The level of bronze liquid in the flattened bottle on the desk went slowly down as I refilled my shot glass. No ice—I wasn't going anywhere near the kitchen. The music continued, a distant pulse, but I could hear the closer sounds of things creeping and scratching in the wall cavities. Every few minutes, I crossed the room to the washbasin and washed my hands with a reddish carbolic soap whose smell reminded me of infant school. In those days, I'd believed soap could make me clean.

Hints of movement on the walls made me jump up and turn on the sixty-watt bulb. At once, the stirring life went back into concealment. But I'd glimpsed the real tenants of the building: woodlice in the damp- bruised corners, slugs under the frosted window. I drained my glass, went back to the washbasin and rubbed soap hard into my face. It couldn't wash away the patches of dead skin. I sat back down, refilled the glass. Stared at the thread-thin worms that writhed slowly in the amber fluid. Put the glass down and turned to look at the brick wall. Its darkness was more than shadow.

Somewhere far away, a clock chimed on a TV set. Voices from another world cheered and sang. The marks on the wall spread outward, then coalesced into the shape of a crooked arch. A doorway that was rotting open. Through it, I could see the clinical golden light of the streetlamps on the frost-streaked pavements. But the air was still and lukewarm. It stank of formaldehyde. I stood up, holding onto the desk as if it could anchor me in the world of health.

The infections that had taken over my skin and gut clamoured for the streets, like lonely youngsters looking for a party. I could stop them. I could kill the body they had infected and keep it safe. But I had some business to attend to. I picked up the bottle and swallowed a choking mouthful of light. Then I stumbled to the wall and rested my hand on the black arch of decay. Something cold writhed against my fingers. I stepped through.

Outside, Snow Hill was the same as before. But now I could see what it was really like. I walked up Livery Street and saw hungry life teeming in rain pools on the canal bank. I saw bodies floating in the water, their heads eaten away. I saw tissue cultures on the walls of abandoned buildings. And lice creeping everywhere, as if the city had a skin. I turned back to the hostel, but couldn't go near the diseased pigeons that huddled in the opening. Then I looked across the alley to the barred factory windows, hoping to see a human face. The lights were out, but some material on the floor glowed faintly. When I saw what they made in the factory, I started to run.

There was no music out here, only the hoarse breath of the traffic. Every car that went past had tinted windows. The air was so cold I felt I had left my skin behind. My breath glowed yellow in front of my face. Something fluttered at me from the doorway of an empty building, tore out some of my hair and spiralled into the cloudless night sky. I rubbed my scalp. Felt blood, and things crawling, and some kind of waste that stung my raw fingers.

The air itself tasted stale, as if it had been used up. I felt a growing tightness in my chest. To stop was to invite contamination, but I stumbled under a railway bridge, leant over and closed my eyes. Rainwater dropped on me. I was about to move on when a hand gripped my shoulder and flung me against the wall.

The impact almost knocked me out. I fell to a crouch and gasped for breath, trying to see through the black cloud that surrounded my head. There were rags underfoot, and crumpled newspapers. Nested into the wall was a piss-soaked duvet with lice streaming over it like the thoughts of an insomniac.

He came at me again, an impossibly thin man with bony hands and white stubble on his head. He gripped my ribs and pushed me back hard. I relaxed enough to save myself a broken spine. He was wearing plastic surgical gloves; I wondered where he'd found them. His eyes were bloodshot. His mouth worked frantically, but no sound came out.

A sick-looking grey rat wandered uncertainly over the duvet, perhaps looking for a place to hide. Saunders kicked at it angrily. I took advantage of the distraction to grab his right arm. The bone was sharp under the bleached flesh. Saunders tried to pull away, staring helplessly at me. I held on as he went into a frenzy of terror, writhing and kicking and biting at my hand. I pulled him towards me and trapped his arm behind his back. He spat in my face. His saliva tasted of bleach.

Slowly, like two drunks at the end of a New Year party, we staggered up the hill together. 'You're safe,' I said. 'Stay with me.' Saunders mimed a bitter laugh. He went on fighting, but I was stronger. When we reached the first canal bridge he went limp, crouched, then tried to flip me backwards into the stinking cut. We struggled in an embrace that was almost sexual. Up close, I could see his skin was so tight it might break. Like a paper lantern. His breath reeked of ammonia.

Somehow, I got him moving along the road again. It was raining hard. There was no traffic in sight. I slipped on a patch of frost, and Saunders kept hold of my arm. I glanced at his face. There was still terror and disgust there, but something else too. He was walking of his own volition now. My hand felt numb where he'd bitten me. The rain burned my eyes and turned everything to a blur. I knew if I stayed here much longer, I'd end up unable to get out of these bitter streets. 'Come on,' I said. To both of us.

We passed the factory, and I kept my eyes averted from its windows. The rotting gap in the hostel wall shone with a faint red light. Something crept across the ground. A pigeon flapped out of the loose bricks, and a rain of lice fell from its wings onto our heads. I took hold of Saunders' thin hand. 'It's safe,' I said, and stepped through, pulling him with me.

The room was exactly as it had been. The same three-bar heater on the wall, the same nearly empty bottle of Scotch on the desk. But the air was freezing cold, though the door was shut. The gap in the brick wall had healed to a blackish smear of damp. There was no sign of Saunders anywhere, except for what I saw when I raised my hands to the glowing heater. Around my wrist, like a white bracelet, the bones of his hand.

BLACK COUNTRY

And time would prove the weapon His crime would be to breathe the air
He would stain the sheets of the Black Country
   – The Nightingales

Clayheath, the town I was born in, is no longer on the map. We moved to Walsall when I was nine, and I never felt like going back. I vaguely knew that it had become a district, and that its boundaries had changed. Then it just ceased to exist as a distinct place, so that by the early nineties it had been absorbed into the Black Country landscape somewhere between Netherton and Lye. The mixture of redevelopment and dereliction had gradually erased it. Even local people I knew seemed to disagree about where it was. Perhaps they weren't local enough.

In the late nineties, my superintendent at the Acocks Green station passed on to me some case notes about an outbreak of juvenile crime in a part of Dudley. Perhaps he thought the stranger aspects of the case would interest me; I was already getting a reputation as the Fox Mulder of the West Midlands police force. A mention of the waste ground near the swimming baths struck a chord in my memory, and I found a couple of the streets named in the report in the A–Z map. Another street wasn't there, however, and it was hard to relate the map to the place I half-remembered. Perhaps it only sounded like Clayheath because I wanted it to.

Something's got into the children was the best the DS at the Netherton station could manage by way of an explanation, while the only adult witness to any of the crimes had offered the comment 'Must be something in the water round here making them yampy.' To which the helpful DS had appended a note: *This means insane, unpredictable or violent.* I remembered the word from my childhood—in fact, it had probably been applied to me on a few occasions. I couldn't remember much about those days, which was fine by me.

To start with, the local primary school had reported a series of unexplained injuries to children: facial bruises, a dislocated arm, a broken finger. The children claimed nothing had happened: they'd fallen asleep in bed or on the bus and woken up having somehow hurt themselves. The school nurse had reported the injuries to the police, who'd made discreet enquiries and learned nothing. The possibility of parental abuse didn't explain the pattern of similar injuries in children from around the area. One eight-year-old girl had offered the confusing comment: 'They all hate me, the others, it was all of them. All of them in one.' Asked to draw her attacker, she'd gone on drawing one face over another until the image was impossible to make out. She'd been referred for psychiatric assessment.

The local toy shop had been broken into via a back window, too small for a normal adult. The cat burglar had escaped before the police could respond to the automatic alarm, taking a random sample of items: toy soldiers, plastic musical instruments, model aircraft, dinosaurs, monsters. A newsagent had been burgled by the unusual process of making a narrow gap in the felt roof, perhaps over several nights. All that had gone was a shelf of comics. Someone had smashed the front window of a hairdresser's simply in order to spray black paint over a displayed photo of a cute smiling child. The discarded spray-can had the small fingerprints of several individuals, all apparently children.

The name Clayheath didn't appear in the report, but one of the episodes detailed brought back strong images of place for me. Someone had gone into the swimming baths early on a Sunday morning and dropped a litter of newborn kittens into the water. Around the same time, their mother had been garrotted and hung from a fence at the back of the waste ground nearby. She was the pet of a local family, and had been missing for a week. The murdered cat was seen and reported by a teenage couple on the Sunday evening. During the day, children had been playing football on the same patch of waste ground. They hadn't bothered to tell anyone about the cat. An autopsy found four small metal objects in the cat's throat: a car, a boot, an iron, and a dog, playing pieces from a Monopoly board.

Finally, the same primary school that had seen an epidemic of injuries to pupils was broken into in the early hours of a Monday morning. All the pieces of children's artwork on the walls had been viciously slashed with a knife. All the mirrors in the school toilets had been smashed. The caretaker, who'd come into the school at seven a.m., claimed to have seen a 'scraggy-looking' child of nine or so, moving so fast his face was a blur. 'Shaking like he was in a fit, all over, had to keep moving not to collapse. And laughing, or pretending to laugh, like when a kid's trying to upset another kid. There must have been a few of them because the laughing was everywhere.' The caretaker had since been dismissed for drinking at work, which cast some doubt over the reliability of his account.

I contacted the Netherton station and offered to help out with the investigation, telling them I knew the school and other local places from my own childhood, and might be able to shed some light on what was happening. They agreed to put me up in a local hotel for a couple of days while I looked around. But the more I thought about going back to Clayheath, the less it appealed to me. It felt like going back to nothing—not in a neutral way, but in a way that might suck me back in and draw the life out of me. The night I was packing up, I asked Elaine whether she thought losing memories could actually change the past. She looked into my eyes and said: 'You should charge yourself rent.'

Driving to Netherton, I decided to stop off in the area I'd identified as having been part of Clayheath. From the expressway, I could see old factories and terraced streets that reminded me of my childhood. I wondered how much of the past was waiting for me to rediscover it. All I could think of was my own recurring dream of another life in which I was a musician, travelling from one country to another, staying in ancient hotels and meeting beautiful, unattainable women. I found the street where the school was, but it wasn't my school: it was a small, flattened building not unlike a secure unit. The houses had been replaced by tower blocks and prefabs, while the high street had become a shopping mall. The location of the swimming baths eluded me. I ended up in Netherton an hour late, confused and tired.

DS Richards, a thin man who seemed vaguely ill at ease, took me for lunch at the local pub. 'No-one seems to know what's going on,' he said. 'It must be a bunch of kids, or maybe a few teenagers who aren't quite the full shilling. You get the feeling they're doing it to make a point. To get attention. Maybe they think it's a joke. We catch them, they'll find out how funny it is.'

'The place has really changed since I was a kid,' I said. 'I'm not even sure it is the right place. What happened to the old school?'

'They shut it down twenty years ago, the building's gone now. Not enough children. The old town was just dying off. It was called Clayheath in those days. Local people never seemed to be well, probably toxic waste or something. The population fell. It just became... well, what you see. A grid reference.'

'It must be difficult living with that sense of a lost community.'

'For the older people, yeah. Not the kids, they take it for granted.'

I swallowed a mouthful of black coffee. It tasted of nothing. 'When I offered to help out, I thought I could find where local kids are hiding. Getting up to things. I was that kind of kid too. But I'm not sure those places still exist.'

'Do you want to give us a statement?' Richards asked, then winked. 'Only joking, our kid. Don't look like that. You never know, there might be something we've missed. Local team aren't exactly the FBI, you know.

'It's a shitty place to live. I don't blame you for leaving. But don't start feeling sorry for the little fuckers that are doing these things. What's important is stopping them before something worse happens.'

The Netherton hotel was quiet and inexpensive, which is what you need for undercover work. A couple of sales reps were talking market access in the bar. Alone in my cell-like room, I pocketed a book of matches (I didn't smoke any more, but the memory of 1970s power cuts stayed with me) and switched on the TV to catch the local news. More firms going out of business, more violence on the streets of Dudley; but nothing about juvenile crime. I switched off the set and at once, as if looking through a window into a darkened room, saw my parents sitting on opposite sides of the living room table, not speaking. And then the narrow bed where I'd curled up with a pillow over my head, night after night, hoping they wouldn't start. Not knowing what to do when they did. The relief I'd felt when my father got a job that took him away from home most of the week. Then discovering that my parents saved up all their resentments for the weekend. The shouting, the bitter silences, the hours of quiet crying, the times when it became violent. The years of it.

I'd suffered from nightmares and broken sleep, been put on a medication that I'd discovered only quite recently to have been a tricyclic antidepressant known for its side-effects. Yes, I'd got up to stuff. Nothing that would make a play on BBC2, but enough to hide my childhood beyond the view of everyday memory. I'd stolen from shops and other kids, defaced library books and posters, smeared my own shit on the walls of toilet cubicles. In family photos, I used to pull faces and pretend I had a stomach-ache. Throughout junior school and the first year of secondary school, I was a disruptive, friendless, arrogant little sod. My parents knew it, and felt it was their duty to keep telling me. If they ever glimpsed the hopelessness behind it, they didn't let on. Eventually puberty gripped me and I turned quiet.

Despite being effectively on duty, I went down into the bar and had a pint of real ale. The two reps were swapping accounts of their one-night stands. It still sounded like they were talking about market access. I was grateful for their voices, which covered up the silence in my head. Maybe that's why heavy metal is so popular in the Black Country. Either that or it evokes some collective memory of the generations of factory work.

A leaflet pinned to the wall of the bar caught my eye: a blues night at a local pub. The date was tonight. That could be a chance to relax after visiting what had been Clayheath. But I'd better get a move on. I drained my pint and went out into the narrow street, the case notes in a vinyl folder under my arm. Richards had told me the number of the bus from here to the swimming baths. He'd also given me a file of press cuttings that I'd flicked through, noticing a photo of the newsagent who'd been robbed. I recognised him.

Perhaps if there'd been more of the old Clayheath still in place, I would have gone on reliving the past. But there was hardly anything I recognised. The swimming baths, badly in need of renovation. The viaduct and the old railway it carried. The grey canal below street level. The derelict brickworks. These were relics, surviving only because there was no profit in removing them. They had lost the town that gave them a purpose. The expressway that cut through the area brought people to the shopping mall and took them away to whatever jobs they had. The tower blocks and prefabricated housing units didn't look like anyone's permanent homes, though no doubt they were. I tried, and failed, to visualise the district as it had been. No memories of any kind came back to me.

With some difficulty, I found the newsagent where the comics had been stolen. The man behind the counter had grey stubble on his head and jowls. He looked too old to be still working. Was this the same shopkeeper, perhaps even the same corner shop? If so, should I apologise for stealing his Sherbet Fountains three decades ago? This probably wasn't the right time. I looked around: stacked copies of *Auto Trader*; bags of loose tobacco; discounted end- of-line food packages; specialist porn. I bought a copy of the local *Express and Star* and let him see my ID card. 'Sorry to hear about the break-in,' I said. 'Any trouble since?'

He shook his head. 'I don't let any kids in here now without an adult. Sometimes I can hear them outside, laughing. Waiting to sneak in when my back's turned. I've seed them hiding between the houses. Watching. Bring back the cane, that's what I say. And in public.' His thin hands were trembling above the counter. I gave him my phone number and asked him to get in touch if he had any worries. Somehow I felt I owed him.

As the streets grew dark, I walked back to Netherton. One question troubled me: why had none of the stolen goods come to light? Local parents would surely be watching their children for anything suspicious. You'd expect a black market with a fairly visible audit trail. Children were no good at secrets. The more blurred and indistinct the buildings became, the more they resembled my state of mind.

Back at the hotel, I ordered a plate of sandwiches and settled down with the press clippings. The only story more recent than the case notes was a mother who'd turned in her nine-year-old son. The police had questioned him for several hours, but released him saying he knew nothing about the crimes. His mother wasn't convinced. 'He's a liar and a thief,' she'd told the local paper. 'He'd cheat at solitaire. His father's a villain.'

Before going out I phoned Elaine to check that she and our daughter Julia were okay. She said Julia still wasn't eating much. 'Do you think she's being bullied in school?' I said that might be part of it, and I'd try to have a chat with her when I got home. 'Remind her who you are,' Elaine said. I didn't rise to it. After I'd put the phone down, I wondered if my habit of avoiding any kind of conflict in the home was making silence a family member, giving it a place at the table, and if that might be as harmful as arguments. Then I decided what I needed was a drink.

The pub with the blues night was just around the corner. It was an open-mic session. Feeling only half awake, I firkled in my weekend bag until I found the small harmonica that travelled everywhere with me. I'd bought it in Stourbridge a few days after leaving home, back in the early seventies. Hadn't played in front of an audience for twenty years. I wiped it with a tissue, checked it still worked. The first note took my breath away, literally.

The next couple of hours passed in a bittersweet haze of whisky, acoustic blues and second-hand smoke. Twenty or so people in a small function room with a coal-effect gas fire—predominantly middle-aged men, with a few women and youngsters. Nearly all musicians. I played a couple of Sonny Boy Williamson songs, though my harp skills were painfully inadequate. The highlight was when a young woman with red hair sang 'God Bless the Child'. At the end, most of us joined in a medley of Leadbelly songs. I felt uneasy singing about racist police officers, but sometimes unease is good for you.

When I left the pub, the cold night air filled my lungs like a cry. I was far more drunk than I'd meant to get. Something was drifting at the back of my mind, impossible to focus on: the image of a hollow face like a dried-out ulcer. I let myself into the hotel and climbed the stairs as quietly as possible. My tiny room seemed to intensify the face of loneliness in my mind. I dropped the harmonica on the bedside table, stripped down to my boxer shorts and climbed under the duvet. But I couldn't get to sleep until I'd curled up on my side, arms crossed over my chest, head thrust deep into the pillows.

I was standing at the edge of the school playground, watching the other kids play some arcane game I didn't understand. No-one came near me. Then I heard laughter through the railings, and turned round. A gang of street brats, not wearing any school uniform. Some of them reached out for me. I ran towards them, jumped the railings without effort, landed hard on my knees, got up and ran with them away from the school, down the grey street, into the park. Dead leaves were falling around us like flakes of skin. Their hands brushed my arms and head as we ran, caresses that were nearly blows. The wind tore their laughter to shreds.

At the back of the park was a chain-link fence with gaps we struggled through into the waste ground. Our feet sank in the muddy grass, but we kept running. Fireweed smeared our clothes with its whitish feathery seeds. The children's faces were pale in the moonlight, but their eyes were black hollows. When I slowed down, they dragged me with them. Finally we broke through a line of ragged trees into a valley where a brick embankment supported the railway line. A train was approaching, black against the moth-eaten grey clouds.

Set into the embankment was a tiny house: a railwayman's cottage. The windows were bricked up. But there was a narrow passage to one side, and a dead tree with a branch close to a window where some bricks had been removed. One by one we climbed the tree, helping each other up, and squeezed through into the lightless room. The children were all around me now, their thin bodies pressed together, and they'd stopped laughing.

I rose slowly from the depths of sleep, still curled up on the bed. The sense of being trapped stayed with me for minutes. I could see a faint smear of moonlight on the curtain. My eyes were wet, but my mouth felt so dry it was a struggle to breathe. I pushed myself off the bed and began to dress slowly, in the dark. Then I reached out to the bedside table and felt until my hand gripped the harmonica.

Outside, it was raining softly. There was no traffic in the streets, though I could see lights moving on the expressway in the distance. I let the dream guide me the couple of miles to where Clayheath had been. Old buildings and roadways were clinging to the new ones like flaps of peeled-off skin. It was cold. I was still drunk, and more asleep than awake. Cats or seagulls were crying somewhere in the night. Soon I passed the derelict school, and walked on through the park. The smell of decay almost made me pass out. More than nature was rotting. The chain-link fence had mostly fallen apart, and I staggered over the marshy ground to the line of bare, distorted trees. My ankles were heavy with mud. My own breath was a rusty wheeze in my ears, a bad harmonica solo.

The railwayman's cottage was still there, unchanged. I pulled myself up onto the dead branch. The gap in the bricked-up window was only large enough for a child. But somehow I forced myself through, tearing my shirt. I was alone in the dark room. There was no sound of laughter. I reached for the book of matches, tore one off and struck it. Then lit another as the contents of the den slowly revealed themselves to me. Every inch of space on the rotting shelves and floorboards was covered with stolen things: dog-eared books, flaking comics, model soldiers and aircraft, soft toys, bars of chocolate, Coke cans, sticks of liquorice. All of it carefully, neatly arrayed, to be gloated over and sampled through the long nights. A secret hoard.

The half-moon passed across the window. Soon it would be daylight. I was sobering up. He was here, I knew, but he wouldn't show himself to me. There was only one way to bring him out. I grabbed a handful of comics with shiny covers, crumpled them and used a third match to set fire to them. A bird screamed with laughter out among the trees. I dropped my harmonica into the burning heap of paper.

The fire spread up the wall, caught the dry curtain. I forced myself back out the window and fell to the stony ground, jarring my ankle. The window breathed out a gust of black smoke. I leaned against the tree, biting my lip against the pain. Something was moving inside the house, like a squirrel trapped in a nest.

There was a sound of falling bricks. Flame licked the darkness outside the window. Then a thin figure leapt onto the tree branch and fell, curled up on himself. I caught him as he tried to get away. Felt the cold and absence of him in my arms. Looked down into his blurred face as his skin creased like a thumbprint, like an image in a sketchbook rubbed out and redrawn. I was in there somewhere. I held him close as his breath faded, as his face broke apart from the inside, until I was holding something blackened and flaky like a rose of ashes.

WITHOUT A MIND

None of this was an investigation. It was personal. Though I first became aware of it when talking with the coroner at the Law Courts about suspicious deaths. He said that people sometimes died for no reason. In the last year, for example, there'd been a cluster of sudden deaths in South Birmingham from previously undiagnosed diseases. 'Sudden organ failure—the heart, the kidney, the liver. No obvious risk factors, no environmental cause. Maybe it's a new trend they'll find a reason for in a few years' time. At the moment, the only medical verdict is that shit happens.'

That wasn't a verdict many people would have disagreed with. It was the early nineties, the nadir of the recession, and emptiness was spreading like an infection through the high streets and trading estates. I was based at the Acocks Green station then, and we were having a bad year. Local crime had jacked up the insurance costs for newsagents and off-licences so high that most of them had gone out of business, robbed or not. The press was blaming negligent policing, while the local authority was slashing our budget.

My own life was a bit jittery at that time. Elaine was trying to combine work with looking after our daughter Julia, and was unhappy about the amount of overtime I was doing. I told her we were busy fighting the crime wave. True enough, but I didn't want to tell her I'd taken out a private loan to compensate for not getting a promotion I'd been relying on. She knew money had disappeared, and hinted that she thought I was salting it away for a mistress or a runner. I'd had no such thoughts—that all came later. There was a phrase from a Springsteen song that wouldn't go out of my head in those days: *debts no honest man could pay*.

One evening I was having an off duty drink with some friends in the Corvid Arms when an old man staggered in, wearing a faded suit. He paused, leaning on a table, then made his way unsteadily towards the bar. As he tried to make himself heard over the jukebox, the barman picked up his mobile and spoke briefly into it. Two security staff came over from the door and informed the old man that he was leaving. I didn't interfere, though the old man was no worse drunk than half the teenagers around the bar. From the doorway his voice rose in protest, then faded. The bouncers didn't return.

A minute later, prompted by a mild unease, I slipped out the door. It was a crisp October night. Between the doorway and a line of cars, a dark figure lay curled on the pavement. Blood was trickling down his face from a gash over one eye. He was holding onto something that looked like a crumpled plastic bag half-full of soft food. As I came closer, I could see blood was draining into it—but not from his forehead. I couldn't make out what the whitish shape was. Surely I hadn't had that much to drink? I reached out, and it backed away from me. Part of it remained attached to the base of the old man's throat.

As blood drained into the creature, its form became clearer. It was something like a human baby, but twisted up and nearly flat, made of some kind of glassy matter or ectoplasm. Its hands were reaching down to its inert victim; the fingers, which were long and slender, were poking into his neck. Blood was flowing through them into the creature's small body. It made me think of a vacuum bag.

The old man twitched and choked as the attacker pressed in harder. Its tiny face had no eyes or mouth. I reached out to try and stop it, or to prove I wasn't really seeing it—and the thing pulled away, covering itself with the blood-streaked feathery tissue it had pulled out from the old man's chest cavity. And then it was gone, crawling faster than a rat, dragging its spoils with it. I looked down at the silent man. Apart from the gash on his forehead and a few small drops of blood on his neck, there was no sign of injury. But he was dead.

As I knelt there, feeling for a pulse, one of the bouncers came up to me and struck my shoulder with his fist. I looked up. He said quietly: 'Any trouble about this and they'll find your little daughter in the canal.' Then he turned and went back into the bar. I phoned for an ambulance.

JOEL LANE

The old man, an Irish Brummie aged seventy-two, was found to have died of natural causes. A haemorrhage had ripped through his lungs like a hailstorm through a leafy shrub, killing him in seconds. There was no damage to his skull, or to the flesh of his withered throat. A past history of pneumonia was suspected. Alcohol was assumed to have been a contributory factor.

A few days later, I was called out to make a shoplifting arrest at a shoe shop in Acocks Green. When I got there, the suspect—a woman of thirty or so—was unconscious in the manager's office. The shoes were all defective stock, heavily discounted. That seemed to make the whole thing worse. An ambulance was on its way, the shop manager assured me. 'She just passed out. Unless she's faking it. You never know, do you?'

The woman, who was very thin, was lying diagonally on the carpet of the narrow room. Her long dark hair was tangled below her, as if under water. I knelt to move her onto her side, and my hand passed through something cold above her face. The light was twisting and corrupting into a figure I already recognised. The creature had attached itself to the unconscious woman's ribs, and its pale figures were starting to redden. I swiped at it and felt a terrible chill bite into my fingers, as if they were covered with frost. But I couldn't get any grip on its translucent flesh. I was dimly aware of the shop manager telling me how the thief had been apprehended. Her story continued as, helpless, I watched the visitor drag out a pulsing mass of tissue and scuttle away to a corner, where it and its prize faded.

'...her before. This time she didn't get away with it.' As the manager finished her account, the office door swung open. Two paramedics rushed in, too late. I didn't have to feel for a pulse to know the woman's heart had stopped.

Karen was one of a group of North Birmingham coppers I used to meet occasionally for an off duty chat in a pub near the Hockley Flyover. We always cleared out sharpish at last orders, before the Friday night lock-in started. One of those nights, Karen told me about the anti-people. It had been a long and stressful week, and despite my financial worries I couldn't resist the lure of their guest ales. I was into my second or third pint when the conversation turned to other people's drinking— always an easy thing to condemn. A senior colleague of ours had recently taken early retirement due to a 'drink problem'.

'It's a way of committing suicide on the instalment plan,' a young officer commented tritely.

'More like bad company—someone hanging on you who won't let you give up your bad habits,' said another.

Karen shook her head. 'Not someone you know. A stranger feeding on you, like a worm. A kind of anti-person.'

'Steady on, wench. You'll be seeing things next. Like Mulder here.' I laughed at that. Had to. Karen applied herself to her thin glass of rosé. She was a small woman with spiky ash-blond hair, very different from Elaine.

When the conversation had moved on, I caught her eye. 'Did you mean that literally?' I asked. 'About the anti-people?'

Karen gazed uneasily at me for a few seconds. 'Have you seen them too?' she said quietly. Her face was expressionless. I bit my lip.

125

A few minutes later, I visited the gents'. My face in the rust-flecked mirror looked sickly and lost. On the way back, I met Karen. She touched my arm. 'Can I have a word?' she said. I nodded.

'You know I work on the Hagley Road? Addicts and prostitutes, it's not fun. The crimes people commit against themselves. Three nights ago, we found a girl who'd been beaten up. By a pimp or a client probably. We called an ambulance and I tried to give her some first aid. Her face was a mess. Later we heard she'd lost the sight in both eyes. Detached retinas, from the beating.'

Karen swayed. Her face was coated with a film of sweat. 'You've had a shock—' I began, but she went on.

'There were two of us, me and another WPC. We were waiting for the ambulance. Just before it came, I saw something move out of the gutter. Like a surgical glove or a plastic bag blowing. But there was no wind. It slipped onto the girl's face, and I went to pull it off but my hand went through it. The blood from her face soaked into it, and I saw it was like… like some tiny flattened child. It was kissing the girl's eyes. She was unconscious. Then it peeled away and just melted into the pavement. I thought I was imagining it. When the ambulance came, I already knew what would happen to the girl. But Jane, the other officer, she didn't see nothing. Am I going mad?'

'I don't think so,' I said. 'I've seen two of them. We need to talk about this. But not now.'

Karen smiled. Her teeth were sharp. 'Yeah. We'd better get back. Or the others will think we're having an affair.'

Did it cross my mind, even then, that I wouldn't mind justifying their suspicions? If so, it was the drink hinting.

We swapped numbers, but I didn't feel able to call her. The anti-people were my personal nightmare, not a secret to be shared. But five days later, Karen called me at my desk in the Acocks Green station.

'I've found a nest of them,' she said. 'Where they hide. Where they take what they've stolen.'

The nest was in Harborne, she said; near the disused railway. 'I used to play there as a kid. When I was twelve, thirteen, I used to go there with boys. It's got memories for me. Yesterday, my day off, I went there for a walk. Just trying to forget about some recent things. Then I saw one of them, creeping under a railway bridge. It was carrying some... trophy, something it had. Then another one followed it. I could almost see through them. Made me think of... shrimps in a rock pool. If they didn't move, you wouldn't know they were there.

'After a few minutes, I followed them. Down in the valley... where there's rotten wood from bonfires, and derelict cars, and stuff. There were dozens of the things, all gathered together, surrounded by fireweed. I think they were praying, but I couldn't see what to. I ran away.'

That evening, Karen's shift ended at nine and mine at ten. We met at the Green Man pub in Harborne, and I drove her to the railway bridge near the fire station. She led me through a gap in the fence. 'This hasn't changed in ten years,' she said. We had torches, but the yellow half-moon was bright enough for us not to need them. At Karen's suggestion, I'd brought something else: a can of petrol.

The railway track was half worn away and overgrown with brambles. I followed Karen down onto the footpath and under the railway bridge, which stank of piss and decay. There were a couple of occupied sleeping bags against the brick wall, but we ignored them. Further on, trees broke up the moonlight like cracks in a window. Karen slowed down, looking ahead carefully. 'It's not far from here.'

A few rusty shells of cars were lined up at the edge of a small clearing. Beyond them, I could see an old mattress and some pillows lying on the remains of a bonfire. Karen gripped my hand. 'Wait.' She crouched behind one of the ruined cars; I dropped beside her. Ahead of us, the pale fireweed and dead bracken were trembling in the breeze. Then I realised the air was still.

I don't know how many of them were in the clearing. It was just a restless folding and corrupting of the light, and a smell like an open wound. Without blood, there was hardly anything to them. Beside me, Karen didn't move; but her breathing told me how afraid she was. I gripped the petrol can and waited. Slowly, as my eyes—or some other kind of vision—adjusted, I could make out their flattened shapes climbing over the pile of charred wood to the mattress. They all left some kind of material there: whitish streaks and lumps of ectoplasm, the ghost organs they had extracted from their human victims.

For what seemed like hours, we watched them put together two figures on the stained mattress. The moon had passed overhead and was sinking through the wet trees when the bodies first stirred. Karen drew in a sharp breath. I thought my heart would stop. The two lifeless shapes rose to a hunched standing posture and faced each other. Around them, the barely visible anti-people crept and prayed on the heap of rotten wood and among the rank weeds.

Still taking shape, the figures pressed together in a slow clinch. I thought they were fighting until I glimpsed a low swelling on one of them that was seeking the other. Kneeling on the mattress, their rough-shaped bodies locked together and shuddered in clumsy passion. Their eyeless faces grew mouths to cry out silently.

Karen snatched the petrol can from my hand, together with the oil- stained cloth it was wrapped in. She flicked a lighter to the cloth, stood up and threw the bundle onto the mound of black wood. It struck the edge of the mattress, which started to burn. The figures carried on struggling even as the fire touched them, as if this was the climax they'd worked to reach. Then the petrol can exploded, scarring my vision. A wave of heat struck me through the car's empty windows. I smelt something burning that wasn't wood or flesh; it made me retch uncontrollably.

Around us, trees and bushes were catching fire. Karen pulled at my arm, turning away. We ran together through the wet undergrowth, hitting branches, stumbling in the darkness, along the footpath, through the bridge, up to the railway line and back down to the road where my car was parked.

I was shaking too hard to drive. We sat in the car for a few minutes. Then Karen pressed her face against my chest. She was crying. I stroked her cropped hair, then slowly lifted her head until it was level with my own. As we began to kiss, I wondered if it was really our own desire that was forcing us together. But that didn't stop my mouth, or my hands.

It was a few minutes past midnight. I drove from Harborne to the Bristol Road, out beyond Longbridge to the silhouetted hills. We parked in an empty lay-by and moved to the back of the car. The radio was playing: a new Massive

Attack song called 'Unfinished Sympathy'. Karen breathed hard, but made no other sound, as I thrust inside her.

Neither of us spoke on the way back through the city. Karen's eyes were closed; she was shivering, though I'd turned up the heating in the car. I was thinking of an incident from my childhood: when an older boy had followed me home from school, spitting repeatedly on the back of my coat. The roads were quiet. The moon was no longer in the sky.

We should have left it there, but didn't. I needed to get past the memory of those desperate puppets and their audience. Karen wanted something from me I no longer had to give. It was hard enough managing my own life, let alone a double one.

We settled it as best we could, with a few furtive dates and a restless night at a cheap Stafford hotel. The night of the fire was the only time we didn't take precautions. We'd just about put the phantom of love to rest when Karen told me she was pregnant.

The waste ground fire had spread a little, but there wasn't much for it to harm. We'd gone back in the daytime and found nothing abnormal, except a bad smell that could have been burnt plastic. The local police had put out an alert for a teenage arsonist.

Karen decided to keep the baby. I won't presume to define her motives. But to some extent, it made the connection between us permanent. And as the foetus grew, my feelings became more complex. It might be a boy, and I'd always wanted a son. Elaine couldn't have any more children. Maybe some day I could acknowledge him. Or her. It was something to look forward to as well as fear.

One night in September, around eleven, Karen phoned me at the station to say she'd gone into labour. I called Elaine and said the station had an emergency. Hoped there wouldn't be too many more lies like that. When I came off shift, I drove straight to the hospital.

As soon as I saw her, I knew something was wrong. Her face had a shrink-wrapped look. She tried to smile when she saw me, but her eyes were focused inward. The maternity ward was uncomfortably warm. I held her hand while a nurse took her temperature and reassured her that all was well and the midwife would be along in a few minutes. 'I need more painkillers,' she said. The nurse hurried off, and I gave Karen a gentle hug. Her breathing sounded torn. I felt sick with guilt, both at being there and at not doing more.

My daughter Julia had been born in another local hospital. It had seemed quite an easy birth—but afterwards, Elaine had lost a lot of blood. They'd had to operate. That was in my mind as I sat holding Karen's hand, watching the sweat trickle down her taut face.

'It hurts,' she whispered. Her lips were cracked. I filled a glass from the jug of water on the bedside table and turned back to her, holding it. A pale, hollow thing was crouching on her belly. I dropped the glass and lashed out at the creature, but felt only a chilly breath. Its long fingers were turning red. Karen was lying still; her eyes were shut.

At that moment, the nurse came back with a syringe. 'What are you doing?' she said to me. 'Did you spill the water?' I stood there, unable to move, as the misty creature drew a small blood-streaked mass head-first from Karen's belly. It dragged its trophy under the bed, where the pool of water was spreading. The nurse pushed me back and applied the syringe to Karen's inert arm.

The labour was protracted and terrible. Two hours later, the midwife delivered Karen's stillborn baby. It was a girl. By then, the mother was fully conscious. 'Can I hold her?' she asked. The midwife wrapped the small corpse in a strip of cloth and placed it in Karen's arms. She looked at the baby, then looked up at me. There was something worse than grief in her face. I looked down at what she was holding. Marked on the dead baby's forehead and cheeks like vaccination scars were the prints of tiny human fingers.

THE SUNKEN CITY

The smudged clip of CCTV footage was taken from outside a factory in Small Heath, a few miles south of the city centre. It showed a street corner before dawn, nobody about. Then a figure appeared: an Asian man in a cheap jacket, hurrying towards the factory gates, late for the morning shift. A delivery van turned the corner at speed and struck the man's right shoulder from behind—making him stagger to the left and then collapse.

His face hit the kerb. The van paused and then carried on.

The man lay half in the gutter and half on the pavement, twitching. Then a second figure, a white man in a long coat, appeared and rushed towards him. He knelt over the injured man, gripping his shoulders, trying to apply mouth-to-mouth resuscitation, but failed. Carefully, he closed the dead man's eyes and laid him out on the pavement, then walked away. His hands were raised in front of his face. Dawn light bleached the scene.

The film clip was broadcast on *Midlands Today*. We were very keen to speak to the man in the long coat, the driver of the van, or any witness to the incident. The inquest was delayed. What we didn't tell the local TV or the press was that, according to our pathologist, the dead man had probably not been killed by his injuries. His shoulder was fractured, but the cause of death was asphyxiation while the heart was still beating.

A search of the area told us little. It was part of the city's industrial hinterland, the factories and workshops interspersed with Asian grocery stores, cheap fast food outlets and a scattering of brothels. There was some nocturnal drug dealing on the streets, but the dead man didn't seem linked to it. He was a machine operator, and there were no foreign substances in his bloodstream—probably he'd not even had time for a cup of coffee. We spent a chilly February night retracing the miles from his bedsit to the factory gates, with no sound to investigate but the mewing of gulls around the Tyseley dump.

Punishment for an unpaid debt was the most likely explanation for the killing. We were deep in the recession of the early nineties; all over the district, shops were closing down, homes were being repossessed. The dead man had lived alone and had no dependents, but his bank account was near its overdraft limit. Everyone owed money. Extracting payment in the form of breath was unusually poetic for debt collectors, but difficult times favour commercial innovation.

The CCTV clip was in the local news for two days without any response. On the third day, we had a call from someone who said he could name the man in the long coat. DC Monk and I drove to the Edgbaston hostel where the caller lived and worked. He was a tall, stooping man with a narrow grey beard. 'I've been the night watchman here for twelve years,' he said. 'What your film showed, he's done it before. Three years ago.'

In his sparsely furnished office, he made us some vile coffee. 'I don't do a lot of entertaining,' he said. 'Not many people talk to me. That's why I remember Corin Ward. Lived here for a couple of years. Used to come in from the pub or down from his room at night, rat-arsed either way, and have a smoke with me. I'd tell him about my software business that wasn't taking off. He'd tell me about his stories and poems nobody would publish. Always said "the herd" couldn't understand someone like him, someone with "vision". Kept going on about how people were just rats, living in filth, fighting over scraps of food. I told him, I know about rats.

'Only person I ever heard him talk about like they meant anything was his first girlfriend. They were fifteen. He said the first time they went to bed, she gave him air. You know, breathed into his lungs. To him, that was better than sex. I thought that was just drunken nonsense, but then I remembered it after what happened.

'There was this girl in the hostel, Nicola. Really thin, quiet kid, didn't have much confidence. She lost her job and got stuck here. Didn't like her family, didn't want them to know where she was. Anyway, she was going through a bad patch financially and sold herself a few times to guys living here. I found out and we had a talk about it. I told her if she started bringing men into the hostel for that, we'd have to throw her out. But if it was just within these walls, I'd keep my mouth shut. We ended up... well, you can guess. But I paid her, I'm no blackmailer.

'One morning I was down here on my own and Nicola crept down the stairs. She was shaking. Her lips were blue. Eyeliner streaked over her face. She asked to talk to me in private. We sat down here and she started crying, silently. Just couldn't stop. She said Corin had tried to choke her. She'd had some business with him. He said he wanted to kiss. Then he had her on the bed and he was clamping his mouth over hers, sucking her breath out so hard her windpipe closed up. She was too weak to fight him off. She was starting to pass out. Then he came and that distracted him, he let go for a moment, she just looked at him and he looked away. She curled up, crying, and when she stopped he'd gone.

'I'm no bleeding heart but there are limits. I had a word with Corin. He didn't want to talk to me, said it was private. I said fun was private, but if I heard anything more about him harming girls I'd call the police. He never spoke to me again, left the hostel a few months later. We've still got his details on file. It's him on the CCTV. The face isn't clear, but I remember the coat. And the way he held up his hands, like he was looking into a crystal ball.'

When we left the hostel, a freezing rain was sweeping through the tower blocks of the Lee Bank estate, which had been in 'redevelopment' for years. Veils crumpled softly over the ruins of 1960s social housing. Tarpaulins flapped from crusts of scaffolding over boarded windows. I could see my breath in front of my face, but it only lasted a moment. DC Monk voiced the question in my mind: 'How many more?'

The hostel records had a forwarding address for Ward: a flat on the Hagley Road that we had to wait until the evening to discover was rented by a young Asian couple. They'd been there six months. The landlord told us the previous tenant had disappeared owing more than a month's rent. We showed him a CCTV still and he said: 'That's him all right. Always looked like he was praying. You should have seen the state he left the flat in. Cost me a small fortune to get it cleaned up.'

'Disposing of evidence,' I said. 'Don't worry. You weren't to know.' Tidy people are the enemies of forensic science.

The landlord's copy of Ward's rent card gave his employer's name and address. He was, or had been, a tile-cutter at a Tyseley workshop. 'Worked mostly night shifts,' the landlord said. 'I could never get hold of him.' Monk and I drove there through flapping sheets of rain: a district as grey and empty as the sky.

Century Tiling was locked shut, no lights behind its wire-coated windows. The small upper windows were lined with black paper. Across the road, gulls were circling in the rain; I could hear their cries, smell rust in the saturated air. We sat in the car and I phoned the station. They told me the factory had gone out of business around the time Ward had disappeared. And one other thing: Nicola James, the girl from the hostel, had drowned herself in a reservoir. He got her in the end.

I drove away, over the railway bridge and up to the Warwick Road. Pages of a newspaper were scattered over the tarmac, blackened by rain. Then DC Monk said, 'Stop.' I pulled over. He looked at me. 'Those windows above the tile shop,' he said quietly. 'They were filthy. No-one could see in.

Why paper them from the inside? To stop yourself looking out… or just to keep your hands busy?' He reached out as if blind. I flinched away and started up the engine.

A narrow alley, reeking of urine, led behind the workshop. The rust on the back door's keyhole had recently been scraped away. There were no back windows. We got into the car, drove a little way up the road, parked and watched. The rain slowed to a drizzle, then stopped. I could see the moon behind a layer of cloud, like a face that never quite had a chance to show itself. It was getting colder inside the car.

by midnight we had another car waiting near the canal bridge. It was so quiet I could hear a train go by half a mile away. Monk was lost in his gloomy thoughts. I was thinking about my wife and young daughter. Then thinking about Karen, my girlfriend, and the night we'd spent together in a Stafford hotel room. How we'd hardly touched apart from making love. And the story she'd told me as we lay there in the dark. About the waste ground in Oldbury where, if you waited in a certain place, you could hear voices drifting in the wind. Like a radio tuning in and out. Afterwards, you remembered what they'd said as if it had happened to you. Couples never went there.

Some time between two and three a.m. a lean figure walked unsteadily down the road towards the tile shop. He was wearing a long grey coat. Holding an imaginary page in his hands, and coughing so hard we could hear him in the car. Monk and I watched him stumble into the passage between buildings. We waited a few seconds, then followed.

Ward had just stepped through the back door when we caught him. The two men from the other car were just behind us. They kept him in the hallway while Monk and I went up the narrow stairs to his hiding place. We could hear him coughing behind us, the worse for alcohol and exposure. The upper room had no electricity: we used our tiny pocket torches to look round. There were candles in bottles, a few dog-eared paperbacks, a bin full of chip wrappers and burger cartons, a sideboard covered with empty wine and spirit bottles, a heap of grubby blankets and pillows, a desk with a black notebook and a torn silk scarf.

Having established there was no-one else up there, we left it all for the forensic team. Ward was arrested on suspicion of murder and attempted murder. He didn't put up any kind of fight. In the car back to the station he sat and trembled, breathing into a cradle of his bony hands. At one point he asked if anyone had a cigarette. We didn't, at least not for him. When we sat him down in the interview room, I thought I saw a look of relief in his narrow face. Almost the only thing he said was: 'You have no idea who you're talking to. I'm a man of visions. My soul is as far above that of the herd as it is above the rats and cockroaches in the sewers.'

As he was clearly suffering from bronchitis, we put a portable heater in Ward's cell. Letting him die in custody wouldn't be a smart move, since a confession was our best chance of nailing him. His face wasn't clear enough in the CCTV film. But in the morning, he was sweaty and desperately short of breath. We transferred him to the infirmary in Winson Green Prison, where he was swiftly diagnosed with pneumonia. From there, the Steelhouse Lane murder squad would deal with him. I moved on to other work, after placing a request with the SoC team: I wanted to read Ward's notebook.

Late the following night, when lack of sleep was catching up with me, DI Maxwell called me into her office. 'You wanted to read this,' she said, passing me the black-covered book. 'Don't think it's much help to anyone. It's not evidence. I don't know what it is, frankly.' Inside the worn cover, there was a title: *The Sunken City*. Then some forty pages of closely written prose. I took it back to my desk. An hour later, I knocked on Maxwell's door and gave the book silently back to her.

What I read, I'm still not sure. Maybe I fell asleep and dreamed I was reading. It was some kind of story about the canals rising, the city under water. Rats and people swimming, silver bubbles escaping from their mouths, the mystery of their breath painting a terrible blue-red sunset. The houses changing underwater, becoming the ruins that their occupiers had always dreamed of. The dreams themselves rotting, bringing people and vermin and weeds together in a morass of toxic desire that would churn and corrode forever in the darkness.

After a restless night, I went to Winson Green Prison to speak to Ward. I'm not sure what I wanted to ask him. I had some insane notion that he could show me the truth of the city. His words had infected me. I got into the infirmary on the pretext that I needed to ask Ward something about the hostel. 'He's not well at all,' the guard said, pointing over to the far end of the room.

In the right-hand corner, I could see a thin figure stretched out on a bed. But there was something in the way: a shifting veil, like a dense cloud of rain. As I came closer to Ward's bed, I thought I could see a number of blurred, misty figures pressing around him. His hands were outstretched, trying to push them away. But they drew closer, like multiple images about to coalesce into one. He was fighting for breath and their faces were all joined to his. I stood and watched. By the time the visitors faded, Ward was still. His mouth was wide open.

INCRY

It was a Friday night in Acocks Green, a deteriorating suburb on the southern edge of the city. The pubs had closed. A young couple, rather drunk, were looking for a place to make love. The alley off the Warwick Road was blocked by overturned rubbish bins. Outside the garages at the top of Shirley Road, a stray cat was slowly dismembering a mouse. The teenagers, who were on their first date, crossed through the car park on the traffic island and looked around. To their left was a coin-operated toilet box. The boy pointed towards it. The girl pressed her face into his chest. They looked around. No-one was in sight. Quickly, they walked to the automatic toilet and the boy reached in his pocket for a coin. They'd have twenty minutes inside; that was long enough. The door slid open. A man was lying on the floor, twisted over, one arm flung out. His jeans were soaked with urine. They thought he was just unconscious until they saw his face.

*

That was in my first year at the Acocks Green office. I was in the incident room that night, and talked to both of the youngsters. They were sobering up fast, withdrawing into themselves. After tonight, I suspected, they wouldn't see each other again. The man in the toilet box had lived locally. His bruises were compatible with his having had some kind of fit or seizure. He'd bitten through his tongue, and then dislocated his jaw. An X-ray established that he'd choked on his own blood. The girl's comment was as much help as anything the hospital gave us: 'His face looked like a scream had torn it apart.'

The next day, the dead man's medical records failed to suggest any medical condition that could explain his death. And CCTV footage showed him going into the toilet box on his own. DC Monk told me the camera had been there for a year, since a man had been severely beaten in the same place. His two attackers had been charged, but there hadn't been enough evidence to convict. Both men had since left the region. Their victim had survived, but was crippled by the attack.

The autopsy recorded no suspicious circumstances, so we filed a report and moved on. But echoes of the toilet box death kept recurring for me. I've always been claustrophobic, hated the idea of being locked in. A drunken friend of my wife once told me I'd joined the force to deny my fear by imprisoning others. I suppose my reaction to her could have been more polite, but I don't like people who think cleverness is a substitute for experience.

That summer, there were a number of unexplained deaths in the streets among otherwise healthy men. None of them were suggestive of violence. Our pathologist called it 'sudden death syndrome'—which I can't say shed a great deal of light on the problem. The other recurring theme was gangs beating people up for the usual reasons. Or no reason at all. I couldn't shake off the conviction that the two things were linked in some way. No doubt being a persecutor of the innocent was affecting my state of mind.

The whole episode might have been forgotten if I hadn't been on a night shift in the Green a few weeks later. I was in uniform, helping to keep an eye on a house whose front window had been shot out from a passing car. After three hours of nothing, I was desperate for a piss. DC Joiner arrived to take over, and rather than walk back to the station I decided to use the automatic toilet around the corner. It was nearly two a.m. and there was no-one about. The machine accepted my coin and the steel door opened silently. The room inside reeked of disinfectant.

While I was relieving myself, a voice jabbed in my ear: *You fucking twisted scum. You vicious little prick. Don't mind handing it out, but you don't like getting it. Do you?* The voice stank of sweat and rage. I felt a hand on my shoulder, a fist jabbing me in the kidneys. Panic gripped my throat. I couldn't seem to breathe. Then I finished, zipped myself up, tried to get to the door. *You won't get away with it this time. Fucking piece of shit bastard lying scum.* A hand gripped my hair, pulled my head back. I turned and struck out at nothing.

Rage moulded itself on me like a skin-tight costume. I fell to my knees, reached out blindly to the panel beside the door. Somehow I pressed the button, got the door to slide open, staggered out onto the empty street and knelt there for a few minutes, fighting for breath. The echo of a cry was trapped in my head.

Carl Bradmore lived on the nineteenth floor of one of the tower blocks on Holloway Head. The smell of disinfectant in the lift made me feel nauseous and close to panic. When I rang the bell, he opened the door almost at once; I'd phoned him to arrange the visit. He was a short, chubby man of thirty or so in an electric wheelchair. He'd been living here for nearly a year, since the attack. Presumably the better security compensated for the more difficult access.

Carl led me into his minimally-furnished living room and beckoned me to sit on the black sofa. 'How can I help you?' he said.

'I need to ask you some questions about the attack on you last year. Can you please talk me through what happened?'

He closed his eyes. 'Just walking home, near midnight. I was in Oxford Road, near the post office. Two young men approached me from either side. I felt a knife in my back. One of them told me to go to a cashpoint. I refused. They marched me to the automatic toilet. There was no-one else in sight. The other man asked me if I came here to get sucked off. I didn't say anything. They started hitting me. I fell down, curled up, trying to cover my head. Something gave way at the base of my spine and I passed out. That didn't stop them.'

Carl was trembling. 'Can I get a drink?' he asked. I nodded and he poured himself a shot of brandy. 'I suppose you want to know why I didn't give in?' I said nothing. 'I thought if they didn't get what they wanted, they were more likely to let me live. I'm not like the brightest of people.'

'What happened after?' I asked. He sipped the brandy slowly, avoiding my eyes. Eventually he looked up at me.

'I was in hospital a long time. When I came out, I got this flat. Had to give up working. I used to be a record producer. My hearing isn't right any more. But friends help me with stuff. I get along. Never saw those two again.'

'Last month, Carl, a man died in the toilet you were beaten up in. Something frightened him to death. I've been there and felt… a trapped rage. Something that went for me because I was there. Caught in its own past. Do you know what I'm talking about?'

A longer pause. He finished the glass and refilled it. Still looking away from me, he said: 'I was in hospital a long time. So many voices echoing in the long corridors. So many dead people. Every night, I dreamt of fighting back. I still do.'

His dream hadn't come true. It had just echoed, distorted. 'An innocent man has been killed. It's got to stop, Carl.'

He looked at me silently for a few minutes. His face was very pale. 'I couldn't stop it if I tried,' he said at last. 'Can you hold your breath in your sleep? but it'll be over soon. Because I'm going downhill. You'd think that was easy in a wheelchair, but it isn't.

'It's not just me. There are the others. The backing vocals. That's where it really comes from. They've been waiting for a chance to come through. And they don't care.'

'Can you hold them back?' I asked.

He tried to shake his head, winced with pain. 'But I'll be one of them. It's harder on the other side.'

'It doesn't seem too easy on this one.'

I stood up and shook his hand. 'Goodbye, Carl. Take care. I hope you find your own voice again.'

'No chance.' He smiled. 'Won't be long now.'

I let myself out. As the door was closing, I thought I heard him call after me: 'Just keep your ears open.' I walked down the stairs, which took long enough for me to persuade myself that nothing out of the ordinary had been said.

Three days later, I was on a night shift in the jewellery quarter. The sky was written over with the blank message of autumn. It was a couple of hours before dawn. I'd been watching the streets, looking out for suspicious activity. But it had been a quiet night. I was looking down over the Victorian cemetery in Vyse Street and thinking about coffee when a faint cry echoed from the buildings. It rose to a scream of fear, then trailed off. I shivered. There was no-one in sight.

Another distant voice cut through the still air. Then two or three at once. The cries opened the night like wounds. They were all around me now, but not coming from the streets: they were in the sky, or else in the unlit tower blocks. They joined together in an atonal chorus that had disturbing power, but no harmony. Then, as suddenly as they had arisen, the voices faded to the restless static of cars on their way into the city.

THE LAST WITNESS

There are crimes of passion, and then there are crimes of impatience. When Tony Forbes marched a journalist at gunpoint onto the mock-Chinese bridge at Brindley Place (or perhaps it was the mock-Italian bridge) and fired a bullet through his throat in front of more than a dozen witnesses, he wasn't driven by overwhelming inner demons. Nor was he trying to make a public scene. He just didn't like waiting.

As a local property developer, Forbes had a reputation for seizing the day and the night along with it. He'd made his money buying up houses and renting the rooms to ex-offenders on probation or rehab programmes. As a result, he'd acquired a team of low-profile hard men who owed him. When he started opening casinos and lap-dancing clubs in Birmingham, the local authorities were so keen to avoid looking his way that he had to place the envelopes in their back pockets.

One time, he couldn't get permission to demolish a swimming baths that was a listed building. He bought the properties on either side, and within a month the baths had collapsed due to ground subsidence. Another time, the owners of a city-centre nightclub turned down a cash offer from Forbes. That weekend, the building caught fire. By the time the fire engines got through the blockade of stolen cars parked around it, there wasn't much left.

The journalist worked for a local paper. He'd written an article about Forbes' business practices, using the paper's disapproval of the sex industry as a platform. After Forbes had spoken to the paper's editor, the reporter had been sacked. But that hadn't been enough for Forbes. I imagined him stewing in his office, turning quiet as the summer day ended, reaching in his desk drawer for a little gun.

A year earlier, a female colleague of mine had interviewed a young woman in hospital. She'd said Forbes had beaten and raped her. That week, one of his building contracts had fallen through. She'd been working as an office cleaner. According to her testimony, he'd been in a state of frantic tension when she'd come in to empty his waste-paper basket. What had triggered the assault wasn't her turning down his proposition. It was when he'd offered her money and she'd still said no. We weren't able to establish whether Forbes had used a threat or a bribe to gain her silence, but she dropped the charges and then left the country with her young daughter.

We were very keen to talk to the witnesses of the bridge shooting. Fourteen gave us statements in the hours following the incident, a long and sleepless night for all of them. A day later, three of the witnesses decided they'd been too drunk or coked-up to have any clear memory of what they'd seen. By then, the *Birmingham Post* had carried a front-page photo of its journalist floating in the canal, his throat torn open.

Within a week, another five witnesses had withdrawn the parts of their statements that related to the description of the killer and his identification from photographs. That left six people—four men and two women—who were willing to say in court that either Forbes or his identical twin had fired the gun. By this time, the businessman had been charged with murder. He insisted it was a fabrication: he'd been in the area, but some distance from the bridge, when the shooting had happened. That meant that sightings of him before and after didn't contradict his testimony. We'd found the gun in the canal, void of bullets and fingerprints.

We tried to keep the identities of our witnesses secret. I still have my suspicions about who in the force was leaking information to Forbes or his gang, but it wouldn't be fair to say. We had Forbes in custody for eight months, waiting to bring him to trial. I didn't see much of him. Not that there was much to see: he was a small, bald man with a paunch that dwindled in his Winson Green cell. His interviews were very dull reading.

Why were we so upset, he wanted to know, about the death of a paid liar? Why were we—and our cronies in the press and the council—paying other liars to testify against him?

The first key witness we lost was a marketing executive of thirty or so. He lost his job after insomnia caused him to make a number of costly mistakes. It also caused him to suffer a fatal heart attack when the weather turned colder. The second key witness, a graphic designer in her twenties, took a possibly accidental overdose of sleeping pills when drunk. Her mother said that she'd complained of bad dreams, and had lost a lot of weight since the summer. In both cases, of course, having witnessed the murder might have led to sleep problems.

The third and fourth witnesses were a teenage couple. Their testimonies were a perfect match, and a sentimental side of me imagined they were too. Certainly being a couple helped them to be resolute about speaking in court. But something went wrong over the Christmas break, because they were found cold in the tiny flat they shared. They'd taken cyanide and died in each other's arms. A note signed by both of them said: *Sorry, we can't go on. This is the only way out of the madness. If we leave it too late they won't even let us die.* As you can imagine, we interrogated Forbes pretty hard over that. But there was no evidence.

As the new year began, we were in daily contact with both of the remaining witnesses. One said he was afraid, but hadn't been intimidated. He wasn't even sure what he was afraid of. The other, a security guard, crashed his motorcycle into a railway bridge and died in an ambulance. There was no frost on the road. The day before his funeral, our last witness was admitted to a psychiatric unit after taking an overdose of painkillers. He was diagnosed schizophrenic and put on a cocktail of anti-psychotic drugs. Obviously, he would not be able to appear in court. We stalled, trying to keep Forbes in custody, but knew we'd have to release him.

I went to see Michael, the last witness, in hospital. He was nearly thirty, a projectionist in a multiplex cinema. In interviews he'd come across as bright, alert and vivacious. Now he was shaky and slow to react. That was partly the effect of the drugs, of course, but something else was behind it. The word that came to mind when I saw his drawn face was *haunted*. His hair was turning grey. We had a coffee in the day room, and I asked him if things were clearer to him now.

'They are,' he said. 'I could never go back to pretending. We're all in coffins, slowly decaying, unable to sleep. The toxic pit is wiping away our faces. How can you go into work, talk to people, when they're already dead? How can you hold someone… or kiss them?' He shivered. 'I didn't see it until a few weeks ago. But it's been there all my life. When you admit the truth, they call it going mad. You wake up and realise you've spent thirty years in the land of the dead. What do I have to *do* to make the visions stop?'

'What are your visions of?' I asked.

'The reality.' Michael's eyes were pits of grief. 'People waking up in coffins, staring, dead but awake. Rats eating their flesh while they sit on the bus. How can you kill yourself when you're already dead? This is the afterlife. The place of desolation. I'm not afraid any more. The end has already come. Nothing ever changes.' He was crying, but only with his eyes.

One of his phrases stuck in my head. 'Where is the toxic pit?'

Michael looked down at the tiled floor. Almost too quietly for me to hear, he muttered: 'It's all that's left of home.'

There was a derelict house in Kings Heath, near the Maypole shopping centre, that the environmental services team had been concerned about for some time. The floor had fallen through, and the rising water table had flooded the basement cavity. The houses on either side were unoccupied, but local people had complained of rats and a bad smell that was unmistakeable if you walked past. The council had been trying to persuade the owner to take action for some time, without success. Lately he'd had other things to worry about. It was one of Tony Forbes' properties, a former halfway house for offenders. No-one had lived there for a dozen or more years.

I drove there on a rainy morning in late January, through the featureless streets of the Maypole housing estate. A few people were around, catching buses to early shifts in the factories outside Birmingham. The rain blurred my view, and it took me a while to find the narrow back road with the ruined house. The front door and windows were securely boarded up, but a gap in the crumbling brickwork on one side—like a cashpoint—was merely stuffed with grey tarpaulins. I'd heard that at one time, local youths had used the house as a shooting gallery. Why was it still easy to get in? The cold had muffled the stink of decay, but when you got close to the house it was an effort to breathe.

With some difficulty, I pushed through the gap and lowered my feet nervously to the floor. This had been the kitchen, though only some damp-blackened shelves and a cupboard remained. I tried not to look too closely at the heaps of refuse in the corners. My torch beam reflected from broken glass and slimy fungus. Damp hung in the air like clingfilm. I pressed two gloved fingers against my nostrils. Something moved behind the inner wall, scratching. It was hard to believe this had once been someone's home.

The kitchen door was hanging from its upper hinge. I stepped through into the living room. At once, a wave of cold nausea hit me and I had to crouch down, holding onto the rotting doorframe. Most of the floor was taken up by a yawning cavity, like an infected wound in an old man's foot. Its edges were streaked with green and yellow mould. The stench wasn't only decay: there was something chemical in it, some kind of toxic waste that had seeped in from the factories nearby. Maybe the source of that waste no longer existed: this pit was its resting place, a museum of pollution.

I crouched there for a while, feeling too sick to move. The walls were crusted with narrow bookshelves, their contents badly damaged and stained. A hanging picture frame held only a dull mass of webs. I stared at the black water a few inches below the splintered edge of flooring. It didn't reflect the light of my torch. I could see a faint, ghostly picture down there: a collection of stills, like a family album. It showed me the life I could have had. The success, the money, the easy sex. Things you want no matter how hard you try to pretend you don't. My dreams were slowly rotting down there. I couldn't look away.

Slowly, I realised the photos weren't just beneath the surface. Some of them were floating. I reached down and lifted a small piece of glossy paper from the foul water. One side of it was smeared with colour, but there wasn't much left of the face it had shown. I pulled out another snapshot, another ruined face. The third photo I picked up was almost blank. I dropped them; they sank, then floated back.

If there'd been anyone here, I would have asked him if he worked for Forbes. Shown him the photo of the businessman that I kept in my wallet. We needed to know who was running his errands. But the only living person here was me. I was conscious of a strong urge to jump into the pit. It would only be accepting what I already knew: that there was nothing for me in the future. But I didn't. I stood up, holding onto the flaking wall, and took out my wallet.

His pale face looked up at me, keen to know why I was wasting his time. I dropped the photo into the black water, then turned and felt my way back through the kitchen and the gap in the brick wall to the street. Cars were passing; children were walking to school. It felt like a film had started running again after being stuck for hours on a single frame.

A week later, our last witness died of a seizure in hospital. We had to release Forbes, as the trial would not be possible. But within a month, he was arrested on a second murder charge. He'd shot a business rival in an argument, then wandered into a canalside pub for a drink. With blood spattered on his jacket and shoes. The barman had called the police. This time we had forensic evidence. But once again, there was no trial. Forbes was judged mentally unfit and committed to a secure unit for a minimum of ten years.

He'd been there for six months when I went to visit him. I had to leave my watch and keys in a safe at the entrance. A male nurse escorted me to his room on the third floor of the warren-like building. He told me Forbes was known as 'the miser' among the other inmates.

Forbes was sitting by his bed, staring through the barred window. It was hard to recognise the smug businessman we'd arrested a year before. His face was gaunt; there were black smudges under his eyes. He'd lost so much weight that nothing fitted him. His hands were shaking, and he kept rubbing them together to disguise the fact.

When he saw me, a trace of hope flickered across his lined face. 'Tell them to pull it down,' he said. 'Talk to your friends in the council. That house, it's got to be demolished. It's infecting the whole area.'

'They demolished it years ago,' I said. 'There's a new building there now.

It's an undertaker's.'

As I got up to leave, Forbes shot me a look of sick despair. I knew that, like the last witness, he'd finally lost the fear. And with it, his inability to wait.

That was twelve years ago. For all I know, he's still there.

DREAMS OF CHILDREN

Just before the end of the last century, I had to interrogate one of the strangest criminals I've ever met. He was a serial witness.

Two men had been involved in a violent argument in the Acocks Green bus station after midnight. One was found dead the next morning, his skull broken on the concrete floor. Another, stabbed in the belly, had crawled out into the street and dialled 999 on his mobile, but died before the ambulance got there. Both were known members of a local gang that handled stolen cars.

The bus station had a CCTV camera. The images were poorly lit, but you could just about make out the two men arguing and then fighting. And with them, but not physically involved, a third man. Who'd watched the fight and then disappeared. In the street, not far from the stabbed man, we found a bloodstained cigarette butt. The blood didn't match the DNA of either of the dead men.

Our witness was a thin man, young-looking, with cropped dark hair. DI Maxwell, who knew a lot about Birmingham gangs, thought it might be Peter Webb—or 'PJ', as he was known then. 'He seems to live on the edge of trouble,' she told us. 'We can't pin anything serious on him. But every bunch of people he's been involved with has fallen apart—violently. He moves from one gang to another, but the result is always bad news. I think he's some kind of agent provocateur. Maybe working for Special Branch. But nobody's telling us anything.'

The only mention of him in police records was five years old. Which would seem to back up Maxwell's theory. He'd been one of a dozen or so people detained after a ruck in a Stechford pub. Three teenage lads were glassed; one needed a blood transfusion. Webb was knocked to the floor and cut his hands on broken glass. Or so he claimed, and no-one said otherwise. One detail from his statement caught my eye. When asked how the fight had started, he said: 'There was no reason. It's just what people are like. Put them together, and that's what happens.'

After much deliberation, we decided to bring him in but not charge him with anything. If he was a police agent, someone might let us know. Though he probably wouldn't. The left hand rarely knows what the right hand is doing.

After a low-key search, we found PJ lurking in Bar Selona. Where the other villains seemed to be giving him a wide berth. He agreed to have a quiet talk with us at the Acocks Green police station. I wasn't sure he was the man we'd seen on CCTV, but he could have been. A slight, furtive-looking youth with bitten lips and dull eyes. He denied any connection with the incident. When we asked for a blood sample, he initially refused. I noticed he was wearing high-quality calfskin gloves. When we threatened to charge him, he gave in and took off his left glove. The hand was pale and bony, and covered with little scars.

His blood matched the smear on the cigarette. I prepared myself to get to know PJ. At once, I realised I wasn't keen to. There was something about him that depressed me and made me angry. His calm denial that he'd been a witness to the two deaths. The near-certainty that he'd smoked a cigarette while watching the stabbed man die. And the strange hint of martyrdom with which he greeted the demand for an interview after the blood test. As if the weight of police brutality had descended on his neatly-cropped head.

At the very least, he was guilty of withholding information. I wanted to put him under arrest, but Maxwell said I'd be threatening his cover. I said he probably didn't have any. 'He's not posing as a villain, he is one.' We were both getting quite angry. I went back to the interview room, where PJ was sitting with a mug of tea. He'd brought out a notebook and was drawing sketches in it, holding a pencil in his gloved right hand.

I asked to see the notebook, and he handed it to me silently. He'd been drawing a sketch of me, naked, standing with my back to a wall. There were open wounds in my neck, belly and groin. A junior colleague glanced at the picture and laughed. 'It's not fucking funny,' I said, and for a few seconds felt so angry I didn't know what to do. I threw the notebook down on the desk. PJ picked it up, wincing as if his hand was too painful to use.

A feeling of helplessness grew in me. There didn't seem any point in talking with him, or with anyone. I asked him to come in and answer some questions the next day. He agreed, with the same air of wounded innocence. Then Maxwell chewed me out for postponing the interview. 'I said don't arrest him, not let him walk away,' she said. 'You'll get nothing out of him tomorrow: you've lost the momentum.' I shrugged. 'What's wrong with you?' When I was alone, I punched the wall so hard the plaster broke.

That night, I dreamt of being back in school assembly. All my colleagues from the police station were there as children. I screamed silently as they dragged me up on the stage, stripped me naked and cut me open with tiny craft knives, laughing violently as I bled from my hands, face and penis. I woke up shaking, my face wet with tears. 'What's wrong?' Elaine said. I couldn't answer. She embraced me, but I drew away and curled in on myself, playing dead.

The interrogation took a long time to go nowhere. Maxwell was busy with another enquiry, so it was just me and my longtime colleague DS Austin with PJ and the branding irons. Interestingly, he wasn't bothered about having a solicitor on hand. 'Don't need some shyster to represent me,' he said. 'Everyone knows I'm on my own.'

PJ's account of the fight at the bus station was strangely detached. 'Those two never got on. They didn't have the discipline to work together.' An argument over money had turned personal, and he'd been unable to stop them attacking each other. Why had he let Gary, the stabbed man, die on the pavement? 'I tried to help him. But it was too late. That's what people like you can't understand.'

I asked what he meant by that. He gave me a bored look. 'You're not as intelligent as your colleague, are you? He knows what I'm talking about. You're starting with the answer you want and working backwards. Someone always has to be to blame. And you've already decided it's me.'

'Why do you draw pictures of wounded people?' Austin asked.

'So that's a crime now?' PJ said. 'Something else I'm to blame for. All the trails of evidence lead to me.' His deadpan selfishness was depressing me. I felt sure I could get a clearer statement from him if Austin would keep quiet instead of pandering to his ego.

We carried on recording PJ's statement about the fight. He seemed to relish the details of violence. 'Gary was bleeding to death. I tried to make him keep still, but he crawled out of the station like a slug, leaving a trail of blood. He seemed to think an ambulance would save him. I had to walk away. I'd already seen one friend die that night. And you ask why I kept quiet about it. You're really not human at all, are you?'

His words made me feel a peculiar kind of emptiness. I was trying to fight that off and concentrate on what exactly he'd done, but Austin broke in: 'Does suffering have a religious significance for you?'

Enough. 'Fuck's sake, can we stick to the facts?' I said. 'You're playing his game. We need to get a statement, not a fucking gospel.'

Austin went pale. 'You're not even trying to understand,' he said. 'You're making it all too easy for him. We have to get under—'

'Like fuck—' I was reaching out to turn off the tape recorder, but my hand clenched into a fist. Austin was already on his feet. I was about to smash him in the face when I glimpsed PJ across the table. His eyes were closed; there was a look of mingled pain and joy in his silent face. His hands were rubbing together slowly, and blood was smeared between them.

In my mind, like a book of sketches, was every humiliation I'd ever suffered. Every time I'd been made to feel worthless—as a child, as a youth, as a man. Behind each image was something I couldn't see clearly and didn't want to. The deformed shape of the human creature. In that long moment I felt myself begin to die. Then PJ opened his eyes, saw my blank face, and smirked.

'You'll be sorry,' the witness said as I marched him down the stairs to a holding cell. Maybe I would. But if his cover was so deep, a night in custody wouldn't break it. Or maybe there was no cover, except plain sight. If so, I'd make him take a look at himself. The CCTV footage hadn't been a fluke. As much as he needed to see, he needed to be seen. I'd taken his sketchbook, which seemed to cause him real distress. While PJ festered in the holding cell, I sat in my office and leafed through it. I was on a night shift, and was pretty close to the edge.

At three a.m. I quietly unlocked the door to his cell. He was standing by the window, awake. By the flickering barred mercury light in the ceiling, I poured the torn-up pages of his sketchbook from a jar onto the floor. He didn't react. I walked out, locking the door behind me.

I don't recall most of what I worked on that night, except that it was violent. Two of our informers wouldn't be heard from again. In Walsall, where DI Maxwell had gone, a lawnmower squad was cutting down the long grass. Crimes of passion were thin on the ground: the smart money was with crimes of profit.

Before dawn, I went back to the holding cell. I don't know what I was expecting. A massacre painted in his blood? PJ was standing at the window, just like before. On the far wall was the reassembled picture of me, the scraps of paper stuck in place, the wounds smeared with red. I stared at it, and began to shake.

The cell was colder than I remembered. Behind my back, PJ said: 'I know what you're made of.' When I turned to face him, my sleep-deprived eyes made him seem almost featureless. Like his own CCTV image. There was nothing I could do but sign the release form. Too tired to drive, I caught a train home and went straight to bed. My dreams were bad, but at least I didn't remember them.

I never saw the witness again. That month, a major turf war broke out between gangs involved in most of Birmingham's organised crime: drug dealers, sex industry traffickers, property developers. When the dust had settled and the chalk outlines had faded, I learned that PJ had left the region. Nobody knew where he was.

Ten years on, I still wonder about him. Was it wrong to let him get away? Where did he end up? Did his hands feed violence, or feed off it? What games are they learning now? I read the papers and look on the Internet, which is probably his new playground, and wonder.

WAITING FOR THE THAW

It was a quiet February morning. The city had been snowbound for over a week, and finally it had thawed enough to rain. An hour into the shift, we had a 999 call from a landlord in South Yardley. One of his tenants had done a runner owing him a month's back rent. The landlord had let himself into the flat and found two dead people sitting on the sofa. Neither was the tenant.

DC Blake and I drove up from the Acocks Green station, past the cemetery and the dark twin towers of the Swan Centre. The landlord, a middle-aged Irish Brummie with no form worth mentioning, met us in the driveway. He owned half a dozen houses in this street, reconditioned terraces divided up into self-contained flats. A nervous-looking woman in a housecoat stood in the doorway, watching us and smoking.

'I haven't seen Mr Dorn in six weeks,' he said. 'He usually pays the rent on time. Flat's been in quite a state, but he's been there. Came round last month and he wasn't answering the door. I came back the next night, still no answer. Left a note. Last week, tried again. Left another note. If he was having problems, I wanted to try and sort something out. He's been a good tenant. This morning, I let myself in.

'There was a funny smell in the flat. Not really bad, but cold. I went through into the living room and there were two people on the sofa. I could tell they'd been dead for a while. Maybe the freeze had stopped them decaying more, I don't know. But neither of them is Kerry Dorn. One's an old man, sixty or more. The other's a boy of eight or nine. Both really thin, like they've starved to death or something. No blood, no signs of a fight.'

An ambulance had arrived while the landlord was speaking to us. He was shivering now. 'I'll take you up there,' he said, then glanced at the ambulance. 'What's that for?'

'Got any better ideas?' I said. The three of us and two paramedics went up to the second floor, where the landlord unlocked a door. At once, I knew what he'd meant by a 'cold smell'. It was like the smell of narcotics, but not the same. Nothing like the smell of decay. It wasn't quite a human smell.

At least the bodies were whole. They were sat together on the couch, wrapped in sheets and blankets. Their faces were grey. Could they have frozen to death? The old man was crouching forward, his skinny back to the arm-rest, his arms around the boy who was sitting with his arms and legs drawn in close. The embrace didn't look like it had been sexual. There was an odd similarity between the two thin faces, like a family photograph. Perhaps that was just them being dead.

The only other item on the couch was a cheap notebook with black card covers. It was half filled with notes in tiny, jagged handwriting. At a glance, it didn't seem to contain anything of practical relevance. I decided to take it back to the station for analysis. As I picked it up, I noticed a few scorchmarks in the battered couch; the ashes of a cigarette or the like were stuck to the fabric.

After taking photos and marking off the crime scene— though unsure if it really was that—DC Blake and I helped the paramedics wrap up the bodies and take them to the ambulance. Then we went for a coffee in the Swan Centre. Patches of grey snow and thin slates of ice were slipping from the roofs; I couldn't avoid thinking the city was shedding its dead skin.

Janet Blake brought me a large cappuccino. I must have been shaking, because she gripped my arm and said 'Not used to this, are you?' She'd been a nurse. I smiled and tried to look as though stiff cadavers were normal company for me. But I couldn't speak. 'Don't worry,' she said. 'They don't care.'

Torn sheets of rain were crumpling against the window. The sky looked too empty to be producing so much water. I gripped the notebook, which felt colder than paper should, and thought of Morrissey's line about *the ghost and the storm outside*.

As I'd suspected, the notebook didn't offer much information. It was apparently the start of some formless impressionistic novel. The author, or narrator, was either drugged or psychotic, though the neatness of the handwriting suggested meticulous control of the writing process. All the rationality was on the surface.

The only significant thing for our enquiry was the recurrent suggestion that some kind of revelation or crisis was just around the corner. If the author was the missing Kerry Dorn, perhaps he'd felt his own breakdown looming. But there was no mention of anyone staying with him, no friends or family. His medical records gave as next of kin: *Unknown*.

What we could establish of Dorn's background made it look like he'd been disappearing on the instalment plan. Good school qualifications but a poor job record. A history of treatment for depression, but no severe episodes. No drug history. His mother had died twenty years before, his father more recently. He'd lived with a girlfriend at one time, but had apparently been single for years.

Lately he'd been working night shifts in a local factory that made plastic gloves, but he'd stopped going into work four weeks before the landlord found the bodies in his flat. For most of that time, he seemed to have been completely alone. It had snowed three times, and each time frozen for days on end. His phone had been disconnected since the late autumn.

I took photocopies of the written pages in the notebook, though for all the sense they made I might as well have copied the blank pages at the end.

The snow has fallen deep on the streets, on the frozen canals, in the bedrooms, into our open mouths. The snow preserves stillness, hides the decay underneath. We're all waiting for the thaw. Waiting for the facades to break down and reveal the truth. Tired of wearing the mask of Prozac or whisky, pretending that when the spoiled meat defrosts it will somehow smell fresh again. The cat in the deep freeze will get up and walk.

Even in winter, you'd be surprised how many people are out on the streets at night. Standing under railway bridges. Walking alone on the Grand Union Canal towpath. Sitting in the doorways of derelict pubs as if waiting for them to open. Silent people gathered in car parks and bus shelters, waiting. I don't really know what for. Some of them look faded or unfinished, you can tell they're not really there.

Maybe they're desperate for some kind of human contact. Like the boy under the viaduct last night who asked me for a blow job. I can't do that kind of thing any more. Feel too old in one way, but in another way back in a state where all I want is to feel safe. The pure loneliness of having nothing to give. I need to be held, but if anyone tried I'd be afraid of them. The only thing that turns me on is walking into an old park toilet that reeks of stale urine and despair. Reading the desperate messages. Nothing to lose.

The psychiatrist said I needed to care for myself. But to do that I'd have to be outside myself. I can feel or survive, that's the choice. The part of me that isn't screaming for comfort is dry and sterile, no longer connected to humanity. How can this scrapheap of needs and reactions be treated as human? I miss my father. Sometimes I think I'll find him out there, walking the streets, trying to find his way home. What they cremated was just a puppet without strings.

The other day, I went walking in Grove Park to feel my father's ashes under my feet. In winter it's like a charcoal sketch of itself. The frozen leaves on the pale grass. The line of poplar trees like guardians of memory. The wide cedar that dropped needles of frost on me as I walked under its skeletal branches. The white bruises on the black ice of the pond. Life waiting to be set free by the melt, to release its long cry of pain. When the meds wear off. I was thinking about Lisa, the baby she'd lost. My sense of relief.

When I'd walked through the trees at the Harborne end of the park, I could look down onto the narrow river that emerges from the ground, trickles on for a mile or two, then goes back under. This is where I scattered the ashes. There was a smell of petrol and decaying trees. I walked alongside the streak of frozen water until it went under a brick road-bridge. There was a group of youngsters waiting there. They were dressed in black ski jackets and jeans, smoking something that wasn't tobacco or cannabis. They looked cold. One of them, a girl, said to me: 'Do you want to free yourself?' I said yes.

She explained to me what it took. Asked what money I had. I told her five quid on me and sixty in the bank. That had to last me a fortnight. She told me to go and get it, then come back. I hesitated. She touched my hand, smiled. A vision flickered over the frozen ground, quick as a flame over a lake of petrol. The city coming to life. Trees, birds, cats. And people. Life everywhere, breathing and dancing and caressing. Even the sky was alive. Then the flicker of vision passed over, and the winter slipped back over the city like the fire curtain when the film has ended.

So I went to the cashpoint. Felt like I was paying for my own grave. But what the fuck else was there for me? With this, at least there was a chance of something. I handed over the notes to the group. They all touched my arms for a moment. The girl gave me a paper twist of powder, a card with some *words in a language I didn't recognise, and a kind of musical instrument like a wooden mouth-organ. I asked if I could do the ritual with them, but she shook her head. 'Alone.' Then she kissed me. Her lips tasted dry and metallic.*

Maybe I'll see them again, when I've freed myself. After the thaw. And together we can help everyone to change. Tonight I'll know.

That was it. No notes to indicate how the story would end. Probably he was making it up as he went along.

A week later, Janet Blake slipped into my office at the start of the morning. 'They've got the test results on the two bodies from the Dorn case,' she said. 'The old man and the boy. I heard from the path lab at the coroner's office. Thought I'd tell you in private, 'cause it's… well, they've screwed up. Makes no sense.

'Dr Murray at the path lab said there's something wrong with the bodies. Maybe they've already been embalmed in some way. They haven't changed in nine days. There's no deterioration, no change in skin tone, nothing.'

'Maybe they worked with chemicals. Have we identified them yet?'

'That's the other fucked-up thing,' Karen said quietly. 'The tissue samples don't match anyone on record. But the two guys were obviously related. Dr Murray said the DNA profiles of the two bodies were so similar, they could have been from the same sample. The two bodies could be the same person.'

That weekend, I went to Grove Park in Harborne and found the narrow stretch of river above the ground. There were no kids hanging around the dark bridge at the edge of the park. But there was a cold smell that suggested pollution in the water. The river was flowing, but as usual it was sluggish. The recent snow had nearly all melted, and the winter trees were glistening with dew. Slowly, and with the marks of decay still visible, the landscape was returning to life.

STIFF AS TOYS

I suppose we've all wanted to do it at one time or another. Not just the outcome, I mean, but the exact process. Like taking himself apart. It happened around four a.m. at the main salvage yard in Digbeth. Peters came alone, got out of his car and climbed onto its roof, then used that to scale the high wall around the yard. He tore his arms and legs on the razor- wire. Up there on the brick wall, streaming blood, he upended a small can of paraffin over himself and flicked his lighter. Then he jumped. Like a small piece of rocket debris re-entering the atmosphere. The rusty metal edges he fell on cut him apart. His hands turned to knotted lumps of carbon. The fire spread through fragments of plastic and leather, but soon went out.

There was nothing much to burn.

How do I know this? Partly from what the pathologist told me, partly from my own imagination. I worked with Peters for three years, before he took early retirement. He'd been in the force a lot longer than me. Lately we'd been talking to him. Overtly for his advice, covertly in case he was involved in some way. Was that Avery being superstitious? Assuming that Peters' breakdown had turned him into someone else? Peters must have realised. But I don't believe that's why it happened. The police were nothing more than half-sighted witnesses. As usual.

Peters didn't work out in Acocks Green. He was a city centre man, with an office at the Steelhouse Lane station. Our local station is a suburban throwback, in between the railway line and the canal: an immaculate red sandstone building with a neatly clipped front lawn. People still talk about Acocks Green 'village', because it has buildings like this. But the façade is only a brick deep. Reality sits inside, a still image of what walks outside. It's getting darker. Too dark to see anything.

The first death was a factory worker, a foreman on an industrial estate in Nechells. He'd been on a late shift and was going out to his car when it happened. Clearly a gangland killing, though we couldn't link him to any organisation we knew of. There was a long wall with some kind of mural painting, a busy civic scene the council had paid for. This foreman's blood was all over it in streaks and swirls, a Hogarth visited by Turner. They'd broken his arms, legs, spine and jaw, then used his body as a paintbrush. No witnesses. The security men in the factory behind the wall didn't hear anything. Maybe the jaw had been broken first.

Nearly a month later, the doorman at a city centre nightclub was found behind the dustbins at the back of a Japanese restaurant. One of those expensive places where they cook your meal on the table in front of you. There was nothing to suggest the restaurant staff were involved, though they recognised him as a customer. At least, from the photograph on his driving licence. Someone had pulled both his arms from their sockets, cracked his skull and removed the pieces as if peeling an egg. All over the West Midlands, we applied batteries to our contacts in the drug dealing network. No lights came on.

Early the next year, the female manager of a sports shop was crushed in the Tyseley car park where she was waiting for her boyfriend. It was him who phoned the police, and we had no reason to hold him once he'd given a statement. Her husband concerned us more, but there was no evidence. It would have taken more than one little bloke, however jealous, to do what had been done to her. About a month later, some charred human remains were found in the Sandwell Valley. It seemed that a body had been carved into pieces, then each piece wrapped in tarpaulin and set on fire. The skull was identified as belonging to a male schoolteacher in Bearwood. What he'd been doing in the Sandwell Valley, apart from dying, we were unable to determine with any certainty.

There was no clear evidence that these murders were linked. But DS Avery, who was working with me on the Tyseley case, thought there were enough common features in the MO to suggest a single gang. Maybe two psychopaths working together. What struck me wasn't just the brutality and callousness of the murders. It was the fragility of the victims. Four strong, physically fit adults. Each one broken, torn or burnt as if it were easy. As if they were brittle things that gave no resistance. We never found a weapon of any kind. In the Tyseley case, the murder weapon could have been a vehicle. But again, no real evidence.

Peters' early retirement was the result of a breakdown. He was a police psychologist, his background a mixture of forensic and social work. A major part of his job was talking to child victims of crime, often abuse. From that, he was drawn into working with child offenders. There was a lot of overlap. I remember him talking about the dolls. His department used to buy cheap dolls from Toys R Us in Union Street. Small ones, boxes of four. They used them to help kids reconstruct things that had happened. It was easier than describing or drawing pictures. Easier for a child to deal with, and easier to codify as a statement. After all, Peters' job was about evidence, not therapy. There was one case of an eight-year-old girl who used three dolls to show the harm her uncle and his drinking pal had made her do to them. Peters had nightmares about that. In another case, a boy in primary school used dolls to show how he and four mates had chased and battered an Asian boy, trapping him between them like hounds with a fox.

'Sometimes,' Peters said to me, 'they'd freak. They'd pick up a doll and break it, throw it at the wall, stamp on it. Dolls are simple things. But the way we use them makes them complicated. A doll is hollow, it can't feel pain. On the other hand, dolls don't heal. If you break a doll, it stays broken.'

The last time I saw Peters was at a conference in Wolverhampton. He looked pale and unslept, bags under his eyes to make a cat burglar jealous. Over a drink at lunchtime, he told me there was no such thing as childhood. 'We all live in a plastic world,' he said, fatigue dulling his eyes. 'Credit cards, software, videos, CDs. They're all kinds of doll. We all live with dolls, buy and sell them, watch and hold them. It's an age of icons.' I vaguely recalled that Peters had a Baptist upbringing.

About a month later, I heard he was refusing to leave his house and had disconnected his phone. After some counselling, he recovered the ability to step outside the front door. But he didn't return to work. Apparently he'd become a total recluse. He didn't have a family; his wife had left him a few years before, and his parents were dead. I sent him a card, inviting him to phone me if he felt like a drink and a chat some evening. He never replied. A constable from Hall Green told me he'd cautioned Peters for reckless driving at three in the morning. Alone in his battered silver Metro, wound up but straight, driving too fast around the nearly empty streets in search of something he wouldn't admit to and maybe couldn't name.

A couple of years went by. Then the spate of murders, and then Peters' apparent suicide. An officer who'd been to his house in Kings Heath described it as incredibly Spartan: no pictures, no patterned wallpaper, everything pure and simple. After his death, a police visit was made to his house. Not a real search, they weren't looking for anything hidden. Just for letters or a diary that might explain what had happened to him. The report commented on how spotlessly clean the place was. He'd obviously become obsessed with hygiene. No pictures or ornaments of any kind. No TV or newspapers. No mirrors. As the report said, the only clue was the hint of paranoia.

Three days after Peters' death, on a Friday night, DS Avery and I were called out to the brickworks in Greet.

It's a small factory with huge windows and a brightly lit interior; you can see it from miles away at night. Behind the factory is an alley where shift workers often hang around waiting for prostitutes. The woman who'd phoned the station was nowhere in sight. I heard an ambulance siren coming nearer as we jumped out of the car. The alley was littered with broken glass, as if several crates of empty milk-bottles had been smashed there. Halfway along it, a man was lying face up.

He looked like he'd been dropped there from a height, though no building was close enough. His blue shirt and expensive slacks were ripped at the sides, and his blood was turning the petals of broken glass from white to red. As we stepped towards him, his hand rose into the air as if reaching for something. His head twisted, stared past us. The eyes were blank. I heard something: a breath, a rustle of hidden movement.

His back twisted, shedding a vest of blood. For a moment, as he died, I could see them. No clearer than reflections in a window or creases in a plastic sheet. A circle of children, watching. Pale faces and thin hands. Nothing more. They were still. The ambulance pulled up next to our car. Two paramedics ran past us. Their boots crunched the fragments of glass like dried leaves.

By the time I got home, my wife Elaine was in bed. Our twelve-year-old daughter Julia was sitting up, listening to a Hole album and drowsily flicking through a make-up catalogue. I reassured her that all was well, Daddy was home safe and she could sleep tonight with no anxieties. 'More violence tonight?' she said. I nodded and she went silently to bed. When she'd gone I poured out a large vodka and drank it while reading the news update on Teletext. In Ulster, a teenaged Catholic girl had been killed in the home of her Protestant boyfriend. In America, a fashion designer had been shot twice through the head. I drank the vodka, chewed the ice and went up to bed. Elaine was asleep.

It was a warm July night, the closeness accentuated by a high pollen count and unprecedented levels of car exhaust pollution. I kept waking up, my limbs tense and shivery, then dropping off again. Some time after dawn, I dreamed of making love to Elaine: a hard relentless fuck, our faces pressed cheek to cheek, our legs thrashing in a perfectly timed disorder. Then I woke up, sunlight glittering in threads on the pale curtain. Elaine was awake too, and we made love just as I'd dreamt it; a little slower and sweatier, but essentially the same. It felt strange. Too much tension, not enough release. As if we were puppets of an impersonal need.

The murder enquiry kept me busy all weekend. It wasn't until Sunday night that I had the chance to visit Peters' house. I went on the bus; my own car was being mended, and I didn't want to use one of the station's vehicles. This was not an official search. I'd talked PC Monk at Hall Green into lending me the front door key. When I got there, it was starting to get dark. The house was in a tree-lined crescent with floppy and vaguely sinister foliage: willow, hawthorn, ash. I let myself in, remembering what Monk had said before about the house being pure and simple. And what Peters had said about simple things. The way we use them makes them complicated. It didn't take me long to find what I was looking for: a stack of furniture and junk obscuring the door to the basement. The door was wedged shut, but had never had a lock; I forced it open. A few rotting wooden steps led down into a small, low-ceilinged room that smelt quite strongly of damp. My lighter revealed a torch on a low shelf, next to the table.

The table was about six feet long and three feet wide. Its surface was covered with small plastic dolls. They were arranged in pairs or small groups. He'd painted expressions onto their faces and wounds onto their bodies. Many of them were broken or contorted, in terrible positions. The battleground could have represented every case he'd worked on. Maybe they were the same dolls. Red enamel paint gleamed in the weak torchlight. I stood there for a while, staring at the little pale figures. The accessories. I wondered what he'd used to mark them: knives, cigarettes, pliers? There were no such tools on the shelf. Only a few bricks in a corner of the room. I used one of the bricks to smash as many dolls as possible. Then I made a heap of the debris on the stone floor and set fire to it. The fumes of burning plastic almost made me pass out.

Eventually the air was clear. Nothing remained but a mat of sticky ashes and a few glowering flecks of dry red paint. I wasn't sure if I was symbolically destroying evil or destroying humanity. We never know. Was my sad little ritual any more superstitious than the rituals of courtrooms and prisons? Was it any more effective? I shut the basement door and put the furniture back against it. Ownership of the house had passed by default to a cousin of Peters who was currently living in the Channel Islands. Nobody would come down here for a while. I mentally apologised to Peters for blemishing his spotless walls.

Outside, it was dark; some rain had fallen. The pavements glimmered a faint yellow. There was a smell of ozone, like a beach tinted with sewage. I didn't feel like waiting for the bus. Rainwater dripped into my hair from the trees as I walked from Kings Heath through Moseley to Acocks Green. It was closing time. White-haired drunks staggered to find their bearings, arguing with the darkness. Cars rushed past at lethal speeds. Girls were picked up discreetly from bus shelters. I kept walking. Maybe it was just in my head, the sound I heard. All the way home: the warm air shaking with a hidden, buried laughter. Plastic laughter. Man's laughter. Manslaughter. Diminished responsibility.

THE VICTIM CARD

He died in the street, about an hour after falling through the smallish front window of his second floor flat. From the scattering of blood, and from some clinical evidence, it seemed his attackers had come down after him. His body had been kicked or thrown about while he was dying. But in all probability, he hadn't known about it. The flat itself told a worse story: broken furniture, shattered wine glasses, blood spattered over the walls with deliberate carelessness. A hammer had been used to smash the window from inside. There was a stink of burnt plastic or varnish; and yards of tape had been pulled out of some cassettes and coiled over everything like dried blood. The disembowelled tapes were all over the flat. There was no sign of breaking in. A grudge killing. This was in the posh part of Edgbaston; well-groomed evergreen trees had shielded his body from the roadway.

The victim's name was Simon Dael. He was twenty-six, worked in marketing. His flat was in a new block, but everyone living around him was much older than he was; and the building itself was surrounded by old houses. This could have helped to explain why the flat was infested with spiders. Both of us at the crime scene noticed this, though it didn't go into the report. Dael's medical records showed that he'd been a solvent abuser in his teens. His lungs were damaged, and he had an uncertain heart action. But if he was easy to kill, why had they gone to so much trouble? Another odd thing about his flat didn't strike either of us at the time: we were too busy cataloguing the evidence of mayhem. But in the car going back, DS Avery turned to me and said it. 'No fucking mirrors.' Unless they were behind his pictures.

That was the start of ten days' work, piecing together the life behind the death. To the police, life runs backwards: it starts with a corpse. It was a cold week in early summer. Rain settled like fine static from a roof of nimbostratus that never entirely cleared. I had other slates over my head: sorting out my marriage, trying to be polite to my wife's boyfriend, trying to persuade my daughter that starving herself wasn't going to make puberty any easier. I could have done with a bona fide killer to interrogate, or preferably several. This case waved them at me, like cards that wouldn't fall into my hands.

The most obvious lead was the death threats. There were three messages on Dael's miniature answerphone. The most recent was a young female voice. *Hello Simon, it's Anna. I hope you're OK. Just thought I'd get in touch again. I was at the club last night. There are some funny stories going round. I wanted to talk to you about them. I think we should talk. Please call me back. You know my number. 'Bye then.* That message had been left at five past midnight, around the time that its addressee lay dying in the street outside. Before that was an older female voice, probably a heavy smoker. *Hello Simon. I hope you're keeping well. Somehow I doubt it. Are you really out, or are you screening calls? Bit late to think of protecting yourself.* (Pause.) *Don't suppose you ever thought of protecting others. You fucking sod. I want you to know, your death is gonna be worse than mine. And I'll know. Because I'm going to see it.* The last few words after that were lost in a fit of asthmatic coughing.

The oldest message was exactly a minute of silence, followed by a few muttered words. The voice was gruff, Welsh, male. There was a lot of interference on the line. *Hi there, it's me. I'm still waiting for you. Don't think you can hide. Don't make me come for you, Simon. You wouldn't like that. This time I won't leave anything. I've had enough of this shit. See you.* Avery thought the call might have been made from a car phone. I thought it might have been made from a basement flat in Hell. We turned over the tiny black tape to the technician at the Acocks Green station. None of the people we interviewed later recognised either of the earliest two voices.

One of several follow-up visits to Dael's flat yielded the key to a small desk drawer. The desk itself supported a tasteful black CD rack. Dael's music collection was culled entirely from the Easy Listening shelves. My daughter Julia would probably have said he deserved to die. The drawer contained a few dozen personal letters, from various places and people. It also contained several used condoms, sealed in plastic bags and labelled with different women's names. Sometimes I hate police work.

The letters were mostly from girlfriends, or ex-girlfriends. They were infatuated, passionate, jealous, hurt and bitter by turn. There were two letters from a woman called Diane, who I thought might match the second voice on the answerphone. Both letters accused Dael of consciously infecting her with HIV; one letter hinted that Diane's friends would make him pay for what he'd done. Both letters were about three months old, and had been posted locally. Neither gave an address. There were several letters from Anna, reflecting a protracted affair and a slightly frosty aftermath; she accused him of insane selfishness. *You want me to be as fucked up as you. I don't think you know what 'genuine' means. First you tell me you're seeing someone else, then you ask my advice about how to please her. You think you can get into my head as easily as you got into my body, but you're wrong*. The address on her letters matched with the 1471 number we'd got from Dael's phone.

Finally, there were three letters from a man called Derek. He appeared to be a former schoolteacher—that is, Dael's teacher. His tone was an uneasy mixture of avuncularity, intimacy and depressive rage. References to 'the old days', particularly some camping holiday where something had happened. *Do you remember the tents shivering on the hillside in the pouring rain? The stars blinking, almost going out? How your tent leaked and you took refuge in the porch of the empty farmhouse? How I found you there at dawn, and took you inside? Don't tell me it wasn't good. We both know it will never be so good again*. The writing was tiny, crabbed, with wide spaces between the words. The most recent letter, dated a fortnight ago, said: *Don't play hard to get. I used to hurt you to make you come off. Is that what you want? Do you want me to make you bleed? To make you as dead as I feel now? It's dark in this room and it smells of loneliness. This has all got to end.* The envelope was postmarked Swansea; there was no return address.

With the letters and packets was Dael's expired passport. It gave his occupation as 'Entertainer'. The photograph showed a fairly handsome young man with a thin face and a haunted look in his eyes. His hair was dark, with a blond streak in the middle. There were no other photographs in his flat.

The suspicion that Derek was in some way a stalker was reinforced by three events in the week following the murder. Firstly, someone broke into Dael's flat in the night, using the rear window above the car park. The intruder searched through every container we hadn't removed, and took the locked desk apart. The next night, the officer on desk duty at the Acocks Green station took a phone call that was almost drowned by interference. He could just make out a Welsh voice, male, saying: *Simon Dael is better off dead. Let him lie. There's nothing to know.* Then the line went dead. He thought it was a mobile phone with dodgy batteries, or maybe a long way off. We couldn't trace it.

Just before dawn, the security camera picked up someone hanging around the station, checking the windows. A short figure, wearing a coat and some kind of soft hat. His face wasn't at all clear. Then he stooped and picked up a bottle, threw it against the station wall. By the time PC Monk had got outside, he'd gone. The glass had shattered hard: the fragments were no larger than hailstones.

After reading through the letters, interviewing Dael's friends was like walking out of shadow into daylight. His address book didn't include anyone called Derek, while next to the name 'Diane F.' there was only a local phone number which turned out to be disconnected; British Telecom records linked it to a minor radio station in Erdington. But there were two Annas listed in the address book, and one set of details matched what we had. Other friends of Dael's listed—from work, from college, from his involvement in amateur theatre and light entertainment—were shocked and anxious to help. But none of them knew anything about the man or woman who might have been pursuing him. Most of them said that Dael 'was a bit secretive' or 'had problems he kept to himself'. The strongest impression I got from them was how gifted Simon was. 'A brilliant actor. He could make you laugh, cry, anything. You always identified with him. He should have been on TV.'

His friends were like daylight: bright, comforting, ordinary. There seemed to be no answers here. I suspected that Anna might know a little more, and arranged to meet her during her lunch break at the museum. They were repairing the dinosaurs and other animal displays after recent flood damage: touching up the hollow fibre-glass or papier mâché exteriors to restore the impression of flesh and bone. Anna led me to her office, shut the door and plugged in the kettle. 'I'm really sorry about what's happened,' she said. 'It's dreadful. Have there been others, the same thing?'

I shook my head. 'We're assuming this was personal. Can you think of anyone who might have had a grudge against Simon?'

Anna looked puzzled. 'Of course. He treated everyone like shit. But I can't think of anyone sick enough to... I

mean, he was a selfish bastard. But that wouldn't justify...'
She shivered. I wondered if she knew about the collection
of souvenirs.

'Actually,' I said, 'he seems to have had quite a few
admirers. I've heard he was a brilliant actor. An entertainer,
like.'

Anna looked warily at me, perhaps aware that to sound
too critical of her ex might place her under suspicion. 'Look,
I don't want to sound bitchy. Simon was talented, but he'd
never have got anywhere. Not in a serious way. Everything
he did was an imitation. Sinatra, Tony Bennett, Gene Kelly,
Michael Caine... he'd have been a good impressionist, but
he wasn't clever enough for stand-up. He just did bits and
pieces: musicals, pantomimes. Sometimes when I phoned
him up, he'd pretend to be someone else. Make me think I'd
dialled the wrong number, then say my name.

'Marketing was perfect for him, really. Hiding behind a
phone, asking clients he'd never seen whether they could
afford not to buy some overpriced piece of crap. I think he
knew he wasn't really a good actor—but that made him
defensive. If anyone ever criticised him or contradicted him,
he dropped them cold. That's why the friends you talked to
have such a high opinion of him. He chose them on that basis.'

Something about this woman made me feel cold. 'So
why did he try to stay friends with you?'

'He wanted to get me back. Maybe he felt something,
behind all the games. It can happen, you know.' She poured
out two cups of coffee, silently composing herself; then
looked back at me. 'What else?'

I asked her about their affair and the breakup. Her
version of events matched what I'd gathered from the letters.

She'd tried to put up with his unfaithfulness until he told their friends about it, and even gone to her for advice about other women. 'I'm not sure if he was testing me, or just being incredibly stupid. He used honesty as a tactic sometimes. *You know, I'm being honest with you so you've got to accept it*. He loved the Oprah Winfrey show. Could never see how two-faced all that stuff was.' I asked her whether he'd talked about an ex-girlfriend called Diane. 'No.' Had he ever said anything about having passed on an infection to someone? 'Never. His health was fine. He never slept well, but I never thought of anything like that. But then, he wouldn't really have told me. We always took precautions anyway. I insisted.'

Did she think he was bisexual? 'Not really. He was quite homophobic. He liked being admired by men, but that was as far as it went. Once, when I told him his acting style was camp, he got really angry.' A flicker of doubt passed over her face. 'There was one thing. When we broke up, I went round to see him. He was drunk. Playing a Sinatra album over and over. He told me people had no idea what he'd been through. That he'd been hurt, abused, exploited. It was too far in the past to be put right. He'd been treated like a doll, a puppet.'

Anna paused. Her eyes were glittering. 'He wouldn't tell me any more than that. He'd finished a bottle of vodka. I was afraid he'd black out. I helped him undress and go to bed. When he was asleep, I left. To be honest, I didn't quite believe him. I thought he was playing the victim card. The next day, he phoned me up to tell me he was seeing a girl at work. They'd driven out to the Sandwell Valley and she'd given him a blow job.' She blushed, angry with herself for saying it. 'Why do I bother?'

'With what?' She didn't answer. 'One other question you might be able to help with. Do you know why Simon had no mirrors in his flat?'

Anna stared at me as if I'd made a sick joke. 'No mirrors? There were mirrors in every fucking room of that flat. It was like being followed around by your own face.'

That afternoon, I drove to Erdington. The radio station was nothing much: a couple of offices in the shadow of Highcroft, a sullen Victorian building that was the only full-scale mental hospital left in the city. Radio Scratching was staffed by two middle-aged blokes (who might have been a couple) and a platoon of volunteers. I vaguely remembered picking up their broadcasts on my car radio at night: soul, R&B, bluebeat, that kind of thing. White DJs in black and blue camouflage. They were instantly on guard when I introduced myself. I explained that I was trying to trace a woman called Diane F. That drew a blank. I showed them Dael's passport photograph. 'Do you recognise this man?'

One of the two bearded DJs shook his head; but the other frowned. 'Is he about twenty-five now? Only ten years ago, there was a boy used to come in here. Dean, his name was. That's him, I think. Yeah. He was into music, knew how to put stuff across, so we let him do a few sessions in the evenings. Brought most of his own records—Dusty Springfield, Marianne Faithfull, Sandie Shaw, all the sixties divas. We'd never play that stuff now. Too nostalgic. Anyway, he came along for a couple of months, then vanished. Always wondered what happened to him.' He looked at me. I said I couldn't tell him. All around us were shelves full of music: dusty cassette boxes, vinyl singles in numbered cardboard sleeves. So many voices, trapped like microscope slides in a hospital.

When I left, it was getting dark. The tall railings of Highcroft projected the image of a barred window onto the road. As I started up the car, a short woman in a dark fabric coat stepped in front of me from between two parked vans. Luckily, I hadn't built up any speed. Her pale hand slapped my windscreen, appearing to spread. She turned to face me, but the setting sun behind her got in my eyes, and all I could see was a reddish outline like a hood on fire. Then she was gone, melting into the shadow of the brick wall.

Elaine had gone out. I cooked myself a bacon sandwich and tried to think it all through. The case, that is, not my domestic problems. Julia was in her room, listening to the Manic Street Preachers; I went up to say hello. She'd taken down all her pictures and put up black curtains; it looked like a cell. There was a chocolate wrapper on her desk, which reassured me slightly. Then Pete Avery rang from the station to talk to me about Dael's autopsy report. Still no sign of Elaine; I drank some vodka, fried an egg in the grease of the bacon and watched a *Newsnight* feature on recovered memory. Then the phone rang again.

'Hello?' The line wasn't very clear; I thought I could hear traffic in the background, or some kind of atonal music. 'Hello? Can you hear me?' Static. Then a series of hard coughs, like echoes.

'Help me,' she said. Maybe the distortion was her breath. 'I've got to reach you…' More static.

'Where are you? Diane?'

'I don't know.' Her voice was clearer now. 'I'm dying. The world is poison. Can you help me? What's your name?'

I could hear a vague fluttering sound, like the beating of wings. 'Are you there?'

'Yes.' My voice sounded hollow in the silence of the dark room. I'd switched off the TV set. 'What's happened, Diane? What is it? If you won't say…' Her breath sounded wet in my ear. I thought I heard her say *Nowhere*; then the line went dead. Straight away, I rang 1471. The machine told me I'd last been called nearly an hour ago; gave me the number Avery had used.

A shadow reached out from the doorway. 'What's she like?' The light clicked on. 'Tell me about her.'

'Elaine, look—'

'It's OK. I don't blame you. Maybe it'll help.' She was wearing a black dress that was sexy without being obvious. Despite the make-up, she looked shattered. 'I hope it does.' I stared at the receiver, afraid to put it down. 'What's up?'

'I don't know,' I said. 'That wasn't a girlfriend, Elaine. It was someone we want to interview. She might be in danger. Or she might be dangerous. I don't fucking know.'

Elaine bent over me and stroked my hair in a weirdly maternal way. 'People have many sides to them,' she said. 'You can be close to someone and still not see the whole person, the other selves.' She touched my cheek. I stared at her silhouette. 'Are you coming up to bed?'

'Later. I need to think. It's work.'

'I love you. Believe that.'

'I'll try.' Her shadow merged with the doorway. The door closed silently. I switched the TV on and sat watching it with the sound off, a glass of neat vodka pressed to my lips. The phone didn't ring again. Some time after midnight I gave up and went to bed. Elaine was sleeping.

I didn't see Pete Avery the next day; he was off working on an extortion case in Leamington Spa. But the morning after that, he came quietly into my office and shut the door. His eyes were underlined. Without speaking, he sat down and looked past me at the window. I looked round, but could only see a green car emerging from one of the station garages.

'Bit of trouble,' he said at last. 'Didn't come to much, but… it's odd. And… well, embarrassing really. Last night, I got home late from this Ronald investigation. I'd just parked my car in the garage and got out when someone came up behind me. He just pushed me against the wall and… cut my trousers open with a razor. Started groping my arse. He was shorter than me, but heavier. His face was just behind me. He had foul breath.'

Avery stared at my desk. His face was red. 'I couldn't throw him off. But I reached up to the shelf above my head, grabbed a flashlight and swung it down at him. He must have been wearing a padded jacket, because whatever I hit was soft. He fell back and I came after him, but it was too dark to see. Then I switched on the flashlight, but he'd gone. I ran outside; no sign of the cunt. I couldn't find the razor either. But my fucking trousers were cut to ribbons.'

I stared past Avery at the framed photographs on my wall, faces drowned in artificial light. 'Have you made a statement?'

'Suppose I'd better. Do you think… that Derek guy?'

'I thought we'd agreed about this case. Don't look for connections where there aren't any. This bugger will have a go at someone else soon. You're lucky he didn't do more with that razor.' Avery was still avoiding my gaze. 'Look, you know how it works. You don't have to nail this guy when it's you he attacked. But we have to. Right away.'

'Sure. I know. Thanks for listening.' He stood up and turned away. 'Oh—Pete?' He stopped. 'Can't say I ever fancied you myself.'

'Fuck off,' he said and left. I downed some lukewarm coffee and set about writing my report on the Dael case. Stressing the established facts, downplaying what we didn't know. It wouldn't enable us to close the case; but it would allow us to give priority to other things. Until, eventually, it dropped out of sight.

Philip Larkin said that what will survive of us is love. It's a beautiful thought, but it's not particularly true. What will survive of us is far more likely to be hatred. Or disgust.

We knew almost from the start that Dael had killed himself. He'd burnt some varnish in a bowl and tripped on the fumes. Some of the damage to his hands and face was self-inflicted, before he smashed the window and jumped through. We found a razor in the garden with bloody fingerprints on it. His blood, his prints. The answerphone messages were another twist in his closed world. Voiceprint analysis confirmed what I'd heard at once: the two oldest messages were the same voice. Dael's. He didn't succeed in convincing me: I'm not a fan.

What came after was harder to understand. At least I thought I could see why he'd taken all the mirrors out of his flat. He stopped needing them. Dael's world was a corridor of mirrors, with himself not the origin but the vanishing point. He'd closed all the doors. He had to do

197

what he did just to convince himself of his own death: he had to be there to shut the coffin. But it didn't work. He's still there in the shadow lives he created. Still lying, still pulling threads, drawing others into his web. He may be only an absence, a silhouette, but he's there. Searching.

One day he'll find me. And I'll kill him.

WINTER JOURNEY

This isn't the easiest of stories to tell. It happened in Fox Hollies, a district where nothing is particularly straight or clear. Before they knocked it down to build another Lidl, the Fox Hollies pub was the business office of a criminal family. More money changed hands in the car park than over the bar. Not far away was a spot—the exact location changed from week to week—where stolen cars were parked overnight. By morning there would be only a bare chassis, stripped inside and out. We had informers there, but it was hard to keep track of things. By the time you cracked open a secret, there was nothing inside and people had moved on.

The centre of the district is just a small cluster of shops between two long parallel roads. To the north, a fringe of trees and a few acres of overgrown park separate the main road from a scraggy housing estate. The local council had commissioned a sculpture partway between the shops and the estate: a pillar supporting a resin fox, its body framed by the outline of a holly leaf. There was something oddly pagan about the image. I used to think it was a shame the fox couldn't tell us what it had seen.

One January in the late nineties, our contacts began to pick up rumours of a homeless boy who was stalking local people, stealing food from the take-away shops, occasionally biting someone or tearing their clothes. The word 'feral' was used more than once. No-one had contacted the police directly, but that was fairly normal for the district. I suspected it was an urban myth being used to explain the wounds of drunken fights or harsh outdoor sex. Still, we kept on the lookout for vagrants and stray dogs in the area. Nothing came to light.

Then an early morning patrol car spotted fresh bloodstains on the children's playground in the north-west corner of Fox Hollies Park. A cat had been torn apart on the concrete. The report suggested an incidence of urban fox-hunting: some local boneheads using a cat for bait, betting on their underfed pitbulls. But the pathologist in the Solihull station said the tooth marks on the stinking remains weren't those of a dog, or even a fox. They appeared to be human.

We found the boy two days later, in the woods near the Spring Road train station. The tracking dogs were reluctant to go near him, but they took us far enough for a torch beam to pick out a thin figure crouching between an oak tree and a factory wall. He tried to run, but we spread out and trapped him against the decaying wall. When the torchlight painted a white target on his face, he froze and shut his eyes. I came towards him with handcuffs, while two other officers backed me with a raised baton and a concealed gun. The boy looked to be about sixteen, his pale face flecked with mud, his clothes torn and grimy. The torchlight caught his narrow cheekbones and bared teeth. Suddenly he opened his eyes, and I saw nothing in them but darkness—as if he was dreaming, his mind a long way away. He didn't move until I grabbed his arm and tried to snap a handcuff on it. Then his back twisted and he fell to his knees. As I knelt to keep hold of him, he leant forward. I could smell rotten meat on his breath, leaf-mould on his skin. I opened my mouth to speak, and he spat into it.

Fortunately, the local press didn't get wind of the story. The boy's identity wasn't hard to establish: a cracked bank card in his pocket was traceable to Mark Knowle, aged eighteen, at an address just south of the Fox Hollies estate. Mark's father, who shared the flat with his son and three dogs more articulate than he was, identified him from the police mugshot. He said Mark had disappeared nearly four weeks earlier, and he'd assumed the boy had just fucked off somewhere. I said he had. Just nowhere in particular.

I had an urgent Hepatitis B jab, but seemed to have no problems apart from a persistent metallic taste in my mouth. Mark crouched in a cell at the Acocks Green station for twelve hours without speaking or sitting down. We couldn't get a response out of him. Eventually our doctor gave him a shot of diazepam, and he relaxed a little. An hour later, he spoke without prompting. 'She gave it to me,' he said. 'It was her. The singer.'

Gradually, in blurred fragments of recollection, he told us about a girl he'd met at the Lady Westminster. That was the estate's main pub, and its weekend karaoke and disco nights drew a crowd of wildly varying age. There'd been a few incidents there recently, but the staff were impressively quick to deal with trouble and the real hard cases tended to go elsewhere. According to the boy, there was a girl who'd sung there a few times. Irena. 'From some country in Europe. She'd come a long way. Don't know what for.'

He'd wanted to buy her a drink, but she wasn't interested. Then he'd followed her out of the pub. 'Couldn't get her voice out of my head. Wasn't going to… just wanted to talk to her. Something inside her that was different, in her eyes. Like the canal at night. She turned round, saw me. Just shrugged. Let me take her into the trees behind the estate. Let me have her.' His voice was slurring. He paused for a few minutes, then said: 'Afterwards. Running. Hungry. Somewhere else. The snow.' He lapsed back into silence, grinding his teeth.

The Lady Westminster got Mike, their karaoke man, to come in and talk to me. He remembered Irena. 'Red-haired wench, kind of pale. Strange voice. Not quite in tune. She did old stuff. The Walker Brothers, David Bowie. Bit miserable for my taste, but the kids liked her. She must have been from Russia or something. Don't know why she was here. Didn't want to know, to be honest.'

I asked if she'd talked to anyone. He shook his head. 'Only to buy a drink and ask me for a couple of turns on the karaoke. She kept to herself. Just wanted to sing. There was this young lad trying to chat her up, but she ignored him. She came here three or four times, then stopped. I don't know where she lives. If she's still around, that is.'

Our enquiries found only that Irena (if that was her

real name) couldn't be linked to anyone who was known to live here or had been reported missing. Of course, girls from Eastern Europe worked in strip clubs and brothels all over the city who weren't registered citizens or visitors. The description we had—a thin girl with pale skin and spiky red hair—drew no response from any of our contacts, legitimate or bent. Which was not unusual.

We also had no idea what, if anything, she might have given to Mark: blood tests and a medical check gave no evidence of any infection. Maybe some bad acid. We were less concerned about that than we were about the possibility that she hadn't consented to the sex, and that worse things had happened to her. But we couldn't get anything more out of Mark. After a week, we had him transferred to a secure unit in Rubery.

I saw the boy when four psychiatric nurses came to take him to the car. He was sedated again, and offered neither resistance nor co-operation. His thin face still had a lost expression, as if he'd come here from a distant place and recognised nothing. Outside, the air was freezing cold and they hadn't given him a jacket. But he didn't shiver. I watched flakes of sleet attach to his face like scars. There was blood on his lips; he must have bitten them.

A couple of days after the transfer, I woke up in the night with a raging thirst. Elaine was asleep beside me. I stumbled to the kitchen, surprised at how much light there seemed to be. My pupils must have been dilated. I filled a glass, but somehow couldn't drink from it; I had to bend my head over the sink and pour the water into my mouth. My throat was burning.

On the way back upstairs, I wondered if Elaine would mind being woken up for a fuck. I hadn't been this hard in weeks. It almost hurt to walk. I touched my erection, and immediately was staring into the boy's dark eyes and watching him lick the blood from his lips. I'd wanted to see him for days before the transfer, had resisted the temptation to pay him an informal visit in his cell. It wouldn't have been professional. Besides, I didn't know what he might do. Or what I might.

I slipped quietly into the bathroom, locked the door and pulled the flush to cover the sounds of my breathing as I brought myself off. My sperm in the toilet bowl reminded me of his spit. His *flob*, we'd have said in school. The cistern held his face. So did the window. So did the doorway. His cheekbones, his damaged lips, his eyes, the darkness behind them. Walking on tiptoe, I went back into the bedroom and picked up my clothes, then got dressed in the hallway.

Outside, the pavement was skinned with frost. The moon glowed faintly through a pale sheet of cloud. I was still aroused, but it wasn't lust that drove me through the colourless streets. It was some impulse I didn't recognise. I was walking, then running, just to be on the move. My throat ached as if I'd been shouting for hours. I ran past the train station, the canal, the building site, the trees that bordered the estate. Then I saw it.

The fox was crouching on a rubbish bin outside one of the tower blocks. Its coat was reddish-brown, streaked with mud. As I approached, unable to keep my breathing quiet, it turned its black eyes on me for an instant. Then it was off, running on the grass at the side of the building. When it reached the gravel car park, it slipped and almost fell. Then it limped away, leaving a smear of blood on the ground. At least, it looked like blood. As I came closer, I could see it was a cluster of metallic flakes. I touched them and held up my fingers, smelt rust.

I chased the fox to the back of the estate and out into the maze of factories and warehouses between Tyseley and Hay Mills. Every now and then it slowed down, twisted in pain and fell, then got up and ran on. It left some of itself behind each time: a fragment of dark inorganic tissue. I had the feeling it was trying to recapitulate a much longer journey within this district, to tell me something. This wasn't about me and the boy any longer. We were just accessories. I thought of the Ted Hughes poem we'd puzzled over in school: the fox entering the mind.

Within sight of the traffic that raced along the Coventry Road, the fox paused on a bridge. Once again, it looked straight at me. I stopped, unable to move, as it leapt over the low wall. A few seconds later, I looked down at the canal. The ripples were still spreading on the black water. The streetlamp highlighted a few metallic flakes on the surface. Suddenly, my exhaustion caught up with me; I gripped the wall and retched several times. Nothing came up but a thin, colourless fluid.

When I got home, Elaine was awake. I told her I'd heard some noises outside the house and gone out to investigate, then chased a potential burglar as far as the Fox Hollies estate. She seemed to believe me; at any rate, she quickly went back to sleep. I lay awake, shivering with tension, until dawn.

The next day, my shift didn't start until twelve. Around nine, I drove out to the secure unit where they were keeping

Mark. My head was full of irrational questions. Where did the fox come from? How many people had it travelled with? Where was it trying to get to? He was no more likely to know the answers than I was.

The traffic on the Bristol Road made the journey painfully slow. I wouldn't have much time to talk to Mark, if he was even talking. Lack of sleep narrowed my vision. Snowflakes were cutting through the air; I didn't think it would settle.

At the clinic, they made me wait in a kind of airlock while they checked my ID against their computer records. Then the clinical manager, Dr Fern, came down to ask why I hadn't made an appointment. I said I was in a hurry. She said 'There's no need to hurry now,' and refused to explain until we reached Mark's room on the second floor.

It was the barest occupied room I'd ever seen. A bedroll on a narrow bunk; a table and chair. No possessions, no pictures. 'Doesn't Mark have any stuff here?' I asked. Dr Fern shook her head. 'So where is he?'

'He tried to break out during the night. The night staff locked him in his room. Another nurse was coming to give him a sedative, but she had several people to see. When she got here, Mark had suffered some kind of seizure. His mouth was full of blood. They took him to the clinic infirmary, and I think he's still there.'

'Is he alive?'

'He was dead before he left this room. The cause of death was severe internal trauma. But according to the doctor who examined him, there were no bruises. The skin was unbroken. It was as if he'd been gnawed to death from the inside.'

Weeks later, Mark's key worker let me see an exercise book the boy had been given in OT to encourage him to communicate. Mark's handwriting was neat and blocky, like an imitation of print. He'd written his name, age and address, then left a few blank pages, then bitten his finger and drawn a crude sketch in smears of blood: a small dog or fox, running. On the facing page, he'd written:

Out the city it never stops the trains the loading trucks the razor wire Tallinn to Helsinki the moon shows different faces but doesn't change running across land tracks in the frozen snow hiding under the skin Helsinki to Odense always cold always hungry like a dream just one step away from nothing Odense to Zagreb staying under cover stealing from bins kitchens restaurants dead gulls on the street Zagreb to Bonn sick all the time spoiled meat nowhere to go no shelter no hiding place am I the fox or the boy who stole it Bonn to Calais what the kiss meant the coat of rust the infected teeth always cold always hungry help me please

SLOW BURN

Everyone knew the fires at the Wren's Nest were the work of untraceable kids with spray cans and lighters. But we had to investigate, if only to make some of them less confident about doing it again. The tracksuited youths huddled on the bare streets of the estate around the nature reserve told us as much by their turned backs as we could have learned from interrogating them. The charred debris of fire-starting equipment among the burned trees and shrubs told its own story. Why wasn't a question for the police, though I wondered at the time whether adolescent rage was enough of an explanation.

When Elaine and I had been courting, we'd come here a few times in the spring of 1981. In those days, the paths were less clearly marked and it was easy to get lost. The limestone cliffs, after millions of years on dry land, still had their own secret geography. The layered ash woods filtered the daylight, made you feel sheltered by some kind of ancient building. Elaine and I walked for hours, holding hands, sometimes pausing to kiss. We searched the exposed rock faces for tiny fossil shells, and chased each other through labyrinths of creepers and ash-fronds. But we never tried to make love there, for a reason we agreed some time afterwards: we both felt watched.

Coming back in the autumn, twenty years later, felt strange. The place no longer seemed peaceful. Black cinders were scattered through the undergrowth, and scorched trees had fallen into the deep gullies. It was hard to see where the effects of fire ended and those of seasonal decay began: dead leaves and black fungus covered everything. Ash trees are called that because of how they look in autumn. The years of police work meant that wherever I looked, I saw places to hide bodies. The sunlight flared randomly off branches as if they were on fire.

Near one of the signposts that guided visitors through the nature reserve, we passed a large wooden effigy of a trilobite fossil. Its ridged surface was charred and split open. The real 'Dudley Bug', which had given the town its municipal symbol, had been found here. The Wren's Nest was high above the surrounding area, though it didn't feel like it. Further on, the footpath led us around the edge of a pool long since rendered inert by blue-green algae. Beer-cans and condoms floated on the dark surface. The limestone rim was yellowed and crumbly like old cheese.

I wondered why Elaine and I had stopped coming here. The place had a way of confronting you with sudden views—sheer hillsides, layered depths—that made you feel on the edge of the unknown. Maybe it was just vertigo. Maybe it had to do with the way our relationship had become focused on the home, on maintaining our own peace and security, not taking chances. If we came here again, it would feel like the end of something.

Most of the fires had started near the edge of the reserve, where the warden's office had been destroyed for the second time in five years. It was a blackened hulk, marked off by 'scene of crime' tape. An earlier police team had already gone through the wreckage, though the fire had started some distance away. The wind blew flakes of ash into our faces. We circled the high metal fence around the disused mines, looking for any discarded items that might hold fingerprints. It was colder out here than among the trees. The bloodshot sun was setting behind the estate.

The old limestone mines had been shut down for decades, due to the effects of subsidence. I'd heard something about a fire in one of the mines, around the time I joined the force. The area was sealed off to stop kids trying to get into them. Looking through the steel chain-link fence, I began to wonder if the fires might have some kind of symbolic meaning. The dark, shapeless buildings inside made me think of ancient burial vaults. Once again, I had the sense of being watched.

This time there was a specific reason. The man standing a little way to my left, who in the fading light I'd taken for a colleague, was looking at me in a rather defensive way. He was aged seventy or so, with a ragged beard and shabby clothes, and his hands were trembling—which could have been due to drink or illness. I nodded to him and said: 'Cold day to be out here.'

'It is. You won't find anything.'

His comment surprised me. 'Why's that?'

He smiled, glanced at the fence, then looked back at me. 'You don't remember me, do you?' I shook my head. 'Morton. You'd recently joined the Birmingham force when I retired. Bad health. I had an accident.' He raised his gloved right hand: the fingers were bent in like the legs of a dead crab.

'Good to see you.' I vaguely remembered his name, but not his face. 'What brings you here?'

'That's a good question.' He cradled his right hand in his left without looking at it. 'I suppose there's not much else to do.'

'Why won't we find anything?'

Morton shrugged; his inert hand made the gesture oddly puppet-like. 'Because you can't see it. There's a lot I could tell you, but I don't think you'd understand. The others didn't.'

He was mad, I realised. But my unanswered questions about the Wren's Nest made me say: 'Do you want to talk? I finish at six, we could have a chat then if you like.' Morton suggested the pub at the north end of the nature reserve. I watched him walk away slowly, bent over, his arms folded against his chest. Maybe he spent all his time here.

Our search team walked down to the Wren's Nest housing estate that bordered the nature reserve. It was a different world. Whole streets of pale terraces were marked for demolition, their windows covered by wire grids. The barking of dogs echoed from concrete walls. Groups of thin youths on street corners eyed us suspiciously as we approached, then turned away. I could see why the local police had needed some external support. Had the arsonists been driven by a hatred of the past, I wondered, or by an obscure need to connect with it?

*

The Crow's Wing pub had originally been an office building of some kind, maybe the local job centre when there were still jobs. It had been refitted with dark red carpeting, the kind whose pattern is more easily felt than seen, and coal-effect gas fires. Morton was sitting at a small table in the corner, next to the silent jukebox. He was smoking a thin roll-up. An empty pint glass was by his living hand. 'Like another?' I asked.

'Cheers. Pint of Banks'.'

There were a few other people in the pub: a man studying the racing page of a newspaper, a young couple talking with hushed voices, a white-haired drunk lost in his own world. I got Morton's pint and a half for myself from the tired-looking barman and returned to his table.

Morton took a deep swallow of beer and shuddered. 'Did you tell your colleagues you were going to talk to me?' I said no. 'They'd have told you not to bother. For once, it's not a conspiracy. They think I'm a lunatic.' His accent was a blend of Scottish and Black Country.

'You might be,' I said. 'Doesn't mean you've got nothing to say worth hearing.'

'I can see a brilliant future awaits you.' He looked at me steadily, then rested his cigarette between the fingers of his dead hand.

'Mad or not,' he said, 'I'm going to tell you why they shut down the mines. People kept going down there and not coming out. They found a few of them in the tunnels, curled up tight, stiff like fossils. Then a tunnel collapsed, killed a whole shift of mine workers. The company said there'd been a fire. That was the only way to explain the state of the bodies.'

Morton closed his eyes, reached across with his right hand to pick up the cigarette. His fingers trembled, and I noticed they were scarred with many small burns. The roll-up glowed white in his mouth, then dull red. He coughed and drained his pint. 'Another?' I asked.

'Cheers.' A few more drinkers, all ageing men, were at the bar. When I returned with Morton's drink, he was looking at a copy of the *Express & Star* he'd picked up from the next table. He pointed to a headline: THEY DON'T BELONG HERE. 'What belongs here doesn't belong in the world,' he said. 'Know what I mean?'

'Not really, no.'

He rolled another cigarette, slowly. The air in the pub was becoming grainy with smoke. 'In 1980, a teenage boy went missing from the estate. His friends said he spent a lot of time out here. We searched the whole area with dogs. On the second day, one of the team noticed that a sealed mine entrance had been damaged by subsidence. There was a narrow gap a boy could have squeezed through.

'It was a long shot, but we had to try. Three of us managed to force the opening a little wider and went down there with torches. It was cold down there, cold and damp—but somehow I felt a heat on my skin, like a fire was close by.

'We found him in one of the side tunnels. Lying on his side, curled up, with his hands over his face. His wrists and ankles were tied up. Some other kids must have left him there. We couldn't be sure it was the missing boy, because the face was terribly burnt. His clothes weren't even scorched, but his head was charcoal.'

Morton paused. His eyes were staring inward; I glimpsed confusion and fear in them. 'What happened then, I'm still not sure. Two of us picked up the body. As we started back towards the mine entrance, the walls around us began to shake.' His hand mimicked the tremor, perhaps intentionally. 'And then part of the tunnel roof collapsed behind us.

'The shock, in a nearly enclosed space, was enough to make me and Finch drop the body. Some debris bouncing off the tunnel wall knocked the torch out of Sumner's hand. He couldn't see to pick it up. We were groping around in the dark when something came out of the tunnel.

'I thought it was a loose rock, glowing with some kind of luminous mould, but then I realised it was crawling over the rubble to get to us. Shimmering like a cold flame. Wasn't human, but it had hands—and a kind of melting white face. It reached out to take the dead boy. I tried to pull him back. Felt something grab hold of my arm. A deep, terrible chill—it made me feel numb all over. I must have blacked out. A few minutes later, Finch was shining the torch in my face. The body had disappeared. There was no feeling in my left hand.

'We didn't know what to report. In the end Sumner told them there was some kind of toxic waste down there, it was too dangerous to explore further. I was in hospital by then. My left hand and forearm slowly changed, over two or three days.' Morton gulped his pint. He was looking pale. 'The flesh turned dark like a bruise, then darker. It started to flake away. By the time they cut it off, it was more like charcoal.

'The official report said I'd been affected by some toxic material that had leaked into the mine from the surrounding rock bed. They built higher fences round the derelict mines to keep people out. Later I tried to tell my superintendent what had happened. He said the poison had obviously affected my mind. I was invalided out of the force. Done fuck all since except come here and wait.'

Morton started rolling another match-thin cigarette. I didn't know what to say. His scarred fingers trembled as they placed the roll-up in his mouth. He thumbed the lighter twice. It didn't catch. Silently, he passed it to me and I lit his cigarette. He closed his eyes and drew a breath, wincing with pain.

'Don't know why I keep coming back,' he said. 'The local boys don't know why they keep starting fires. It's a ritual they don't understand. But I'll tell you one thing. Whatever we saw down there had no intention of getting out into the world. It was a misfit, an exile. It had come out of the fire.'

When we left the pub, I offered Morton a lift. He shook his head, pointing to the footpath that led back into the nature reserve. There was a moon, so I expected he could see where he was going. Though perhaps he could find his way in the dark. I walked down into the estate, where my car was parked. The smell of smoke remained with me as I drove back to Birmingham.

A week later, I heard that Morton had been found dead in the Wren's Nest. A heart attack, apparently, with the cold finishing him off as he lay among the rusting ash trees. I went to his funeral, along with some of my older colleagues. He had little by way of family and friends left. A sense of chill made me leave as soon as the service was over.

A few nights after that, I went back to the Wren's Nest. I had some irrational notion of finding what he'd been looking for, or paying tribute to his search, or giving his spirit the chance to talk to me. People I know dying always knocks me off balance. You don't get used to that.

It was a bitterly cold night. Rain in the daytime had left the ground muddy, and stars of frost were glittering in the beam of my torch. I walked carefully up the wooded hillside to the limestone cliffs, and on past the blue-green water. The gullies on my right were featureless pits; they could have led to the depths of the earth. The chill soaked through my overcoat and gloves, made my skeleton want to curl up like a foetus.

At last I reached the open area where the blackened warden's office stood near the steel fence that enclosed the mines. People were scattered around the fence, alone or in groups. More were coming from the woods all around. The moon was glowing through a hazy scar tissue of cloud. I could hear voices, but not words.

There were white-haired men with bottles, teenage boys and girls, and some rough-looking people in between— travellers maybe, or just off the estate. Some of them had built a mound of fuel: charcoal bricks, newspaper, rubbish soaked with lighter fluid. The crowd began to gather round it, and one of the old men lit a match. It flared up, died back down, then burned steadily. The crowd pressed in around it, warming their outstretched hands. I felt it was Morton's funeral pyre. Maybe the others did too. Despite the heat, my hands were numb.

The fumes were getting to me, or some of the youngsters were smoking weed. I could feel myself becoming detached from everything except the fire. My mind was floating like a curled-up flake of ash. The more I gazed into the red and gold heart of the flames, the more I could see. The faces of people I'd lost. A map of the place where I'd grown up, only ten miles from here. Letters and runes.

Other people were pressing behind me, their breath stale with alcohol and decay, eager to be shown what to do. And then I saw it.

Held in the flames like a reflection in water, a pale shape was forming. It had a thin, spineless body, but its hands were wide and reaching towards us with bloodless fingers. Its face was a swirl, a thumbprint, without eyes or mouth. I could hear its voice in my head like the roaring of a great fire. *Wait. Do nothing. The land will burn. The time will come.* And as we all stood watching, it showed us what would happen. Then, one by one, we turned away and walked back into the night.

THE RECEIVERS

People don't talk about it now. They've forgotten, or pretended to forget, just how bad it was. New people have moved in, and new businesses have started up. 'Regeneration' would be putting it a bit strongly, but most of the damage has been repaired. Or at least covered up. As for the madness—well, nothing healed it, so maybe it's still hidden. When you've seen what people are capable of, it's hard to believe that they can change.

To begin with, it was nothing out of the ordinary. The local branch of Safeway reported a sharp increase in the level of shoplifting. No-one had been caught. In the same week, a Warwick-based building firm reported the theft of a truckload of bricks. Ordinary items are the hardest to track down. Once they go missing, it's already too late.

At the time, a much more serious theft was concerning us. A former local councillor whom we'd been investigating for corruption had died of blood poisoning at Solihull Hospital—the result of a ruptured bowel, apparently. I don't think we'd ever have got enough on him for a conviction. We'd just closed the case when his body went missing, three days before the funeral. The security guard at the mortuary swore he'd not seen or heard anything. But there was clear evidence of a break-in, in the form of a missing windowpane. Not broken: missing.

I won't tell you the ex-councillor's name. It's all over Birmingham in any case, on plaques set in hotels and shopping arcades and flyovers. He'd have attended the opening of an eyelid. I don't even remember what party he belonged to. It doesn't matter these days. He'd been cosy with the building firm that had some materials nicked. That was the first hint I got of how this might all be connected.

That October was hazy and overcast, the clouds dropping a veil of warm rain. I remember things were difficult at home. Julia had just turned eighteen, and Eileen was torn between wanting her to stay and wanting her to move in with her boyfriend. It was a kind of territorial thing. Julia was too old to stay in her room when she was at home: she needed the whole house. As usual, I tried to stay out of it, using my awkward working hours as an excuse to keep my distance. I believe in peace and harmony; I've just never been able to accept how much work they need.

It was a while before the police in Tyseley, Acocks Green and Yardley Wood got round to comparing notes on recent theft statistics. What we were dealing with was an epidemic of shoplifting. No-one much was getting caught, and the stolen goods weren't turning up anywhere. Most of it was basic household stuff anyway, hardly worth selling on. Shoes,

DIY equipment, frozen food, soft-porn magazines, cheap kitchenware, bottles of beer. If there was an organisation behind all this, what the fuck were they trying to prove? Of course, we had our doubts. Rumours of invisible thieves were a gift to dishonest shop staff—or even owners working a scam. It was happy hour on the black economy.

To start with, we encouraged shop owners to tighten up their security. A lot of younger security staff got sacked and replaced by trained professionals, or by hard cases from the shadows of the hotel and club scene. Suspects were more likely to end up in casualty than the police station. We put more constables on the beat to cut down on burglaries. But stuff still went missing—at night or in broad daylight, it didn't seem to matter. Cash disappeared from pub tills. A couple of empty freezers vanished from an Iceland stockroom. A junk shop lost a shelf of glassware. It made no sense. Walking out of the Acocks Green station at night became an unsettling experience. There was hardly anyone around. The barking of guard dogs shattered any sense of peace there might have been. Dead leaves were stuck like a torn carpet to the rain-darkened pavement. The moon was never visible. Every shop window was heavily barred or shuttered. Slogans began to appear on metal screens and blank walls: 'HANG THE THEIVES', 'THIEVING GYPPOS', 'SEND THE THIEFS HOME'. I must admit, I laughe out loud when I saw someone had painted with a brush on the wall of the station car park: 'WHO STOLE MY SPRAY CAN?'

People were being shopped to us all the time, but we never got anywhere. Without the stolen goods, there was no evidence. Some of our informants seemed to feel that evidence was an optional extra when it came to prosecution.

Being Asian, Black, European, unusually poor or new to the area was enough. As the problem escalated, letters started to appear in the local evening paper accusing the police of protecting criminals, or insisting that the homes of 'suspicious characters' be searched regularly. *If they have nothing to hide, they have nothing to fear.* In truth, we were questioning a lot of people. And getting a lot of search warrants. We were even catching the odd thief. But not as odd as the ones we weren't catching.

Julia really summed it up one evening, during one of our increasingly rare family meals. 'It's like some children's gang,' she said. 'Nicking all the things they see at home. Then hiding somewhere, dressing up, smoking cigarettes. Pretending to be their own parents.' She looked sad. Playfulness was slipping away from her. I wondered if she could be right. Maybe it was some whimsical game, a joke played by kids or the members of some lunatic cult. But the consequences weren't funny. People were getting hurt. Homes were getting broken up.

I remember the day, in late October, when I realised just how serious things had become. I was interviewing some people who'd been involved in a violent incident at the Aldi supermarket on the Warwick Road. A Turkish woman shopping with two young children had been attacked by several other shoppers. She'd suffered a broken hand, and her four-year- old daughter was badly bruised. No stolen goods had been found in her bag or her bloodstained clothes. She told me a young woman had started screaming 'Stop thief!' at her in the toiletries section, near the back of the store. People had crowded round, staring. A man had grabbed her arm and held her while the young woman started throwing jars of hair gel at her. Someone else had knocked her down from behind. She'd woken up in hospital, and it had been a while before she'd found out that her two children were safe.

Then I talked to the young woman who'd thrown the jars. She was only nineteen, a hard-faced AG girl with china-white skin and hair tied back. She chain-smoked throughout the interview, flicking ash over the table between us. Her answers were mostly monosyllables, but a few times she interrupted me with sudden outbursts. 'She wouldn't let go of her little girl. That means she was using her as a human shield.' And later, 'Are you a copper or a fucking social worker? Wake up and join the real world.' I don't think she really heard a word I was saying.

A couple of days later, a tiny padded envelope was sent to the Acocks Green station. It was full of crushed stink bombs. The smell lingered in the building for days. Groups of neo-fascists took to patrolling the streets in combat jackets, led by dogs on steel chains. Meanwhile, the thefts continued. In desperation, all the local police stations joined forces in a massive raid on the homes of suspects. We found next to nothing. But local racists used the operation as a cover for their own little *Kristallnacht*. Asian shops were broken into and smashed up, and a few homes were set on fire. We were caught off balance, too busy hunting for stolen goods to stop the violence. I still wonder if our superiors knew what was going to happen and turned a blind eye.

November was unexpectedly cold. It never seemed to become full daylight. The frost made everything slippery or tacky, difficult to handle. Car fumes made a smoky haze above the streets. I spent the days and nights rushing from one crime scene to another, from thefts to fights to arson attacks, my hands and face numb with cold and depression. It felt like the meaning was being sucked out of everything. Julia's boyfriend moved to Coventry to start a new job. She started moving her own stuff over there in batches, a suitcase at a time. It was strange to find things missing—pictures, books, ornaments—that I'd come to take for granted as part of the house. Maybe Elaine was letting Julia take some things that weren't strictly hers, just to avoid arguments. I felt too tired to mediate between them; all I wanted to do at home was sleep. Without Julia there, filling the house with her scent and music, I was reminded of how things had been before she was born. When Elaine and I had first set up home together. Maybe we could get some of that back.

It was maudlin retreat into the past that sent me to the allotments in Tyseley, a dull photocopy of the district I'd lived in as a child. The allotments occupied a strip of land between an industrial estate and a local railway line that only carried freight trains. There was a patch of waste ground at one end, with some derelict railway shacks and a heap of rusting car bodies. It was overgrown with fireweed and pale, straggly grass. I'd spent a lot of time in places like this at the age of ten or eleven, getting into fights and spying on couples. Somehow I remembered them as having a kind of mystery, a promise that was never fulfilled.

It was my day off—either Monday or Tuesday, I'm not sure. Another chilly, overcast day. I'd been walking around Tyseley all afternoon, trying to make sense of things. How quickly it had all changed, once the fear had taken hold. I wasn't immune either. How easy it was to blame. How hard it was to know. In some way I couldn't understand, the police were being used. Not to find the truth, but to cover it up. There was a time, I thought, before I was caught up in this. There must be a part of me that can stand outside it. The light was draining away through the cracks in the world. By the time I reached the alley at the back of the allotments, a red-tinged moon was staring through the ragged trees.

I was so far up my own arse by then that the first time I saw the child, I thought he was one of my own memories. The light was fading anyway; his face was indistinct. He was reaching through the chain-link fence from the railway side. I remember his fingers were unusually thin and pale; they seemed too long for his hands. He glanced at me without making eye contact. His eyes were large and very dark, but his skin was so white it seemed translucent. His brand-new ski jacket made him look bulkier than he probably was. Something about his posture suggested need. I wondered what he was looking for.

A flicker in the half-light distracted me. Another child, ducking behind the derelict shacks. Then a third, somewhere beyond the fence. I realised I was surrounded. But I felt more tired than scared. There was a smell in the air like ash and burnt plastic; probably there'd been a bonfire nearby on the fifth. The evening light felt dry and brittle, like old cellophane. There was no colour anywhere in this world. I could see a double exposure of my own hands as I moved from side to side, trying to catch one of the paper-faced children. The way they jittered and grabbed and hid reminded me of silent films. I wondered how far they'd go to become what they appeared to be.

It was getting too dark to see anything much. I stumbled to the end of the line of shacks, where three old brick garages backed onto an alley. I'd been here a year before, investigating the beating of an Asian boy by skinheads. There was a smell of mould and cat piss. No-one was around. I glimpsed two of the film children in a garage doorway, pretending to be a courting couple. I lunged at them, but caught only a rusty metal screen. One of them touched my wrist with soft fingers. It took me a few seconds to realise that he'd taken my watch. My mind kept asking me what was wrong with the garages. I looked around the alley in the unreal glow of city lights reflected off the clouds. Three garages. When I'd been here before, there'd only been two.

I hardly said a word at home that evening. Near midnight, I came back with a torch and a spade. The children were gone. The third garage had been clumsily knocked together with bricks of different sizes, mortar slapped on to cover the gaps. It was a faux building. Made from stolen materials. I prised the metal door loose and stepped inside. The ground was soft under my feet.

between the uneven walls, every kind of stuff was heaped up: clothes, food, cushions, magazines. All of it beginning to moulder. There was a pane of glass attached to the inside of the brick wall. Beetles stirred in the waning light of my torch. I saw bags of pet food that had been torn open by rats. Flesh gleaming from the damp cases of porn videos. Soft pizzas rotting in an open freezer that couldn't be plugged in here. My foot slipped on dead leaves, and I put my weight on the spade.

Have you ever dug into a cat litter tray and realised what was buried under the wafer of soil? The blade sank inches into the ground, then lifted a sticky wedge that smelt like a museum of disease. I pushed my left hand against my mouth and bit down. My torch fell and stuck, its light reflecting from pale spots in the exposed slime. Metal glittered. A face swam into view on a scrap of paper, then vanished.

I dug for a while. The ground was full of cash: crumpled fivers and tenners, verdigris-covered coins, all slippery from the layer of nearly liquid excrement they'd been buried in. I gagged and retched any number of times, but I hadn't eaten since lunchtime. Daylight seemed a long time ago. Eventually I got down far enough to reach a number of yellowish, brittle sticks wrapped in dark cloth. There was nothing left of his flesh. I did as much damage as I could with the spade, then covered up the fragments with the strange earth I'd removed from them. The contents of the garage had drained my torch; I doubted it would ever work again. I left it there with the other rubbish.

The moon's small, bloodshot face peered at me as I stood in the allotments, wiping my shoes with dead leaves. I thought about the power of damaged lives. How a corrupt politician might try to come back, feeding on money like a vampire on blood. How he could attract followers desperate for an illusion of normality. No wonder the police couldn't make a difference.

Money talks. But you wouldn't want to hear its accent.

As I walked home, the streets around me were deserted. The sodium light gave the pavement a faint tinge of gold. There were no thieves, no vigilantes, no children, no beggars. If anyone had got in my way, I'd have killed them. I needed someone to blame. We all do. But there was nothing except a smell of shit, and an icy chill in the air.

WAKE UP IN MOLOCH

It started with the machine in the garden. Though I suppose it had been going on for a while before that, and perhaps a long time. If you live around here, you take certain things for granted. Birmingham grew out of the Industrial Revolution, so in a sense it owes its life to the machine. It was inevitable that sooner or later, we'd have to give something back.

In the autumn of 2002, an unusual death was reported to us. A man in his fifties had died while mowing the lawn in his back garden. His widow, who contacted us, was convinced it had something to do with a bizarre machine in the garden next door. Of course, we assumed this to be the familiar mechanism of displaced grief: blaming the loss on some mysterious external agency makes it easier to accept, at least to begin with. The neighbour's machine appeared to be some kind of inert urban sculpture: a dark mound of pistons, cogs and levers with no energy source and no imaginable purpose. He said it was there to frighten off potential burglars.

We were expecting the post-mortem to indicate a natural death. When the coroner told us the cause of death was exposure to poison gas—of a kind not used since the First World War—we were round there within minutes to confiscate the machine. But it had gone. The owner said he'd taken it to the rubbish dump at Tyseley. Only the threat of a murder charge made him go there with us and point it out among the rusting cars and mouldering sofas.

The HSE officer took charge of the machine, and established that it contained various chemicals which, over a period of time, would drip together and generate occasional bursts of toxic gas. I spoke to a guy there called Spencer who described the machine as 'a mechanical compost- heap that, left to its own devices, could be relied on to kill everything in the garden'. At this point, I recalled that the garden it had been placed in was essentially a dirt yard: any grass and flowers had been removed, and the only tree was dead.

The owner of the machine, a Mr Ford, claimed he'd not tampered with it in any way since purchasing it. He'd bought it from a scrapyard in Warley that had advertised in the *Evening Mail*. It sold chunks of rubbish as 'unusual garden sculptures'. When we asked him for the scrapyard's details, he admitted that they'd actually sold the machine to him as a 'rat and fox killer'. He'd bought it purely for its appearance, not realising that it didn't need fuel to operate.

The scrapyard proved impossible to trace; in recent months the area had been levelled prior to redevelopment, and there was no record of any salvage company. According to the site record, the land was leased by a religious organisation called the Union of Body and Spirit. We arrested Ford on a charge of manslaughter. Over the next few months, as we worked with the HSE to put a case together, we were in some danger of getting lost in legal and scientific technicalities. But I was asked to liaise with the family of the dead man, take full statements from them and keep them up to date. That helped me to remember what this meant. That, and the look of nausea on Spencer's face when he'd told me about the machine.

The CPS held onto the case files for six months before grudgingly approving the prosecution. The trial was more than a year after the death. It lasted five days. Spencer and I sat through the whole tedious process. The prosecutor ignored most of the scientific evidence we'd spent months assembling, and reduced the case to a handful of soundbites about Ford's lack of regard for his neighbours. The defence argued that the machine had given every appearance of being safe—the very point we'd worked so hard to disprove, though the prosecutor didn't seem to care—and devoted an entire day to questioning character witnesses: Ford's wife, his grown-up son, his colleagues in the TV repair shop he ran, the friend who'd been best man at his wedding in 1963. By the end of the day, it was clear that Ford was such a great bloke I wondered why he hadn't been given the freedom of the city.

The not guilty verdict surprised no-one, except Spencer. Like many specialists, he couldn't see the spin for the facts. 'Why are Birmingham people so utterly blasé about machines?' he said helplessly. 'We let drivers who kill children off the hook because these big cars are hard to steer on wet roads. We let engineers who run generators inside

closed buildings off the hook because carbon monoxide
has no smell. There are so many machines around us
that we don't know how to be afraid of them.' I thanked
him for all the work he'd done; then I went to speak to
the dead man's family on the steps outside the courtroom.
They were subdued, just going through the motions, as if
nothing they saw was real.

A few months before the trial, there was another peculiar
death. A teenage couple went into a Bordesley Green
industrial estate late at night to find somewhere quiet. Their
date never reached its conclusion. As they walked together,
hand in hand, past the chain-link fence of a warehouse that
stocked alarm systems, the girl stopped and turned her
head towards the boy. When he leaned down to kiss her, he
saw that one side of her face was covered with blood. He
caught her before she fell, but she was already dead.

The A&E department at Heartlands Hospital found
several small fragments of twisted metal in the left side of the
girl's head and neck. We were notified and sent in the city's
bomb squad, who established that the shrapnel had been fired
from behind the warehouse fence by a crude security device.
I saw a photograph of the machine: it was something like a
black shrub, with cameras instead of flowers. The company
that owned the warehouse claimed to know nothing about
any such weapon. The site's caretaker had apparently done
a runner overnight; the only personal items he'd left in his
office were a cracked mug and a wall poster showing the
workings of a generator: a steel core wrapped in copper wire.

As we searched the site for fingerprints that might help
us to trace the caretaker, a distant roar filtered through

the plasterboard walls. It was a Saturday afternoon, and the match at St Andrew's had just ended. We marked off the crime scene and called it a day. Outside the estate, thousands of jubilant fans were keeping right on to the end of the road. An Asian shopkeeper was dragging in his advertisement boards before anyone could walk into them. He smiled at me. 'Have the blues won again?'

'The blues always win,' I said. It had been a long day. It was going to be a long night. And at the end of it all, I knew, there would be no result. Even if we tracked down the caretaker, what local jury would care about some teenager who shouldn't have been there? It didn't matter that the estate itself had no gates. They hadn't broken into anything. They were just looking for a place to make love. If Jason Voorhees lived around here, they wouldn't make films about him: they'd just give him a job in security.

Just after the trial of the neighbour, I took a weekend off to unwind. But as usual when things get to me, I didn't go anywhere. Elaine went to visit her mother in Redditch on Sunday morning, and I spent the day wandering around near home and feeling brittle. Everywhere I went, newspaper boards kept me up to date on the local car industry: Jaguar announcing closures at Coventry, Rover in crisis talks with the unions at Longbridge.

In the afternoon I drove across the city to Grove Park, where Elaine and I had walked a few times in our courting days. The pond was still there, the cedar tree, the ornamental garden. And in the distance, blurred by mist, a line of poplar trees flanking the road. Driving here, I'd seen a display of wreaths at the crossroads outside the park gates. It was a cold day, but kids were chasing around like there was no tomorrow.

The familiarity of the park hurt me. I wanted it all to be different, because everything else had changed and this island of memory felt abnormal. I walked around the pond, letting its stink of rotting vegetation dissolve the last twenty years. Nothing was visible under the cloudy surface. On the far side was a patchwork of rhododendron and other shrubs. And beyond that, an area of grass with some black tree I didn't recognise.

As I walked towards it, I realised it was made of metal. It had tiny red fruits like cherries, the lowest some four feet off the ground. The leaves were arranged in whorls, like crooked black wings. A kid on a bicycle rode past and stopped under the tree. He looked about seven years old. As he reached up to pick one of the berries, I tried to shout 'Don't'. No sound came out. With a single tug, he pulled the fruit off the branch. It blew up in his hand.

By the time I reached the boy, he was unconscious. Red scraps of his hand were stuck to the metal tree like wet blossom. I carried him a few yards away from the metal tree, then took off my sweater and tied it around his arm to slow the bleeding. What was left of his right hand kept shaking, as if he'd had an electric shock. I pulled out my mobile and phoned for an ambulance. As I did so, a blur of movement beyond the shrubbery caught my eye. A small man in grey overalls, running away. The park keeper. If I went after him, the boy would be left alone. The ambulance service forwarded me to the police, and I described the running man. By the time the ambulance arrived, the boy was dead.

At least we caught the park keeper. He was at home, packing a suitcase, when two officers knocked at his door. When they finally broke in, he was just sitting there on the carpet, with the full suitcase beside him. He was rewiring a plug. When they searched him at the station, they found a small enamel badge in his shirt pocket. It showed a coil of wire wrapped around a steel rod. Underneath were the words: THE UNION OF BODY & SPIRIT.

The factory was in Netherton, part of the unique patchwork of urban villages and gravel meadows that make up the Black Country. The park keeper had told us where to find it. The threat of a life sentence had opened his mouth. He'd called it the temple. In the sodium haze of pre- dawn its windows glowed red from its dull brick walls. DC Avery and I had driven up from Birmingham to check the place out; three squad cars would arrive in an hour to take whatever action was needed.

We used wire-cutters to clear a gap in the coils of razor-wire above the spiked railings at the back of the factory. Inside the fence, I climbed the rusty fire-escape while Avery kept a lookout. There were no windows at ground floor level, but the rosette-shaped glass panes some twenty feet above the gravel yard looked down on the factory floor. I wiped some of the grime off the thick glass and peered through, wondering if there was a night shift. There was.

The light inside was murky, and I couldn't see very well. Some kind of machine occupied most of the floor. It looked rather like a giant steam engine turned inside-out, with pistons and wheels and chains moving at the surface. Its black chassis was ribbed and pitted like a fossil, and gleaming with oil. I couldn't see what the machine was doing. There were dozens of workers around it, holding onto its various surfaces and protrusions. They were all naked.

Despite the evidence of movement, I couldn't hear any sound from inside the window. Various components moved repeatedly back and forth or round and round. The workers held onto parts of the machine and brought themselves into contact with it. Some of them were female. Hands, faces, breasts, stomachs, cocks, feet. Whatever part of themselves seemed to need comfort. The machine stroked them, oiled them, tore them. Their blood ran down their bodies and the sides of the machine, onto the dull floor. I closed my eyes.

'Are they in there?' Avery said when I climbed down from the fire-escape. I nodded. 'What they doing?'

'Worshipping.' The morning air tasted of rain and petrol and broken stone. I pulled out my mobile and dialled the station to ask for more backup.

By the time the shops were opening across the road, we'd arrested everyone in the factory. But in the end, no-one but the park keeper went to prison. We couldn't prove that the Union of Body and Spirit had made the killing machines, and what I'd seen through the window was people inflicting injuries on themselves. We were able to put the factory out of business, but I dare say the worshippers found another temple. If you grow up around here, you take certain things for granted.

When I got home that night, I couldn't talk to Elaine or even hold her. I drank some whisky but it didn't calm me down. There was a sound in my head, like a chant I couldn't quite hear. Its rhythm eventually lulled me into an uneasy sleep. Then I woke up in the dark, the red glow of a blast furnace trapped behind my eyes, and I could finally hear it. A name being chanted over and over, until it was the only thing in my head. *Moloch*.

POINT OF DEPARTURE

At the back of New Street Station, a concrete block holds a staircase leading down to one of the nearby streets. Birmingham city centre is built on a steep hill, so you often need stairs to get from one street level to another. This particular staircase contains three flights of stairs, each with a convex mirror to let people walking down see if anyone is waiting for them. In winter the staircase is freezing cold. The crude tracery windows have no glass. There's a persistent smell of urine, chemical solvents and human decay.

In my late teens, I sometimes caught the train into Birmingham on a Friday night. I remember running up that staircase a few times, very drunk, eager not to miss the last train back to Wolverhampton. One time I slipped on the wet stairs and fell hard, then vomited from shock and the miasma of the rancid stairwell. I still managed to catch my train, but I remember feeling that I had contributed to the place's toxic atmosphere. The mirrors would remember me.

Nearly twenty years later, a young woman was found dead on the second landing of the staircase. Her purse was missing, and two rings had been wrenched off her fingers. By then I was in the Birmingham police force, part of the team at Steelhouse Lane. The pathologist told us the victim's body (which had been found shortly before dawn) had been robbed an hour or two after her death. The cause of death was a heart attack. She'd taken barbiturates during the night—probably bought them in the station, then gone to the staircase to take them. Some bruising on her hands and left shoulder suggested that she'd fallen. There was no serious injury. Unless she'd been scared to death, no-one had killed her.

Searching the concrete stairwell with two colleagues after that incident brought back memories from my teens. Little seemed to have changed here. Perhaps the stairs and the landings were a little more worn, holding more of whatever got spilt onto them. We'd sealed off the building, including the upper flight of stairs that led via a corridor to the Palisades shopping centre. I'd heard stories over the years of violence on the two landings, including a drug dealer and his mate setting two pitbulls on a rival—one from each end of the staircase, trapping him in the middle. Not much of him had been left.

That story and the stale ammonia fumes must have got into my head, because my own memory of falling on the staircase included images of being attacked by a dog. I remembered treating an infected bite on my arm. I had to check afterwards that there was no scar, but by then the false memory had faded. The other thing that confused me during the search was that whenever I glanced at one of the convex mirrors, I seemed to glimpse a blurred shape flapping its wings as it came up the stairs towards me. Just for a moment, and then the mirror showed only the empty stairs. It was a trick of perspective, or of flaws in the mirrors, but every time it happened I felt a brief wave of nausea. It was early December; our breath made scars in the frail mercury light.

The search revealed nothing new. Afterwards, I crossed the road to the Electric Cinema—which, at that time, had window dummies in contorted positions on its balcony. The two daytime staff members told me they'd never seen anything strange happening in or around the entrance to the staircase, but that people sometimes came into the cinema looking disturbed or 'out of it'. It was an art cinema, after all.

That night, I dreamt of climbing the same double-twist staircase towards a pale waterfall on the top flight. I wasn't sure it was just water, but thankfully I woke up before the torrent could reach me. It was coming from the station car park, and something made me sure its origin was the station itself. I woke up feeling cold, then rushed to the bathroom to throw up. A dog was barking somewhere behind the house. I went back to bed, and lay there awake until daybreak.

Over the next few weeks, two people reported being attacked on the staircase behind New Street Station. But neither of them was injured, and their stories were both so far-fetched that we suspected drugs were the source. The first was a middle-aged sales manager staying at the Comfort Inn. She'd got off her train and walked down the staircase with her suitcase late in the afternoon. Then, she said, a group

JOEL LANE

of five or six Eastern European youngsters had tried to frighten her into giving them money by cutting each other with knives. She'd curled up and closed her eyes, refusing to watch. Eventually they'd given up. 'The stairs were covered with blood.' DC Joiner went there shortly afterwards and found a single trail of small blood drops, more suggestive of a nosebleed than of violence.

The other story came from an elderly man who said a 'foreign girl' had approached him in New Street Station and offered him sex for money. When he'd declined, she'd followed him into the stairwell and trapped him on the first landing, then tried to strangle him. He blushed saying this, and muttered: 'I didn't mind. In fact it got me off.' He'd passed out, he said, and woken up minus his wallet. The medic at Steelhouse Lane said his throat showed no trace of recent bruising.

It seemed to me that both 'victims' were dreamers rather than fantasists. I mean that their dreams had happened to them like real events. But where did the dreams come from? I remembered hearing that some kids had been found sniffing solvents on the upper flight of stairs, between the station car park and the Palisades, a few months before. The strange idea occurred to me that their hallucinations were trapped between the mirrors, unable to break free except by hi-jacking the people who passed through.

Then just before Christmas, a teenage boy called Paul C. was admitted to the City Hospital A&E department, suffering from blood loss as a result of multiple dog bites. He'd been found unconscious in Station Street, a few yards from the stairway. There were vicious bites on his hands, arms, legs and neck. He nearly died, but recovered after a blood transfusion and a ten- hour coma. His estranged mother visited the hospital, but his still more estranged father didn't.

I spoke to Paul while he was recovering in hospital. He said he'd been on his way to the station when a pack of dogs had attacked him on the second landing of the staircase. 'Pouring down the stairs,' he said. 'I don't know how many of them. Nine or ten. They just kept coming.' I asked him why he was going to the station at a time (midnight) when no more trains were due. 'I was looking for male company,' he said without embarrassment. 'Haven't got the money for clubs.'

By then we had a CCTV camera installed on each landing in the stairwell. The film showed Paul, wearing a leather jacket, climbing the stairs and then backing off with his hands raised to protect his face. He fell back against the wall. His hands shaking, growing dark with blood. Vague shadows around him that looked like flaws in the film or the camera lens. More blood spreading on his jeans. Getting up, trying to run away, falling down the stairs. Blood spraying from his wounds. The whole time, no-one and nothing else there.

A week later, I went to visit Paul in his Erdington bedsit. We went for a walk along the main road to Spaghetti Junction. The bites had healed incredibly fast: no more stitches, just a few dark streaks on his pale skin to show the wounds that had nearly killed him. We stood under the concrete flyover, with traffic roaring past overhead, and I told him no-one else had seen the dogs. Where did he think they'd come from? 'Out of the station,' he said immediately. 'There are people there all night. Whatever they want, it's

243

not to be there. True? Some of them are waiting for trains, or waiting to score, or waiting to sell themselves. They all have needs. That can be powerful. What happens if…'

He paused, staring at the pale graffiti-marked pillars, the damp-stained concrete underside of the junction. I noticed a scar under his left eye. 'All those dreams, broken, ruined. What if they come together? I tell you, it's going to be worse than you can imagine. They'll just pour down the stairs and into the street. There won't be anything a bunch of coppers can do.' He smiled nervously. 'You can't arrest human nature. Some day, the dogs will break free. They'll kill and eat and fuck and shit all over the city. And you won't even be able to see them on CCTV.'

'I hope you're wrong,' I said. 'But I'm not going to tell you your idea's ridiculous. We both know it isn't.' I shook his hand. 'Watch out, lad. Be careful with those guys. Dogs aren't the only predators on the streets.'

'They'd better watch out for me,' he said. I watched him walk up the steps onto Slade Road, his leather jacket flapping like vestigial wings. He glanced back and waved, then walked on, still limping. The winter sky behind Spaghetti Junction was a far richer blue than the insipid 'sky blue' of watercolour paintings. But the landscape itself had no colour and no vitality. It looked like a corpse.

The gap between Christmas and New Year is always a heavy time for the police. I didn't get any leave until the first January weekend, when the three of us—me, Elaine and our daughter Julia—went to stay with her parents in Leicester. It was a quiet break. We walked through the frost- covered park by the university, and along New Walk:

a mile-long avenue with old buildings on one side and bare, delicate trees on the other. Lying in bed with Elaine, I wondered if she and I had a shared dream. My own dreams seemed too lonely, too driven by fear and need, to be hers as well. But perhaps the marriage gave my dreams a shelter, a space to form in, like the clearing a fox makes in the undergrowth before it goes to sleep.

I had to work on Monday but Elaine didn't, so I came back on my own by the last train. It began to snow while I was still in Leicester: wet, heavy flakes that marked the landscape like brushstrokes. The temperature fell through the evening, and the snow clearly wasn't going away. I should have left early, but I was drinking with the family, enjoying a normality I couldn't reach on my own. Luckily the trains were still running—but the last train took over two hours to get to Birmingham New Street, and by then the streets were blank with snow.

The station concourse was nearly as crowded as on a Monday morning, but no-one was going anywhere. I waited in the taxi rank for another hour, along with a dozen other people. No vehicles were coming into the city centre. Snow continued to fall, covering up the dirt on the roads and buildings, erasing footprints within seconds. Drivers were abandoning their cars and looking for shelter. It was too cold to walk the streets; by now the snow was a foot deep.

I went back to the railway station. Groups of young people, dressed for a different season, were huddled around the heating vents. Couples were warming each other with kisses; groups were arguing about what to do; loners were curled up, trying to sleep. Two police officers I didn't know walked through the concourse. I decided not to identify myself: there was nowhere they could take me, and they didn't need my help at the moment. In fact, I'd never seen so many people behaving themselves after closing time. It was like some kind of unspoken amnesty. In the waiting area, a hundred or so people were sitting like a cinema audience, gazing at the destination board. Which listed the next morning's arrivals and departures. I sat there for a while, watching the people around me go to sleep one by one. It was a strangely intimate experience. Blurred images drifted through my head. I saw an army of travellers all dreaming at once, their dreams projected through the stairway onto the white screen of the snowbound city. *It's going to be worse than you can imagine.* Slowly I became very afraid of the still people. Where had they come from? What did they need? What might their dreams turn into? My legs and back ached as I stood up and dragged my feet out of the concourse and through the car park, which was jammed full of inert cars, to the concrete stairwell.

The weak mercury light showed me the wet grey stairs and the swollen mirror on the top landing. I walked unsteadily down the first flight, then paused and looked back. The reek of piss and ammonia grew stronger every moment; perhaps it was coming from the past, not the stairs. Another smell joined it: something animal, like the muddy fur and rank breath of dogs. I was so afraid now that I couldn't move, though I tried and tried to get away. My body pressed itself back against the concrete wall. My eyes moved slowly up to the mirror. It held only a grey swirling chaos of sleet or feathers or scales, pouring down from the station.

My mouth was dry. I saw my own breath in front of my face, and wondered if it was the last one. Something brushed past me. I crouched by the wall and covered my eyes. There was a sound of rushing, a broken rhythm like trapped birds. More things brushing past me, but not attacking. I looked up.

There were two or three dogs on the stairs. They were crawling weakly, and flickering like a double exposure. Above their pale heads, I could see wings beating. Slowly the dogs faded, and the flying shapes became clearer. They were people, but their arms were bony frames holding skin and feathers. One by one they swooped down to the landing and past me to the exit on Station Street. I followed them down the stairs and saw each one framed by the doorway, rising in the sodium light, wings outstretched, flying up through the snow and above the black rooftops.

Paul had seen only the dogs. Maybe his sense of the common dream was different from mine. Or maybe we were both wrong.

BLIND CIRCLES

When a lorry driver in north central Birmingham takes the wrong fork at Perry Barr, he or she comes upon a lonely and faceless country.

The Aldridge Road passes the City Cemetery and bears north-east into a wasteland of garages, factories, scrapyards and expressways. The only sounds are dogs barking and cars backfiring. The roads widen, as if fattened by their diet of oil-soaked rain. The trees fade away and the colour washes out of the skyline, leaving only a blank repeated motif of tarmac, breeze- block and concrete. It's a screen saver of a district.

At a roundabout with more exits than a roundabout ought to have, the driver has a choice of heading west towards Walsall or east towards Sutton Coldfield. A mile either way from the grey factory-farm of the Kings Road estate, a more normal West Midlands landscape begins to assert itself. Stopping for a drink, or even a meal, becomes an idea that one can contemplate without panic. With the slight drop in altitude, the air seems to be a little easier to breathe. Afterwards, the driver may learn that he has been through Kingstanding.

Before things really kicked off there, it had always been a trouble spot. Vicious fights every weekend. Racist attacks, arson, gang murders. Industrial decline has made a mess of north Birmingham in general. But Kingstanding had something else, a vibe of imprisonment that was hard to explain in terms of familiar issues like unemployment and lack of resources. Being at once the highest and the most northern district of Birmingham, it had something to prove. Little gangs of scarred and tattooed Kings Road lads patrolled the district at all times, looking for trouble. They claimed to be enforcing the law, but they'd smash up anyone whose skin, face or attitude didn't suit them. They wore camo gear to make themselves more visible.

In the autumn of 2002, I was sent over to the Kingstanding Circle station to cover for an officer on sick leave. They had two other people ill at the same time, so they'd asked for help. I drove there early on a Sunday morning, and just had time to register the grey vacuum of the area before I had to clock in and start interviewing some of the hard cases they'd kept in overnight. The first one was a lad named Terry. He'd attacked an anti-war stall in the Circle that was set up by four students from UCE. Smashed the stall, broken one of their faces.

Terry was wearing a combat jacket over a 'No Surrender to the IRA' sweat-shirt. He introduced himself as 'Terry McCann, Aryan Defence Militia, National Front, UVF', and gave a Hitler salute. The Aryan Defence Militia were the gang of losers he hung around with at weekends, patrolling the streets. He was a skinny boy with a pale web of scar tissue across the left side of his face. Seeing him reminded me immediately of the thugs who'd bullied me in secondary school. I wanted to punch him, which didn't help me to interview him effectively.

As usual with that type, his remarks were a mixture of scrambled knowledge and pure fantasy. 'We need to police this area. The police are all nigger lovers. The Macpherson Report said they have to be, there's no room for white patriots in the Force. They proved it yesterday, they let those nigger lovers put up a stall here. Students. Do they fucking live in Kingstanding? Do they know what we've been though with the Pakis and the niggers and the asylum seekers?'

'And the Jews and the gypsies,' I said. 'Don't forget them.'

'You don't live here, do you?' His face tightened with hatred, became almost childlike. 'I've never seen you here before. What gives you the right to come here and tell us how to behave? What do you know about Kingstanding?'

'I know the law. We're here to uphold the law. It doesn't change from one street to another.'

'There's only one law. That's the law of racial survival.'

I took a deep breath. 'We've got a statement here from one of the lads you attacked yesterday. I want you to read it and tell me if there's anything you disagree with.' Terry nodded. I passed him the statement.

His eyes flickered over the page, without focusing. Suddenly, he spat on it. I snatched it back. 'It's not written in English,' he said flatly. 'It's written in nigger lover language.'

I nodded. 'I'll read it to you, okay?'

'Fuck off. I can fucking read. There's something wrong with my eyes.' He looked at me for a moment, then looked away. I'd taken his bloodshot, unfocused gaze to be the effect of lack of sleep.

I held up a copy of the *Police Gazette*, with a headline about arson. 'What does that say?'

'It says you're a nigger lover.'

'Look son, you're really pissing me off. You're facing two assault charges. If you don't watch out, you'll be looking at six months in prison.' 'Good job I won't be able to see them then, isn't it?'

We took a statement from him, but he needed help to sign it. His friends were waiting for him outside the station: three guys with camo jackets and dogs on long leads. I stood in the doorway, watching as they led him away. He didn't seem able to find his way home alone. The other lads had scars worse than his, and one had 'NF' tattooed on the back of his head.

By the end of the week, the Kingstanding station was still three officers down. I was needed back at Acocks Green, so they arranged for more cover. The three sick officers were all men. It hadn't occurred to me to ask what was wrong with them.

It was over the winter that things really began to change. I kept in touch with DC Bestwick at the Kingstanding station, who was bewildered by the situation. 'Some kind of epidemic. All these guys slowly going blind. Maybe it's an infection carried by dogs. I swear they're using their guard dogs as guide dogs.' Within three months, several dozen cases of blindness were reported. Mostly among violent lads who were known to the police. They were still drinking and fighting, guided by their mates, but at least they weren't patrolling the streets any more.

There was something else, too. Kingstanding wasn't the kind of district where strangers were allowed to breathe easily. In fact, they weren't allowed to breathe at all. But several newcomers had been spotted among the Kings Road estate crowd, blending in as if they'd always belonged there. In fact, Bestwick said, they were as popular as if they'd just come out of borstal. 'There's four or five of the bastards. Dunno where they've come from. Male, white, fair-haired. I mean really white. Albino, maybe. Always surrounded by a gang of Kings Road hard cases who are buying them drinks and fucking cigarettes. Maybe they're the Ku Klux Klan.'

That wasn't as facetious a remark as it might sound. Bestwick was from near Manchester, where the BNP were starting to burn holes in the map. I'd always thought the fascists were a threat at a personal level, unable to affect things on any bigger scale; but Oldham and Burnley had shown that the BNP were capable of taking over a town, once their *agent provocateur* tactics had set communities at each other's throats. In October, fifty NF supporters had marched through Kingstanding. And where they went, the boot boys and the arsonists were bound to follow.

In January, I drove up there while off duty. Traces of frost glimmered on the pavements like slug trails. Half the shops in Kingstanding Circle were boarded up. I waited for twenty minutes, then saw two guys coming over the hill from the cemetery. They were wearing combat jackets and dark glasses. They both had Alsatians on leads. Were they blind, or did they just feel like walking slowly? No doubt they'd trod the same street every day of their lives. Something Bestwick had said came back to me. 'Kingstanding people always say, if you don't live here you can't understand. I always thought that was bullshit. But it's true now. They've made it true. If you don't live here, there's no way you can understand what's happening.'

I waited to see one of the pale newcomers, but none of them came. Every couple of minutes, an HGV or fuel tanker heading out of Birmingham made the road vibrate and the surviving plate-glass windows tremble. A sign above one of the boarded-up shops said WINDOW BLINDS. I thought, *How do you make a window blind? Turn away from it.* My hand turned the key in the ignition, and five minutes later I was out of there.

Five weeks later, I was back. It was night, and from the Kingstanding Road I could see the city's lights spread for miles ahead of me: Newtown, Aston, the city centre. This district was a crow's nest, a vantage point for anyone who wanted to watch over the city. It was still midwinter here: the ground was tacky with frost, and the air was thin and sharp. Through the layers of traffic noise, I could hear dogs barking.

There was some kind of political meeting going on tomorrow night. Bestwick hadn't been sure of the details, but it was a fairly safe bet that it wasn't the SWP. There'd been no leaflets or posters, but everyone seemed to know about it. Some movement calling itself Light of the North—Bestwick was sure it had to do with the blond strangers. 'North as in Nordic, Aryan. Maybe they're a heavy metal band.' And maybe not. The meeting was at a local primary school.

I parked my car by King's Standing Wood. No wonder they had masculinity issues around here. The trees were grey and angular in the moonlight, like girders in some vast warehouse. There was no-one on the streets. I let myself into the caretaker's office at the back of the school. This had taken some persuasion, but the caretaker had a cottaging history that he didn't want the school to know about. At night all cats are grey.

Through a gap in the blinds, I surveyed the school car park and the street beyond it. The window was just open. There was a smell of burning, not fresh; maybe the remnants of a November bonfire. The flickering of car lights in the distance was the only movement. And then, around midnight, I saw one of them. A pale man with hair like frost. He was wearing a thin denim jacket, but didn't appear to be cold. He glanced around the car park, then looked at the school. Quickly, I stepped away from the window. When I looked out again, he was walking calmly away in the direction of Kingstanding Circle.

After that, it happened every hour. They were clearly patrolling, or at least watching the streets. As far as I could tell, there was no-one else around. Not even a stray cat. The white men—and Bestwick was right, they were probably albino— had a kind of blank, restless purpose about them. Like they had passports to the night. Their cold wakefulness got into my head and overcame any thoughts of sleep. I could see why they might have a following in this place. Somehow, they embodied the idea of surveillance. I had a confused sense of territories shifting, a different world being mapped out around me.

Some time between three and four, I heard the first unexpected sound of the night. A scratching at the door, and a faint whimpering caught somewhere between the need to be heard and the need to remain silent. I couldn't see anyone or anything through the window. Tensing myself to be ready for trouble, I opened the door an inch. Nothing. A few inches more. A slanted face poked into the gap. A dog. I let it in and it stood on the doormat, shivering. An idea took shape in my sleep-deprived brain. The dog could be my disguise. What else were dogs for?

The moon was a fraction short of its profile the night before. The sounds of distant traffic permeated the stillness, like nocturnal voices in a tenement house. As far as I could judge, the crowd gathering in the school car park consisted entirely of blind men and their dogs. Some had walking-sticks and dark glasses; others just gazed blankly around, waiting to be tugged or guided. Nobody spoke. I waited between two cars, with the dog crouched tense at my feet. The glasses turned every face to a sepia photograph. A wedding party from an old family album. They couldn't see me, but I hoped their dogs wouldn't betray me as a stranger.

The school door opened, and one of the pale men came out. The first one I'd seen the night before. 'Leave the dogs here,' he said. There was a trace of something Baltic or Scandinavian in his voice. 'Just leave them. Come inside.' One by one, the blind men dropped their leads. The dogs stayed where they were, trembling from cold or tension. Their owners shuffled towards the open doorway. Two of the white men caught their arms, guided them calmly into the school.

I shut my eyes as I approached them, so they wouldn't realise I could see. The hand that gripped my coat sleeve felt as light and hard as bone. I tripped on the doorstep and almost fell. The interior of the school was as stark as the exterior: no paintings or photographs, no signs of children's presence. I wondered if it had closed down. There were a few more of the blond men waiting inside. About seven in all. I couldn't tell them apart, but that was the dark glasses limiting my sight. And I had to be careful not to look directly at anyone.

Chairs had been set up in tidy rows to occupy the school hall, as if for a parents' meeting. I thought momentarily that my own junior school had been built on a much larger scale. I'd thought the same thing when I first took my daughter Julia to school in Acocks Green. Nearly fifteen years before. We're never ready for change, but we get used to it, and then we're not ready for things staying the same.

It took a while to get everyone seated. I wondered why we all had to face the same way, when none of us could see. Order? Three of the newcomers sat at the front, behind a small table. Evidently they took 'right of assembly' literally around here. One of them rapped on the table. 'Good evening. We are here tonight for one reason. Law and order.' His thin voice cut through the silence of the hall. He made the words sound like the names of unfamiliar deities. 'Not the bogus law and order of the Government and the police. We all know whose agenda they serve. We stand for true law and order. The law of our race. The order of nature. Day and night, winter and summer, man and beast. We are the truth. And you are the army.'

I half expected the audience to respond with a co-ordinated Nazi salute. But they sat there like crop-haired statues, waiting for the next word. The speaker stood up. He was very thin, I noticed. The glasses meant I couldn't see his eyes properly. For some reason, I was glad of that. 'Kingstanding used to be a white area,' he said. 'Britain used to be a white country. And they will be again. Together we will cut out the tumours of corruption and deceit. The doctrine of racial equality and the cancer of race mixing. The Jewish lies and the poison of Islam. We will cut them out. We will burn them out.' The most disturbing thing was his total calmness, and the lack of any reaction on the part of the audience. How had they come so far from the human world? Bestwick was right: I didn't understand.

The other two men behind the table stood up. 'Are you with us?' one of them said. 'Or are you with the appeasers and the liberals and the bureaucrats who've sold out your heritage? Are you with the shit at the bottom of the multiracial swamp? Or are you rising into the Light of the North?'

The response came: 'Light of the North!' Some fifty voices, all bellowing at once. I shouted with them, so as not to be suspected; but the words came easily, and I wondered how many fascists started by just trying to blend in. 'Light of the North!' we repeated, and the old walls echoed the vowels. A few of the dogs outside began to bark.

The pale man who'd not yet spoken put his hands to his face and breathed on them, as if trying to thaw them out. When he opened his hands, something was glowing between them. A thin flame, dead white, like a burning strip of mercury in a school chemistry lesson. I forced myself not to look at it. I wasn't supposed to see anything.

'Come forth to receive the Light,' he said. 'One at a time. Wait to be taken forth. Wait… and see.' The shimmering flame obscured his face. The other two men came down to the front row of chairs. Each of them took a blind man by the arm and led him towards the colourless fire. More of the dogs were barking now, and I could hear a faint scratching at the door.

As the first of the believers approached the flame, his face seemed to lose all expression. The stranger's white hand drained it of features. When the flame moved away, the face was a blank mass of scar tissue, like an unfinished doll. The believer fell away to one side of the stage. His body made no sound when it hit the floor. The stranger's hands danced in the air, and the flame between them was so bright I couldn't have looked at it without dark glasses. The second believer approached the stage, one hand feeling the air in front of him.

The blind men continued to respond to the strangers' touch, rising two by two to the stage and the white flame. The limp bodies piled up on either side. I tried not to see too much, but my eyes refused to close. I was sitting near the edge of the third row. How long before I was grabbed and taken to the starving light? And what would they do to me if I resisted? The worst thing was that I didn't want to resist.

The only sound I could hear was the barking of the dogs outside. It was getting louder, but it didn't seem relevant. They were thumping against the door now, their soft mindless bodies unable to breach the security of the building. We'd deal with them, and everyone, later. For now, the only reality was the white flame and the scar of its light. The power, the need. Two more believers were taken and drained, their form released into the light, their husks dropped. Then two more. I could smell burning, but it wasn't like any burning I had smelt before. The air in the hall was as cold as ice.

Something hit the outside of a window to my right. And again. Glass splintered. The barking was suddenly much louder. More glass fell inwards, and dogs poured through the gap. I could see their breath white in the air.

As more dogs leapt in behind them, they attacked the holder of the flame. He fell, the pure light in his hands becoming a prism of twisted colours. The dogs tore at him. The other pale men backed off, panicking. The territories were changing again. I reached up to my face and slipped off the glasses. What the dogs on the stage were ripping apart had no blood. He was white all the way through.

Another window broke, and more dogs came in. Every dog in Kingstanding must have been outside the school that night. One by one, the strangers were torn to colourless shreds. The dogs didn't eat whatever passed for their flesh: they killed and moved on. The blind men— those still alive—were on their feet, calling out to each other or their dogs, trying to make sense of this chaos where everything had been so simple. The floor was littered with broken glass.

I didn't want to stay. I didn't want to help the survivors or clean up the mess. Above all, I didn't want to look at the featureless waxy blobs that had been human faces, the inert bodies scattered around the stage like props. I walked out into the hallway, found the bolt on the school door and slipped it free. Leaving the door open, I walked back to my car. The streets were empty. Apart from the traffic, of course.

My car was still where I had left it, on the edge of King's Standing Wood. The moon was clouded over, but the accumulated light of cars and buildings hung over the trees and made their branches just visible against the bare ground. I got into the car and fumbled with the ignition key. My hands were shaking too badly for me to drive. A streetlamp showed me my own face in the rear-view mirror. I watched the reflection of my breath clouding the still air. After a while, the interior of the car warmed up a little and my breath was clear. I sat there, not moving, until dawn began to creep through the trees. Then I started the engine and drove home.

FACING THE WALL

I was in the police force for twenty-four years. Started as a constable, finished as a detective sergeant. If you asked me why I quit, I couldn't tell you. There isn't a why. There's just what happened. But everything falls apart, so perhaps it doesn't need much explanation.

Do you remember the spring of 2003? Nobody knew why we'd gone to war in Iraq. We were dropping bombs on a capital city for reasons everyone knew were false. I suppose the weapons of mass destruction were like angels: you knew they were a myth, but somehow it would bring bad luck to say so. There was a sense of things having their own momentum: the war had to happen because it was happening. It was the end of something we didn't even have a name for.

In March of that year, some builders collecting a pile of scaffolding found a dead man underneath it. His blood was all over the back wall of the warehouse, a former church in Digbeth. I got drafted into the investigation team because they were short-handed. Most of the South Birmingham police were too busy raiding mosques and arresting mouthy teenagers as terrorist suspects to bother with a murder.

The dead man was thirty-five, divorced, lived alone. He'd been a cook in one of the Digbeth cafeterias. The cause of death was a number of vicious stab wounds in his back, made with something like an ice-pick or a loose railing spike. We doubted this had been the punishment for a dodgy bacon sandwich. His clothes were in a neat pile a few feet away. There was no blood on them.

The absence of a murder weapon was matched by the absence of any reason for him to be there. I thought it was a gangland execution: he'd been marched into the warehouse and forced to strip before being pushed to the wall and murdered. But none of our local informers had heard anything about it. The dead man had no form. Traces of Ecstasy in his bloodstream might mean he was linked to drug dealers, but only his age group made that remotely unusual.

There were two bits of evidence that looked more promising. The first was a scrap of paper in his wallet with the names of some local escort agencies and massage parlours. The second was a note in the pathology report that minor injuries on the body—cuts, lash marks and burns— had been inflicted weeks or months before his death.

Around that time—just before or just after the body was discovered in the warehouse—my wife left me. Things had been difficult between us for years, but I'd hoped that when our daughter left home we'd be able to reach a balance. However, no sooner had Julia moved into her boyfriend's flat than Elaine decided our house was no longer a family home. I was more confused than bitter, virtually a spectator to the end of my marriage. If there'd been a crisis, a terrible row, a betrayal, I could have found a way to heal the rift. But how Elaine and I behaved didn't seem to matter. The process had a momentum of its own.

By the time we'd divided up the house contents and I was trying to convert the living room into a bedsit for purposes of mental regression, it was already summer. Climate change had become an inescapable fact, and the city felt like a vast iron box with the sun trapped inside it. There had been two more deaths by stabbing, all of them solitary men found in desolate industrial buildings. I was working long shifts, and drinking at home to try and get my emotions over with as fast as possible.

A young couple had moved into the house next door. I got into the habit of listening for them late at night, if I was at home. When they made love I'd press my whole body to the wall, arms outstretched as if trying to embrace the vision. I thought of her orgasms as rare moths I was trying to catch. It took me weeks of eavesdropping to realise that she wasn't getting there, only faking to excite her partner or herself. Once I began to listen for it, I was saddened by her frustration. The magic seemed to be beyond everyone's reach.

The second dead man had been found in a disused factory in the Jewellery Quarter. He'd been stabbed twice in the lower back, once on each side of the spine. The pathologist said it might have been a botched attempt to remove his kidneys. He didn't have a donor card, but he was carrying a membership card for a 'gentleman's club' half a mile away. It was near the Hockley Flyover, in Great Hampton Street. I bet the owner was chuckling for weeks after he made that purchase.

My visit to the parlour was as low-key as possible. I waited until the Madam was alone, then showed her my ID. She called one of the scantily- clad girls to take over the door, and led me into a tiny office with a wall safe and a phone. 'We've never had any trouble here,' she said. Her face was blank, but her hands were trembling.

'I'm not looking for trouble,' I said. 'Just some information.' I showed her a photo of the dead man. 'Do you recognise this guy?' The report of his death hadn't yet appeared in the papers.

She nodded slowly. 'Seen him here a few times. Don't know his name.'

'Can I talk to someone who...'

'Went with him?' She opened a ledger and flicked through the last few pages. They were covered in tiny, neat handwriting. 'Oh.' She closed the book. Looking away from me, she said quietly: 'He saw Maxi. A few times. She's only here by appointment. Bit of a specialist.' She gave me Maxi's mobile number.

As I got up to leave, she said: 'Come back if there's any... other way we can help you.' I didn't respond to her smile. As I left, one of the girls was showing a punter out. Her costume was revealing at the front; at the back, it was nothing but a couple of strings. My face flushed as she opened the door for me. The other man walked off hastily. It was getting dark; the office buildings across the street reflected the lamplight from their dusty upper windows. Old-fashioned stone carvings made the roofs appear to be carrying vines, exotic birds, and black roses.

I wasn't asked to interview Maxi the 'specialist'. Which, given my state of mind, was perhaps a good thing. I caught a glimpse of her walking into the station: a tall woman in a dark blue trouser-suit. My boss, DI Hargrave, talked with her for a couple of hours. Later, she told me Maxi was a dominatrix.

'Williams paid her to tie him up and beat seven shades out of him. There's a basement room under that parlour with no windows. A punishment room. But she refused to go on seeing him. You know why?'

'He asked her to kill him.' The thought hadn't occurred to me before that point; but as soon as I said it, I knew it was true.

'You know what this means? He could have been complicit in his own killing. And so could Morris. Serial manslaughter. Or gimpslaughter.' Hargrave glanced down at the interview notes, without focusing. 'Maxi says she gave Williams a phone number she'd picked up off the Internet. Some organisation called Maze. Sort of a contact group for masochists. I've tried the number. Disconnected.'

'Maybe they kind of… died out.'

'I don't think so,' Hargrave said. 'To kill like that takes something unusual. Whoever did that won't let someone else top him. Not without a fight.'

'Reminds me of that case in Manchester. The young guy who was killing senile pensioners. Said it was wrong to keep them alive.'

Hargrave shook her head. 'He was just a pathetic madman. This guy's something else. He's a real monster. He'll go on until he's stopped.'

When I got home, near midnight, I couldn't sleep. I poured myself a large whisky and sat at the computer. The words 'masochism', 'pain' and 'punishment' all brought strings of interesting sites, but nothing I could connect with the two deaths. 'Maze' got me nowhere. I began to trawl sites of wounds and murder victims while getting more and more drunk, convinced that the answer was hidden somewhere in the computer. Or somewhere in my own head.

I began to think about the time, a dozen years before, when Elaine and I had gone into the maze at Longleat. I'd been convinced I could work it out, but we'd never even found our way into the inner section. At the third or fourth sighting of the same landmark, Elaine had wanted to give up. But I'd insisted on searching further, until it was getting dark and we had no choice but to leave.

The backstreets of Digbeth and Hockley were mazes. Old industrial districts, part redeveloped and part derelict, with no consistent street plan or identifiable centre. They were the key financial districts of the black economy. Stolen cars were driven there and were in fragments before the dawn. Every business seemed to be a front for something else. And there was no point appealing to Neighbourhood Watch groups for information. Hardly anyone lived there—at least, hardly anyone who had a home.

Three of us spent a few weeks doing the rounds of saunas and massage parlours in the West Midlands. We were looking for anyone who recognised Morris or Williams, or had heard of Maze or any similar organisation. After a while, my memories of these places began to blur into a generic impression, like the franchises of a retail chain. The reason the police tolerate massage parlours is that they minimise the visibility and disruptive effect of prostitution, not that they minimise the exploitation or the danger. There's a difference.

One girl asked me if either of the dead men had had a tattoo. 'I heard something about Maze,' she said. 'The members all have a small tattoo on their backs, just above the belt. It's made with blue ink. The ink they used to use in fountain pens.' No such tattoo had been found in either case; but then, the skin area in question had been gouged out from both men.

Needless to say, I didn't avail myself of the facilities at any of these places of recreation. Even though I could have done with a jacuzzi at the end of another hot day out on the streets. And I could have done with some other things too. Elaine leaving had changed what I was capable of.

After a month of struggling with my sense of what was appropriate behaviour for a police officer, I drove up to Stafford and visited a parlour there. Without my ID. I expected a brutal experience, but was surprised at how kind and friendly the girl was. Driving home, I began to realise that affection was not what I had wanted. The facts of reality called for something more violent. I was mixing work and pleasure even then, though I didn't know it.

Hargrave was right. At the end of July, a third man was found in a car repair garage in Witton. He'd been pretty much torn apart, painting a collection of machine tools with blood. Once again, the murder weapon was apparently missing. A search of his house revealed a new factor: the bloke was gay. Not that it made much difference. A new set of contacts, websites, venues; but the same kind of death and almost certainly the same killer.

Looking for a tattoo seemed ridiculous when you'd seen the crime scene photos: bits of him were scattered over several yards, and his lower body had to be reconstructed with the help of computer modelling. However, now the guys in the path lab knew what to look for, traces of a small design began to appear. The ink was blue-black, and scar tissue under the skin helped to define the shape of the tattoo. After a few days, they had an image they were at least fifty percent sure of. It was a bull's head.

The third case brought me an answer. I found it in my own time. At Boots, a barely lit male pick-up joint on the edge of the city centre, I met a man in a leather vest whose ex-lover had belonged to Maze. He told me a story in his bedroom. It was a story I'd heard before, or rather read as a child. Afterwards, I let him do what he wanted. It didn't matter.

Nothing mattered except finding the killer. And I did find him. It took five months. Along the way I picked up a few scars and bruises, a broken rib, and a small tattoo at the base of my spine. I played games devised by lonely men in their basements and garages, and learned to feel my way through the maze of their inarticulate need. Of course, I had to leave the police force. I couldn't afford for rumours to get out— either at work or in my new life. Some of my old friends seemed to decide I'd changed too much. But I never lost sight of my goal.

On a dark morning in midwinter, I found him. He'd killed at least five more people by then. Meeting him wasn't something that happened by chance. You needed contacts, rituals, payments. He moved from place to place, but was always at the heart of whatever you were trying to get into. At that time, his home was an industrial estate in Nechells. A labyrinth of new factories that had never been used and old terraces that should have been empty but weren't. I found him by letting him come to me.

When I first saw him, my impulse was to turn and press myself against the wall. We were standing in a disused office where squatters had left heaps of charcoal and filthy blankets. The plaster had fallen from the back wall, exposing neat brickwork. The moonlight through the barred window showed me his silhouette. He didn't speak as he walked towards me. I realised he was mute. My fingers trembled as I unbuttoned my shirt.

His raw breath in my face was semen and blood. He looked at me. I couldn't see his eyes. Then he stepped back and waited. I turned to the wall and dropped to a half-crouch, one leg bent. My right hand was unzipping my boot as he charged. I turned back with the knife in my hand. He was strong, but I was faster.

The moon was down and the building was pitch-dark when I found my way back out, carrying the trophy of my fight. Leaving another unsolved murder, and a body they had no chance of identifying. As I climbed over the gate to the alley that led to a junkyard that led to a narrow street, I muttered a prayer for all the defeated souls who'd given themselves to him. All the shut-down strangers. The men who'd travelled so far into ruin they couldn't wait for death to catch up.

I had to keep moving after that, on the run from his followers. I drove to Wales and drifted from one small town to another, then caught a train to the south coast of England. It's February now, and the estuary where I'm staying is choked with blackish lumps of ice. In the spring, who knows? I might catch a ferry and head east across the continent, maybe ending up in Greece. Or even Crete.

Every night, I kneel in the dark and open the wooden box I've carried with me from Birmingham. It's the only possession I've kept, apart from a little suitcase of clothes and a few maps. I lift up the thing in the box and... worship it, I suppose. It's easier to worship what's dead. I've used bleach and formaldehyde to reduce the smell. I don't want trouble with the police or hotel authorities. And of course, without the body, it's nothing much. Just a slightly decayed bull's head.

If you want to know who I am, there's your answer. I know who I am. I'm the man who killed a god.

ACKNOWLEDGEMENTS

Thanks are due to the editors of the following publications, in which some of these stories first appeared:

'My Stone Desire' in *Black Static* #1, September 2007
'Still Water' in *Supernatural Tales* 11, Spring 2007
'Morning's Echo' in *The Seventh Black Book of Horror* ed. Charles Black, Mortbury Press, 2010
'The Hostess' in *Crimewave Eleven: Ghosts*, 2010
'Beth's Law' in *British Invasion* ed. Christopher Golden, Tim Lebbon and James A. Moore, Cemetery Dance Publications, 2008
'A Cup of blood' in *Supernatural Tales* 8, Autumn 2004
'Even the Pawn' in *Crimewave Ten: Now You See Me*, 2008
'A Mouth to Feed' in *Shades of Darkness* ed. Barbara and Christopher Roden, Ash-Tree Press, 2008
'Black Country' (pamphlet), Nightjar Press, 2010
'Incry' in *New Horizons* issue 6, winter 2010

'The Last Witness' in *Where the Heart Is* ed. Gary Fry, Gray Friar Press, 2010 'Dreams of Children' in *Under the Radar* 7, January 2011

'Waiting for the Thaw' in *Weird Tales* #359, Winter 2012

'Stiff As Toys' in *Scaremongers 2: Redbrick Eden* ed. Steve Savile, Tanjen, 1998 'The Victim Card' in *Midnight Street* issue 3, Winter 2004

'Winter Journey' in *Black Static* #5, June/July 2008

'The Receivers' in *Dark Terrors* 6 ed. Stephen Jones and David Sutton, Gollancz, 2002

'Wake Up in Moloch' in *PulpNet* (online), 2005

'Blind Circles' in *Fusing Horizons* issue 2, spring 2004

'Facing the Wall' in *The 3rd Alternative* issue 38, summer 2004

Some stories have been slightly amended for this edition.

Joel Lane was the author of two novels, *From Blue to Black* and *The Blue Mask*; several short story collections, *The Earth Wire*, *The Lost District*, *The Terrible Changes*, *Do Not Pass Go*, *Where Furnaces Burn*, *The Anniversary of Never* and *Scar City*; a novella, *The Witnesses Are Gone*; and four volumes of poetry, *The Edge of the Screen*, *Trouble in the Heartland*, *The Autumn Myth* and *Instinct*. He edited three anthologies of short stories, *Birmingham Noir* (with Steve Bishop), *Beneath the Ground* and *Never Again* (with Allyson Bird). He won an Eric Gregory Award, two British Fantasy Awards and a World Fantasy Award. Born in Exeter in 1963, he lived most of his life in Birmingham, where he died in 2013.

INFLUX PRESS

Influx Press is an independent publisher based in London, committed to publishing innovative and challenging literature from across the UK and beyond. Formed in 2012, we have published titles ranging from award-nominated fiction debuts and site-specific anthologies to squatting memoirs and radical poetry.

Lifetime supporters: Bob West and Barbara Richards

www.influxpress.com
@Influxpress